A SPARK OF STORMS

AN ALADDIN RETELLING

HEART OF THE QUEENDOM
BOOK 1

SUSANNAH WELCH

Cover Concept and Design by MoorBooks Design
Editing by Nia Quinn

eISBN: 978-1-958568-08-8
Paperback ISBN: 978-1-958568-09-5
Hardback ISBN: 978-1-958568-10-1

www.susannahwelch.com

ALSO BY SUSANNAH WELCH

Heart of the Queendom

A Spark of Storms

A Spark of Nature (Coming Soon)

City of Virtue and Vice

Dance with the Wind

Dance with the Night

Dance with the Dawn

Fight with the Wind

Fight with the Dark

Fight with the Heart

For Kent,
A true fairy tale prince

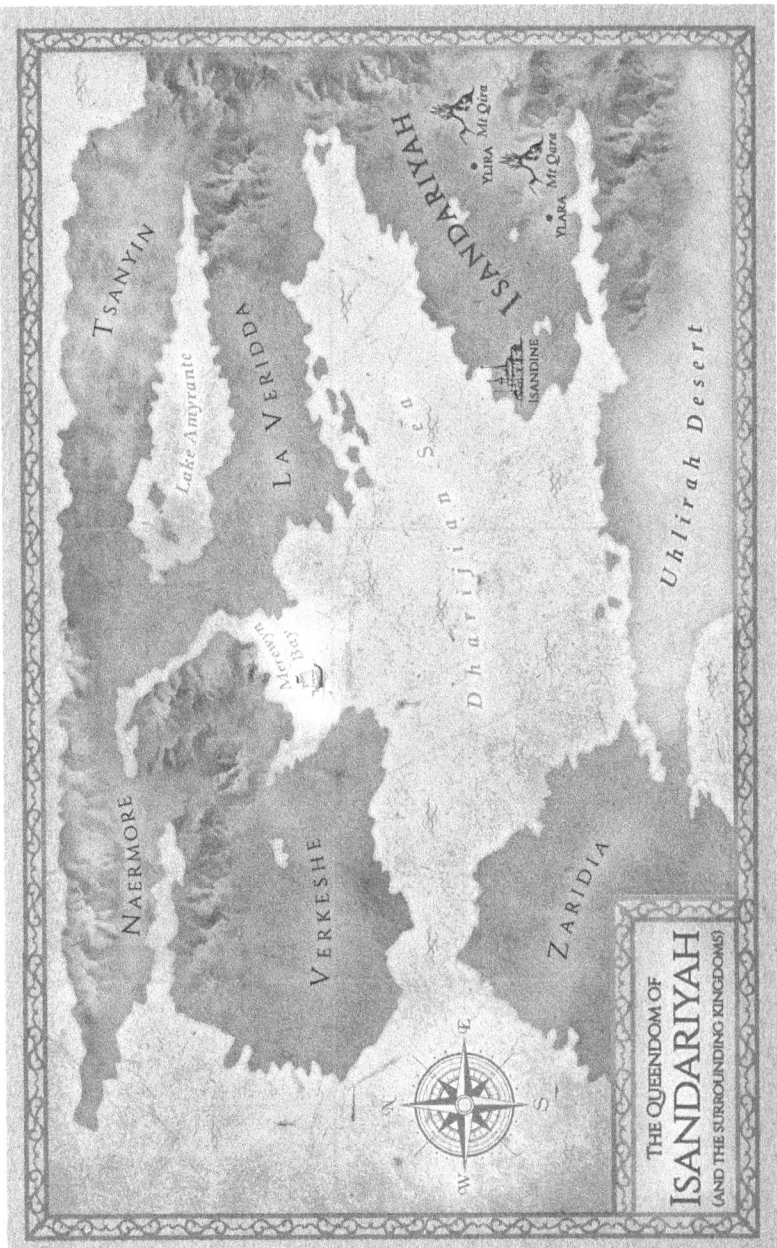

THE QUEENDOM OF
ISANDARIYAH
(AND THE SURROUNDING KINGDOMS)

PART I

1
—————

Alanna strategically adjusted her corset and headed for her target. Her delicate heels clicked on the cobblestone road as she wove through the slow-moving horses and darting pedestrians. Her thick black hair was pulled up into a twist, but she swirled her finger around a smooth ringlet and rested it gently against her bare shoulders. The layers of petticoats and thick satin threatened to overheat her, but her eyes never strayed from her target on the other side of the cobbled road.

The broad man stood in the middle of a crowd of adoring sycophants in the shadow of the palm trees lining the busy promenade. He ran his fingers through his softly curled mahogany locks, leaving his hair even more perfectly coiffed. His tailor had highlighted his muscular build with a green velvet jacket, wide in the shoulders, nipping in at his narrow waist.

Wearing velvet in the tropical heat? Only rich people had that sort of vanity.

Rich people. And people like her.

Though the man was surrounded by admirers, his eyes

scanned the busy street, always looking for one more fan. Alanna didn't know his name, but she sized him up from a distance. He was exactly what she wanted.

He was Alanna's target, but as she closed the distance between them, she turned herself into his target instead.

Alanna tripped over a perfectly good brick and tumbled directly into the path of an approaching carriage. The man in green velvet caught her smoothly in strong arms, whisking her out of danger.

She stared up at him, wide-eyed, her breath coming in short gasps thanks to the tight corset. "You saved my life," she whispered as she clung to him, sagging against his muscular body, one breath away from spilling out the top of her tight bodice.

The man's eyes swept over her golden brown shoulders. "It was my pleasure." He drew the last word out in a way that set her teeth on edge.

She covered her disgust with a tiny little pout. "That was scary! Thank the Twins you are so strong!" She ran her hands down his shoulders, squeezing his arms. "You have so many muscles!"

The man flexed his biceps under her hands, and she found it difficult not to laugh. No matter how many times she said the line, it always surprised her how well it worked.

"Good thing I was here to rescue you. Are you sure you're okay?" He made a show of looking her up and down for injuries, but Alanna didn't miss where he focused most of his attention.

She took another heaving breath for good measure. "I'm just shaken up. Thank you for holding me while I catch my breath."

"I'll hold you as long as you need." Though the words sounded sincere, he pulled her close enough to give him a good view of everything she had on display. She giggled, her hands curling around his waist.

His lips twisted in a patronizing grin. "What's a little lady like you doing out here by yourself? It's too dangerous on this busy street for someone as young as you."

She bit her lip, which not only helped her hide her grin, but also drew his attention to her rosy lips. "I'm not young! I'm twenty-one." The only true thing she'd said so far. "And I'm not alone. I'm here with my twin sister. Should I go get her? We owe you so much for rescuing me."

The man's eyes lit up with undisguised glee. "Yes, go get her!"

Alanna smoothed her hands down his arms, caressing the skin on his wrist before clasping both hands in hers. She spoke in a throaty whisper. "I'll be right back."

She stepped onto the cobblestone road, throwing him one more flirty look over her shoulder while twirling her loose tendril of hair with her finger. All her moves were carefully calculated, but her playful giggle was real. Her targets never remembered the old saying that a bird in the hand was worth more than two in the palm tree.

He licked his lips as some of his entourage slapped him on the back, congratulating him on his good fortune. He absently rubbed his hand over his wrist, and his eyes widened, then fixed on her face.

Alanna chirped in surprise at the fury in his eyes. She shoved the man's watch and coin purse further into her pocket, then lifted her skirts and ran.

Perhaps stealing the man's watch at the end had been a bit too brazen. She pushed aside the analytical thought and focused only on landing each step on the cobblestone road precisely. Even in heels, she thought she could beat the hulking man in a foot race; however, a twisted ankle would spell disaster. She skidded around a corner and ducked into a narrow alley. A few men lounging in the cool shadows followed her movements with raised brows as she ran by.

She barely avoided running over a child who watched her with an open-mouthed stare. The man in the velvet coat shouted as she slid through a gap in a metal fence onto another busy street. The edge of her skirt caught on the fence with a sharp *rip*, and she cursed quietly.

She pasted a relaxed smile on her face and blended into the crowd strolling through the outdoor market. Fancy ladies had no reason to sprint through the streets, but her deceptively calm stroll felt as if a target were painted between her shoulder blades.

She slipped into the shadow of a vendor's stall filled with brightly colored fabrics, then hid behind a fluttering sample of silk and peeked out onto the street. The man in the velvet coat squeezed himself through the gap in the fence with a glare. His eyes scanned the street, and his head swiveled from side to side. When he turned away from her, she let out her breath in relief. Her heels were extremely uncomfortable, not to mention expensive, and she didn't want to ruin them by sprinting any further.

"Can I help you, my lady?" The silk vendor watched her with wary eyes.

She laughed lightly, then dropped her voice to a conspiratorial whisper. "I'm hiding from my husband. He told me no more expensive fabric." She slid the silk through her fingers as she looked up at him through lowered lashes. "You won't tell him I'm here, will you?"

The man's lips curled in a knowing grin. "Of course not. A lady's business should be her own."

Alanna nodded regally, then tucked the smooth tendril of hair behind her ear and did some shopping.

Alanna loosened her corset and took her first deep breath in hours. Her shoulders strained as she untied and unhooked herself, then she threw the corset onto the threadbare mattress on the floor.

"I don't know who invented these contraptions, but it definitely wasn't a woman."

She rubbed her sore ribs as she sat on the wobbly crate that served as her chair. After wading through the layers of petticoats, she finally uncovered her patent leather shoes. Her nimble fingers unbuckled them as quickly as she could without ripping her delicate stockings.

"Ah ..." she sighed, wiggling her liberated toes. "As soon as I can find shoes that actually fit, we need to snatch them immediately."

Alanna removed her sparkling earrings and laid them carefully inside the rough-hewn wooden box. They were fakes, of course, but so finely made they looked authentic, and she didn't feel safe wearing them all the time. She hid the box inside the crooked drawer of her dresser.

She reached into the petticoat pockets and pulled out the fat pouch of coins. The coins jingled as she plopped the bag on the rickety dresser, and the sound drew her companion to her side.

"I knew that would get your attention," Alanna said with a grin. "You are such a mercenary, Bibi."

The small white monkey hopped onto the dresser and peeked inside the pouch. The monkey's careful little fingers lifted out each coin, depositing them in neat stacks.

"Not a bad haul," said Alanna when Bibi had finished her accounting. "It's lighter by several silver coins because of the fabric I bought. At least I found a color to match this dress so I can patch the rip." Alanna began pulling the pins out of her thick black hair and gave the monkey a questioning glance. "Aren't you going to help me with these pins?"

Bibi plucked at her fur and wouldn't look up.

Alanna narrowed her copper eyes suspiciously. "What did you do?"

Bibi ducked her head, then jumped off the dresser, scampering to her little shrine. She picked through her collection of shiny rocks, feathers, and ribbons until she found what she wanted. She hopped back onto the dresser and held the treasure out to Alanna.

"A ladies' ring? When did you take this?" Alanna studied the ring, impressed at the quality, but it didn't lessen her irritation.

Bibi fidgeted with the pale blue ribbon on her neck, unwilling to look at Alanna.

She gave Bibi a stern frown. "I've told you not to steal anything when I'm in the middle of a con! Proper ladies don't own monkeys, and if you get in trouble, I'll blow my cover trying to help you."

Bibi skipped over to her shrine and started organizing her feathers.

"Now you're ignoring me?" Alanna huffed, but examined the ring. "This is an actual sapphire ... I guess I can't be too angry."

Bibi abandoned her shrine and jumped onto Alanna's lap. The monkey flopped onto her back, offering her belly in an inviting way.

Alanna's irritation fled as she rubbed the soft white fur. Bibi tickled Alanna's fingers so carefully, she almost didn't notice when the monkey snatched the ring back out of her hands.

Alanna laughed. "It appears I'm not the only one who falls for the belly rub trick. Whoever you stole this ring from, I hope she learned her lesson not to pet unusual animals in the marketplace."

2

After Alanna made her way out of the cloud of petticoats, she pulled on a short top of draped fabric and flowing cotton pants gathered at the ankles. She sighed in relief at the infinitely cooler fabric. The rich were the only people who could wear satin and velvet comfortably, since they could afford homes with tile floors and cleverly built vents to pull in cool air. Alanna, and the rest of the people as poor as her, needed practical clothes for the oppressive tropical heat.

She stepped into her soft slippers, frowning at the leather pulling apart at the seams. She could fix ripped fabric with her own needle and thread, but leatherworking was beyond her skills. The stack of coins on her dresser would continue to shrink.

She gathered up the petticoats, corset, thick satin dress, and too-small shoes and looked them over for any signs of wear. Luckily the rip wasn't as bad as she'd thought, and she disguised it by adding an extra drape of the expensive fabric she had purchased. Once all the clothing met her exacting standards, she polished the patent leather shoes until they shone, then grabbed her old satchel and carefully placed a blond wig inside. She unlocked the heavy deadbolt on her door and stepped into the open air of the theater's roof.

The tiny shed on top of the roof had been her home for over fifteen years. Before becoming her home, it had been an aviary, but the bird shelter had been unused for decades. Alanna didn't know if the theater had once housed the birds as messengers or as actors, but it held enough perches for dozens of birds. Now it only held Alanna and Bibi.

Alanna looked out far beyond Isandine's city walls at the two volcanoes in the distance, the dwellings of the Twin Goddesses, Qira and Qara. She offered a prayer to Qira the Trickster, thanking her for assisting her in a quick getaway, and promising to offer a sacrifice in the shrine on her behalf.

Instead of climbing down to the neighboring roof as she usually did, she quietly opened the heavy door that led inside the theater and crept down the narrow spiral staircase. The iron staircase was in an unused area backstage, so no one noticed her as she tiptoed into the costume closet. She hung up the dress and petticoats and tucked the shoes back into their home on the bottom shelf.

A powerful voice sang onstage, and the lure of the rich notes drew her out of the costume closet through a server's passageway into one of the viewing boxes for the rich patrons. The voice was stronger now that Alanna was in the audience, and she sank low into the tufted love seat to listen to the rehearsal.

The woman onstage wore an elaborate costume of gold lamé and feathers and sang a song of lost love to a theater of empty seats. Despite it just being a dress rehearsal, she sang as if the theater were packed. Not that Alanna ever watched the performances when there were people around.

The first time she had watched a rehearsal, she'd been with her mother. They had been in the same box seats she sat in now, except, with Alanna being seven years old, her mother couldn't stop her from leaning against the railing, watching the whole performance with wide eyes.

Alanna had loved the beautiful costumes, the music, and all the drama, and she'd fallen in love with the theater. She couldn't pry her eyes away from the beautiful dancers twirling across the stage.

She had whispered to her mother, "Someday, I'll perform in this theater."

Her mother had gazed on her with eyes sparkling with delight. "Child, you're so clever, one day you'll *own* this theater."

Alanna smiled at the memory of her mother's eyes, clear and bright. She choked down the lump that threatened to rise in her throat and slid out of her chair to leave.

The theater director stood in the doorway with crossed arms.

"I heard someone was skulking around backstage," he said. "I should have guessed it was you."

Leland was only a few inches taller but much thinner than her. He wore a velvet jacket reminiscent of the wealthy man she'd met earlier, but Leland's was clearly a cheap knockoff. He was wheezing from his walk up the stairs to the box seats—he rarely moved from his spot in the audience where he spent most days yelling at the performers. Even though Alanna wasn't a good fighter—she usually charmed her way out of situations or just ran—she was probably stronger than this man.

She shouldn't be physically afraid of him, yet Alanna still froze like a trapped animal.

"Good afternoon, Leland." Alanna adopted the character she always played with her landlord—courteous yet bland, with shoulders hunched to hide her curves.

"You've always been so polite." He rested his hand

against the doorframe, blocking her escape. "When your mother first brought you here as a child and begged me to let you live on the roof, you stood with downcast eyes. A perfect picture of a demure little girl." He gave her a long look up and down. "You aren't a little girl anymore, though."

All her confidence from earlier had fled, her mind careening back to the fear in her mother's voice as she taught Alanna how to deadbolt the aviary door.

He gave a low chuckle deep in his throat. "I can't believe your mother left you alone in a theater as a child."

Alanna fought down the memory of the first night she had woken to wheezing just outside her door ... the overwhelming scent of alcohol ... the rattling lock ... her muffled cries for her mother with the covers pulled over her head ... and the eventual grateful prayer to the Goddesses when the drunk man stumbled back down the stairs to bed.

He stalked closer, backing her against the edge of the love seat, and he laughed. "Your mother must've been crazy."

A flash of anger strengthened her spine, and she hissed, "She wasn't crazy."

His eyes widened at her harsh tone. She used his distraction to slide out of his trap against the love seat, then darted for the door.

His low voice caught her before she could escape. "Your rent is going up."

Alanna didn't turn to look at him. She knew what she'd see in his eyes—the usual proposition to live at the theater rent free, in exchange for keeping her door unlocked.

A dark shiver crawled across her skin, but she still didn't turn around.

His voice sharpened. "I guess you could always find somewhere else to live."

She clenched the doorframe for support. He knew she

wouldn't leave.

Couldn't leave.

Alanna unclenched her hand and faced him with a pasted-on smile. "I'll pay the rent, Leland." She hoped her carefree voice was as convincing as the actresses rehearsing onstage.

Alanna left him standing there, his lips pinched tightly as he wheezed through his nose. She strolled down the hall until she was out of sight, then sprinted down the stairs, through the theater lobby and out the front door.

As she leaned against the stone facade, she scrubbed her hands across her eyes, trying to wipe away the tears. She should find somewhere else to live. Somewhere safe and with cheaper rent. But how could she leave the home her mother had found for her so long ago?

What if her mother came back and Alanna was gone?

Deep down, she knew the idea was ludicrous. Her mother was not coming back. But picturing her mother as she discovered the empty aviary brought fresh tears to Alanna's eyes.

"Are you okay?" A gray-haired woman laid a gentle hand on Alanna's arm. At her touch, all Alanna's tears dried up as if they had never been. She turned to the woman with an instinctual smile on her face.

"Thank you for your concern. It's proof I'm good at my job." She gave a sweeping gesture toward the theater, as if that explained it.

The woman blinked, her expression unsure.

Alanna pulled the blond wig out of her satchel, settling it over her thick black hair. "Just another role, you see?" She winked, then walked down the street.

She didn't dare a final glance over her shoulder at the woman. Alanna was pretty sure this was her least convincing role of the day.

3

Alanna tucked a few stray strands of dark hair under her blond wig. She normally wrapped her thick black hair in a tight scarf underneath her wig, but she was anxious to get inside the monastery and didn't want to take the time to do it properly. Besides, she didn't think this target would even notice the difference.

"Good afternoon, Sister." Alanna pressed her palms together near her chest and bowed. "Might I be permitted inside to spend a few moments in quiet contemplation?"

The scholar's lips softened in a peaceful smile. "Of course, my child." She clasped her hands within the sleeves of the white robes worn by the women of her order and bowed in return. "All are welcome to seek the blessings of the Goddesses."

Alanna knew better than to retort that while all might be welcome to visit, only unmarried, childless women were permitted to become one of the queen's special order of scholars.

She passed through the vestibule into the cloister. On her right, the covered walkway's intricate columns provided a view into the central courtyard filled with trees, flowers, and shrines for quiet contemplation. On her left, massive doors led further into the monastery, where the scholars worked devising new technology for the queen. Aqueducts, telescopes, and wonders of architecture and agriculture had been discovered by the queen's scholars. Alanna held no ill will toward the scholars.

The queen was another matter.

Alanna found her target on a worn stone bench in the shade of a mango tree. A book lay open on the woman's lap, but her attention was focused on a red bird on a low branch. The bird shook out its feathers, and the woman watched it with a serene expression.

Alanna moved quietly, so as not to startle the bird or the woman, and took a seat on the same bench. "It's a beautiful bird." She tried to keep her voice casual, but the words came out strangled.

The woman's eyes didn't leave the bird as she said, "Their wings are so fascinating. Such a miracle of science."

Alanna looked at the open book in the woman's lap. Alongside a sketch of an outstretched bird wing were complex mathematical formulas calculating trajectory and lift and surface area. The pages were aged and worn. They hadn't been written in for some time.

Alanna spoke softly, as if the woman were a bird that might be startled if she said the wrong words. "You enjoy studying birds?"

The woman's copper eyes shimmered, and Alanna bit her lip to hide how much joy it brought her. "Studying birds is my life's work. When the queen offered asylum to women scholars throughout the world, I risked everything to make it here."

Bitterness crept into Alanna's voice. "You gave up much for the queen."

A shadow slid across the woman's eyes. "Yes ... but I had little choice."

Alanna ground her teeth, angry at herself for causing the darkness in the woman's gaze. She pitched her voice in a reassuring tone. "I'm sure the risk will be worth it."

The woman's eyes cleared, and she nodded slowly. "Yes, someday I will provide my daughter with the life she deserves."

Alanna's breath hitched in her throat. "Your daughter?"

The woman twisted her thick black hair absently, unaware that she shouldn't mention her daughter while wearing the white robes of her order. "She's only seven years old, but she's such a clever girl. Beautiful and compassionate and feisty."

Alanna didn't want to accidentally break the fragile moment, so she didn't risk moving to wipe away the tears streaming down her face. "You love her very much."

The woman smiled, her eyes still on the bird. "She's my world. I would do anything for her."

Alanna stared at the woman's face, so familiar, yet lost to her forever, and drew in a shuddering breath. "I don't know if anyone will ever love me like that again."

The woman finally turned and regarded her with clear eyes. "Love yourself as you are, and others will do the same." She tucked a stray lock of the blond wig behind Alanna's ear with a soft hand.

Alanna stopped breathing, savoring each heartbeat, until the cloud passed back in front of her mother's eyes.

The woman blinked, confusion on her face as she squinted at Alanna. "Do I know you?"

Alanna's lips trembled as she shaped her mouth into the semblance of a smile. "I've seen you here before."

The woman began wringing her hands. "Something is not right ... Something ..."

Alanna clasped her mother's hands between her own and spoke to her as if soothing a child. "Everything is okay. You're safe here in the monastery with the birds. See the beautiful red bird up there? Aren't his wings so fascinating?"

The woman turned toward the mango tree, and once she spotted the bird, her hand-wringing ceased. "Yes ... fascinating ... Truly a miracle of science."

Alanna gently placed her mother's hands back on the open book in her lap, then crept out of the monastery alone.

4

As soon as she exited the monastery, Alanna ripped off the blond wig and stuffed it into her satchel. She had learned that it confused her mother to see a grown version of Alanna when she believed Alanna was still a child. The blond wig helped, but her mother still usually ended up in distress.

Every time she left, she considered never going back. Her mother always appeared calm when she arrived; it was only after finding Alanna familiar that she became overwhelmed. Perhaps Alanna should just let her mother live out the rest of her life in a fog of peace and leave the scholars to care for her. She had to admit, the scholars did a good job caring for her, despite her mother's inability to contribute to their community anymore.

But of course, the scholars should care for the sick among them. The scholars had no families of their own.

The queen had seen to that. Just because she had remained unmarried all these years didn't mean her scholars should be forced to do the same. Plus, the queen had seven sons by seven different men. Why couldn't she have allowed Alanna's mother to keep just one child?

The wind whipped through Alanna's hair, which was disheveled from her wig. Fallen leaves scattered in the wake of her furious steps, and petals fluttered off the trees as she stormed by. She stomped down the cobblestone street, her eyes fixed on the ground, until strong arms grabbed her, pulling her out of the way of an oncoming carriage.

She shook her head out of her daze as the carriage sped past. The moment reminded her of this morning, except she hadn't seen this carriage at all, and the arms were completely different.

The woman's bare arms were strong yet not overly muscled. She wore a bright blue vest with matching leather pants tucked into shiny black boots. Gold bangles with strange markings circled her wrists, and gold chains of different lengths shifted around her neck when she moved. Her leather outfit marked her as someone from the north, but her deep bronze skin implied she might be a native of Isandariyah. However, her pale pink hair thwarted all Alanna's guesses about the woman's ethnicity.

"You saved my life," murmured Alanna, flustered that the words she'd spoken to the man this morning were actually true this time.

The woman set Alanna securely on her feet, then smoothed her pink hair back into her high ponytail. "If those horses had trampled you, your blood would've spilled all over my new boots." Her hot-pink lips quirked into a grin.

Alanna let out her breath in a wild laugh, then swayed on her feet, suddenly light-headed.

The woman took her firmly by the arm, leading her to a stoop and depositing her on the stair. "Are you okay? You're crying." She wiped a soft thumb underneath Alanna's eyes.

The gesture was so reminiscent of Alanna's mother, her tears threatened to drown her again. Instead, she sat up straighter, rubbed her eyes, and pasted a smile on her face. "I'm just grateful for your rescue. I should go."

Before she could stand, the woman tugged her back down. "I think you'll sit here until that lie of a smile is actually true."

Alanna blinked, unsure what to say.

The woman leaned back and pulled a pipe out of her pocket. Alanna watched the woman's unhurried motions with fascination. The woman lit the pipe, took a few small puffs, then offered it to Alanna.

Alanna's eyes widened. "Umm ... No, but thank you."

The woman shrugged, then lounged against the stoop, legs outstretched, as if she didn't have a care in the world. "My name's Geeni."

It took a moment for the words to register. "Geeni?" Alanna repeated the name, trying to give her mind time to catch up.

"Well, it's actually Ginevere, but that's a little too serious for most casual conversations, don't you think?" She winked. "And you are?"

"Alanna." The name popped out of her mouth before she realized what she'd said. It had been years since she had given anyone her real name.

"Alanna," the woman repeated. "A traditional name from La Veridda."

"Um ... I—" She shook her head, trying to pull one of her usual aliases into place, but failing.

Geeni took another slow pull of her pipe. "Many women fled La Veridda when King Ruzgar occupied the country. Asylum granted by the queen saved a lot of lives."

"The queen saved lives, but there was still a cost," Alanna snapped. Then she bit her lip, angry she'd let some of her true feelings slip out.

Geeni raised a single pink eyebrow, then laughed. "No

need to hide your distaste for the queen for my benefit. I disagree with her on quite a few political issues." She exhaled a long trail of smoke. "So, what do you do, Alanna?"

Since all her roles had failed her, she answered with a hint of truth. "I acquire resources from smug men who assume my pretty head doesn't contain a shred of common sense."

Geeni's eyes widened, then she slapped her thigh, laughing loudly. "A girl after my own heart! I assume it's a lucrative business, considering how many men of that sort I've met in my lifetime." She chewed on the end of her pipe absently as she considered Alanna, then she leaned forward suddenly. "Perhaps you can help me with something. I'm in need of an actress."

"Um … I do know a few actresses—"

Geeni chuckled. "I'm not looking for a professional. I'm looking for someone who knows how to hide what she's feeling, and if she has a hint of bitterness toward the queen, then even better. Plus, the job pays well."

Alanna narrowed her eyes. "What's the job?"

"I need someone who can fit into an alias that will allow her to walk freely in the palace. She needs to know how to be funny and charming and utterly sincere."

Alanna raised her own eyebrow. "And?"

Geeni grinned. "She needs to keep her ears open, listening for any interesting rumors." She pointed at Alanna with her pipe. "This actress will need to keep her head while surrounded by seven dreamy men. There's no time for any relationships on this job."

Alanna snorted. She had conned countless men over the years. She was a professional, and there was no way she would fall for someone while she was on the job.

She crossed her arms. "And?"

"And …" Geeni drew out the word. "As she makes her

way deeper into the palace, she will pick up something the queen took from me long ago."

"The queen stole something from you?" Alanna stared at the unusual woman. What could the queen possibly have taken from her?

"Well, not from me personally, but from my family. Bring my family heirloom back to me, and I will grant you anything you wish."

Alanna dropped her voice, suddenly aware of all the random people passing by. "Anything?"

Geeni leaned forward, her jade eyes intense. "What is it you wish for, Alanna?"

She pictured her rickety dresser packed with gold coins, enough to buy a small farm of her own. She imagined a peaceful place with her mother outside on a bench, watching the birds. When her mother turned to look at Alanna, recognition lit up her face, and she smiled.

Alanna whispered, "I wish to be unforgettable."

Geeni's eyes sparkled. "Darling, your wish is my command."

5

After Geeni made her proposition, Alanna stopped by Qira's shrine and offered her sacrifice to the flame as she had promised. She wrote her prayer on a stolen scrap of paper, one of Qira the Trickster's favorite sort of offerings. Her prayer thanked Qira for the quick escape and asked for a sign whether she should take Geeni's job. The dream of finally moving her mother out of the monastery and onto a peaceful farm felt so real, and if Geeni could really offer her that, perhaps the risk of stealing from the queen would be worth it.

She threw the prayer into the fire at the center of the shrine, sweating from the tropical heat and the holy flame. The fire originated at the heart of Qira's volcano and continued to burn thanks to the unceasing offerings of her people. Qira's sister Goddess, Qara the Wise, had her own shrine with her own flame, but from the first moment Alanna stole something to eat, it was clear who her patron Goddess would be.

As she left the shrine, she put on the face of an invisible girl. Not overly happy and innocent, or she'd be seen as a target. Not scowling and purposeful, or she might be seen as a threat. She blended into the crowd, becoming a bland, insignificant girl, losing herself in the rush of people.

She stopped at a street vendor, picking up a meat pie with some of the coins she had stolen. The meat was unidentifiable, but spicy and greasy and absolutely perfect. She leaned against a wall, watching people pass by, wiping the grease off her chin.

Her hand paused midwipe.

At the stall across the street stood a startlingly handsome man. He appeared to be in his late twenties. His skin was slightly paler than her own, a light bronze to her warm brown, and his dark hair curled in loose waves, long enough to brush the stiff collar of his shirt.

The stiff collar was the first unusual thing she noticed. He was dressed in an unbleached linen shirt and a pair of gray work pants a gardener might wear, but something about them seemed off. The pants were just as neatly pressed as his collar. Most laborers didn't take time to press their clothes before work, not even if their work had brought them to the marketplace for the day.

The unusual man leaned over to speak to the older woman selling scarves in her stall. Her wrinkled face lit up, and she clasped his hand warmly. Alanna was too far away to hear their conversation, but the woman told him a long story while the man nodded, a thoughtful expression on his face.

Alanna was so caught up in their exchange, she almost didn't notice the young woman standing right next to her. The young woman sized up the unusual man with a predatory gleam in her eyes.

She didn't blame the young woman for considering it. His strange clothing marked him as someone with money, despite his attempt to hide it. The kindness on his face as he spoke to the old woman proved he could be manipulated if the story was good enough. And the fact he was the most gorgeous man she had seen in her life? Well, that would make the con a downright pleasure.

Even though she recognized the man as an easy mark, it wasn't jealousy that flared to life in her chest, but instead an odd protectiveness. The young woman only took a single step before Alanna grabbed her by the arm, jerking her close enough to whisper in her ear.

"Not that one." She whispered in the darkest, most menacing voice she could. "Walk away now, and I won't have to use this blade pressed against your side."

The young woman's eyes widened, and she gave the man one more hungry look. Alanna growled slightly, squeezing her arm tighter. The young woman sighed in defeat, walking away without a backward glance.

Alanna huffed out her held breath, relieved the girl had fallen for her trick. The "blade" was just a small pair of sewing scissors she kept in her pocket. Even if she had an actual blade, she had no idea how to use it in a fight. Luckily, her bluff had worked before she got herself trapped in a role she couldn't play.

She grinned, savoring her victory of protecting the unusual man, when he dropped the old woman's hand and stared down the street in panic. Alanna followed his gaze to the source of his alarm.

A gray-haired man in billowing black robes walked down the center of the road, flanked by five of the queen's soldiers. The man's dark brown skin marked him as someone from Zaridia—not unusual, since the queen recruited her henchmen from everywhere. His gray braids flowed down the sides of his face, mixing into his long gray beard, which reached nearly to his waist. The soldiers' boots clicked loudly, but it was the regular thudding of the staff held by the black-robed man that sent a spike of fear into

Alanna's heart. He had a heavy presence about him, as if he pulled all the air toward himself, making it hard to breathe.

Alanna could easily slip into the alley a few feet away and disappear before the bearded man even got close. But when she glanced again at the unusual gorgeous man, a terrifying realization clicked into place.

The black-robed man was coming for him.

The odd protectiveness filled her again. She raced across the street, dodging the terrified people scattering to hiding places of their own.

As she approached, the man's eyes flicked from doorway to alley to horse-drawn wagons, finding nowhere to hide. She stepped in front of him, and his eyes snapped to her face.

She caught his soft gasp, then all her thoughts narrowed to his eyes. His irises were the color of twilight, blue with hints of shifting colors on the horizon. His dark eyelashes blinked slowly as he looked at her, and she forgot what she had come to tell him.

A child bumped into her, running to his mother's side, and Alanna's attention widened to the world around her. She remembered the imminent approach of the black-robed man and held out her hand.

"Come with me."

The gorgeous man stared at her extended hand in confusion, but understanding quickly dawned on his face. He looked back into Alanna's eyes, and she was nearly carried away in their twilight depths again.

His hand in hers jerked her fully awake.

"I'll follow wherever you go," he said.

His solemn words startled her, threatening to drown her in his distracting stare again. But instead, she gripped his hand tightly, and they escaped into the secret depths of the city.

6

———————

Alanna had escape routes planned from every location in the city. On occasion, she needed an emergency getaway when a plan went sideways, so she knew every twisting alley and secret staircase that could get her back home safely.

As she towed the handsome stranger along behind her, she realized her mistake. All her escape routes took her home. She led him into the alley behind the theater, but hesitated before showing him the way up.

He didn't know the reason she stopped, but he glanced over his shoulder, studying the road behind them. His dark eyebrows crinkled in concern, and stress tightened the muscles around his lips.

She sighed and made her choice. "Follow me."

His lips quirked up in a heart-stopping grin. "I told you I'd follow wherever you go."

Her breath caught in her lungs, and she tried to blame her inability to breathe on their wild dash through the city. She cleared her throat and began to climb.

The climb wasn't easy. It involved pulling herself up onto window ledges and shimmying along drain pipes before finding the exact handholds that let her climb to the tallest part of the theater. She had briefly considered taking him through the theater's front door and seeing if she could con her way past the director again. But this way, anyone inside the theater could honestly say they hadn't seen him. And no one except Alanna knew the complicated path to the theater's roof.

No one else except this man.

She pulled herself onto the ledge of the roof with him close on her heels. Once they stood safely together on the roof, Alanna grimaced. She hadn't thought beyond escape. She had led a strange man into her private space. What was she supposed to do now?

He spun in a circle, taking in the view of the city on all sides. The theater was one of the taller buildings in the city, but his eyes snagged on the tallest structure of them all.

The queen's palace stood like a gleaming beacon in the late afternoon sun. At this distance, Alanna couldn't see the soldiers who patrolled the castle walls, but they were there. The man turned away with a quick shake of his head. Did the palace remind the man of the soldiers chasing him?

She wanted to ask him about the soldiers and the man in the black robes, but all her questions died on her lips as he took in the view of the rest of the city with a lazy smile. She asked what she needed to know above all else. "What's your name?"

He whirled sharply with a startled expression. "My name ... um ... You can call me Jay."

"Jay." She tested out the name, and he broke into a wide smile.

Her breath hitched. She wanted to hit herself for being so flustered over a guy, but she couldn't stop herself from staring into his eyes again.

"What's your name?" His voice was deep, and resonated with a warmth that made her feel safe.

"Alanna." She breathed out the word on a contented sigh. She bit her lip, cursing herself as a fool for giving out her real name twice in one day.

He whispered, "Thanks for rescuing me, Alanna." His eyes lingered on her lips, and suddenly, the late afternoon sun felt warmer than she ever remembered.

She had led him to her home and given him her actual name. She had not only broken her own strict rules, she had put herself in a situation where she could get taken advantage of.

Taking advantage of lovesick fools was *her* job.

She stepped back, tucking a stray lock of hair behind her ear in an attempt to pull herself together. "It's no big deal."

"Really?" He gave a fake innocent look. "So, you regularly rescue men and lead them up here?"

"What? Of course not!" Her indignant reply caused him to laugh, which stirred the panic rising in her chest.

Of course she didn't bring men up here. She shouldn't have brought him. She needed to put on the familiar character from this morning. That woman was giggly and silly and could get a man to do whatever she wanted, even if what she wanted was for him to leave and forget the location.

She tried to reach for that woman's high-pitched laughter but couldn't find it. The only voice she could find was her own, and that one was unprepared for this situation.

Jay finished his study of the view and walked closer to the aviary.

She grabbed his arm. "Where do you think you are going?"

"I'm just looking around," he said playfully. "Are you hiding secrets up here?"

He slipped out of her grasp and opened the aviary door with a dramatic push. His teasing grin faded as he looked around her room, her old mattress on the floor and the broken scraps of furniture, and realization spread across his face.

"You live here?" he whispered.

Since no one had ever seen her room, she had never been embarrassed about it. Until now. Her lips tightened with a fierce pride. "Don't you dare pity me."

"I don't pity you," he said solemnly, all traces of his grin gone. "I just ... This isn't where I imagined you lived."

She crossed her arms, her rising indignation the first sense of strength she had felt since she rescued him. "And where exactly did you imagine I lived?"

"I guess somewhere similar to where I live ..." His eyes refused to meet hers. "Well, maybe not exactly like where I live."

She started to ask where that was, when Bibi suddenly swung down from her perch overhead. She hung one-handed from a rail that used to be for birds, but had now become Bibi's personal playground.

Jay's startled gasp brought a true laugh to Alanna's lips. It wasn't the fake giggle she usually made around men, and when Jay smiled, her stomach flipped over in a disturbing way.

"Who is this pretty girl?" Jay reached out a careful hand to Bibi, who reached back with her feet and one free hand.

"Keep a firm grip on your jewelry and anything shiny. She's a fancy girl who likes fancy toys," said Alanna with a fond grin at Bibi. Then she mentally kicked herself for admitting something so close to the truth about her profession.

Jay didn't seem to notice anything strange about Alanna's confession. Instead, he pulled something out of his pocket and handed it to Bibi. Alanna couldn't tell what it was, but Bibi released her grip and hopped over to her glittery shrine, turning the object over and over in her hands.

Jay giving a gift to Bibi warmed Alanna's heart in a way she hadn't expected. She walked inside to hide her face, her feelings a confusing mess. A gorgeous man was standing in her doorway, and she had no idea what to do. What did normal people do in situations like this?

"Can I offer you something to drink?" The words felt foreign to her, probably because she had never spoken them in her life.

He turned to her with a graceful smile. "That would be lovely. Thank you."

She handed him a glass of water from her small pitcher. She watched him drink, unsure what to do next.

He looked at her over the top of the glass, slowly lowering it. "Aren't you going to have some, too?"

Heat flooded her cheeks as she stared at the glass in his hand. "That's my only glass."

His mouth dropped open, but he recovered quickly. "Thank you for sharing it with me."

As he handed it back to her, his fingers brushed against hers with a shock, and she dropped the glass.

Jay dove for it, barely catching the glass before it hit the ground. He smiled up at her, clearly relieved her single glass was still in one piece. A lump formed in her throat at the sight of him crouched on the floor in his neatly pressed work clothes, so obviously not what he seemed, so not like her at all. She pushed past him and walked outside to watch the sun's slow descent toward the horizon.

The glass clinked as he set it down carefully, and he

ducked out the aviary door. He didn't speak, just observed the sunset at her side.

The sky had shifted from blue to golden pink when she finally spoke. "I don't know who you are, but it's obvious you're pretending to be something you are not."

He raised an eyebrow. "What makes you say that?"

She laid out the facts as if she were a magistrate passing judgment. "You wear the clothes of a laborer, but they haven't seen a bit of labor in their life. The style is nondescript. Almost *too* nondescript. It would be better if your clothes definitively marked you as a gardener or a plumber or a street sweeper. Then when people see you, they would know exactly where you belong. Once you fall into a neat category, you become invisible." She eyed his clothing critically. "These clothes are too generic, so it's unclear where you fit."

He appeared to hold his breath for several moments, then whispered, "It's unclear where I fit ..." He stared at her as if she had uncovered something deeply personal about him, despite her point being the exact opposite.

"Who are you?" she asked.

His eyes tracked the sun as it sank behind the tallest towers of the palace. "Have you ever wanted to be someone else? Just for a single day?"

"I dream about being someone else every single day." She had never said the words out loud before, and her honesty confused her so much she couldn't meet his eyes.

The silence between them grew. She'd revealed so much about herself in one sentence. She felt more exposed than when she led him onto the roof, than when he saw her mattress on the floor, than when he held her only glass. She had laid bare her heart to a total stranger, and she didn't know how to escape.

She felt him watching her, his quiet presence begging

her to look at him. She was afraid to meet his gaze, fearing she would find pity. He lifted a hand to her chin, slowly tilting her face until their eyes connected.

Clicking boots and the slow thudding of a staff rang through the street in front of the theater.

Alanna and Jay both dropped to the ground, crawling to peer over the facade's edge to the street below.

The gray-bearded man and his soldiers stopped in the middle of the street. People scattered out of his way, but he barely glanced at them.

Alanna's whisper was the faintest trickle of air. "Who is he?"

"He's the queen's royal advisor." Jay's eyes were locked on the black-robed man. "Some believe he is a wizard."

"A wizard?" Alanna studied the man's wrinkled face, trying to detect any signs of magic. "Magic is real?"

Jay narrowed his eyes at the wizard. "I guess that depends on who you ask."

Just then, the wizard's eyes flicked upward, directly to where the two of them crouched.

They both pulled away from the edge, shifting to lean back against the facade with a thump. Alanna drew in a sharp breath as she imagined the wizard invading the roof, her room ... and then dragging Jay off for his nefarious plans.

A storm of anger roared to life in her chest. Her heart had already been battered by the flood of emotions of the day, but now her heart was a whirlwind that couldn't be contained. She would protect Jay from that wizard, no matter the cost.

She turned her focus from the storm in her chest to the literal storm brewing overhead. The previously clear sky swirled with a sudden tempest. She risked a glance over the facade; the few people who hadn't already run from the wizard huddled in doorways.

The wizard waited in the middle of the whirlwind, his black robes billowing around him, as calm as if he were the storm itself. The longer Alanna watched, the fiercer the wind grew, until his soldiers could barely stand in the rough winds. But the wizard remained firmly planted, his staff rooted to the spot.

Jay got to his feet and glared at the wizard. Alanna was mesmerized as Jay struck a regal pose, his hair barely ruffled by the wind at all.

The wizard narrowed his eyes, then nodded. He faced the raging wind and strode away from the theater, the soldiers staggering at his side. At the end of the street, the wizard turned for one last look. He shook his head, but continued walking, and the wind faded into a soft breeze of relief.

The lingering breeze wrapped around Alanna, sending a cool chill down her neck. Jay turned toward her, and the last trace of wind blew through his dark curls before flying away.

Alanna could barely breathe as the people found their way back into the street, talking about the strange storm. She drew a ragged breath. "Did that wizard send a storm to attack us?"

Jay eyed her, appearing to weigh his words carefully. "I don't think that storm was attacking us."

She rubbed her arms, trying to warm herself after the chill wind. "It sure felt like an attack."

Jay's eyes traced the street where the wizard had walked, then glanced up at the palace. "I should go," he said abruptly.

Alanna had wanted him to leave from the first moment

he stepped on the roof, but now, she was reluctant to see him go. "What if he finds you and sends another storm?"

He looked at her as if seeing her for the first time. "Thank you for rescuing me, Alanna. I hope we meet again someday." He took her hand in his, then bowed, pressing a delicate kiss against it.

Before she had time to register the shock of the unexpected kiss, he had swung his leg over the side of the roof, climbing back down the way they'd come. Once he was out of sight, she went inside, sinking onto her mattress with a sigh, and touched the back of her hand with gentle fingers.

She kicked herself for being a foolish girl. Sighing over a boy was ridiculous, and she needed to get over it and get back to work.

She considered the job Geeni had offered. A job in the palace was more risky than her usual quick cons, and the consequences of being discovered trying to steal from the queen would be severe. Plus the queen's royal advisor was apparently a wizard. The sudden storm that had formed around him sent a spike of terror through her heart.

Geeni had told her if she wanted the job, to meet her at the dress shop closest to the palace the following morning. The strange woman's proposition was just too risky, so tomorrow Alanna would avoid the area around the palace entirely. She would continue as she had before, charming unsuspecting men out of their money.

Bibi hopped down beside her on the mattress, still playing with the gift from Jay.

Alanna sat up and held out her hand. "What shiny thing did he give you, Bibi?"

The monkey reluctantly handed her the bright silver coin.

Alanna grinned. "Silver, eh? He must have thought you were a pretty girl to give you a full silver piece." She flipped the coin in the air, caught it and placed it faceup on her palm. Unlike gold pieces stamped with the likeness of the queen, each silver coin was stamped with the face of one of her seven sons.

She peered closer at the face on the coin, and jerked back. How had she not noticed it earlier? The strong line of his jaw and his soft curls, perfectly captured in smooth silver. Her mouth fell open, and Bibi took the chance to steal back the coin.

The coin marked with the face of Prince Jaemin.

She leaned back onto her old mattress, a slow smile spreading over her lips. Qira the Trickster had given her a sign. She would take Geeni's job after all.

PART II

7

_____

As Alanna drew closer to the dress shop, the shadow of the palace loomed. The soaring towers of glittering quartz blocked out the sun rising in the distance, and the cool shadow sent a shiver of doubt into her mind. She didn't know what she was getting herself into. Had she made this decision in haste? She hesitated outside the dress shop, but before she could open the door, Geeni flew out and dragged Alanna in. Bibi barely had time to hop inside before Geeni closed the door behind them.

The dress shop's shades were shut, and the room was dimly lit, with only a few candles burning. Mannequins in ball gowns stood at attention throughout the otherwise empty room.

Geeni grabbed a pale pink corset and a pile of petticoats off a countertop and tossed them to Alanna. "We don't have much time, so I hope you are skilled at lacing up a corset quickly."

"Um ... Geeni, I'm not sure ..."

Geeni's jade eyes locked on hers. "You have questions I can answer, however, we have a ticking clock here. If there's a chance you want this job, you need to start dressing and ask your questions as we go, okay?"

Alanna ran her fingers across the pink corset and petticoats in her arms, the clothing more delicate and beautiful than any costume she had ever worn. It couldn't hurt to put it on while she discovered more about the job. She stepped out of her simple clothing and pulled on the first layer of undergarments, checking herself in the large mirror. "What exactly is my job?"

"Your job is precisely what I told you before. You keep your ears open for any interesting gossip and take back what was stolen from me." Geeni leaned against the counter and began packing tobacco into her pipe. Bibi hopped onto the counter and fidgeted with the blue ribbon around her neck as she watched Geeni's movements with fascination.

Alanna fastened the corset hooks, one after the other. "And what exactly am I stealing? Is this some precious treasure that will get me killed?"

Geeni struck a match and lit her pipe with a gentle puff. "It's precious to me, but most people would consider it common." She coaxed the tobacco into a warm ember, then surveyed Alanna with serious eyes. "It's a book."

Alanna's hands stilled on her corset. "A book? You want me to sneak in and steal a book?"

Geeni grinned. "Simple enough, right? Just a little book the queen keeps in the family library deep within the palace. You'll have to be charming enough to win an invitation inside. Think you can do that?"

Alanna huffed, flipping her black hair over her shoulder. "That's all? Listen for gossip, charm my way into the family library, and steal a book?"

Geeni strode to Alanna's back and tugged her corset strings tight. She bit her pipe between her teeth so she could speak around it. "That's all. In return, I will pay you well and make all your wishes come true." She winked at Alanna in the mirror.

Alanna exhaled sharply as Geeni tugged the corset and knotted the laces firmly in place. As Alanna wiggled, trying to settle her bits into more comfortable positions, Geeni grabbed a pink taffeta gown off a mannequin and commanded, "Arms up!"

Alanna raised her arms obediently as Geeni lowered the sparkling dress over her head. She had thought Geeni might sneak her in as a chambermaid or a serving girl, but as she swam through the layers of skirts, nausea rose in her chest. She spoke loudly from inside the cloud of taffeta. "You said you had an alias for me. Who exactly am I supposed to be?"

Geeni settled the shimmering pink fabric over Alanna's shoulders, then set to work on the row of tiny buttons along her spine. She peeked over Alanna's shoulder in the mirror and said around her pipe, "You're a princess, of course."

Alanna had been running her fingers across the shining fabric and suddenly stopped. "Excuse me?"

Geeni finished with the buttons, then circled Alanna, examining her work. "You're a princess. Princess Aliyabeth of Naermore, to be exact."

Alanna blinked at her stupidly before finally finding her voice. "I look nothing like the people of Naermore! No one will believe I'm their princess."

Geeni raised an eyebrow. "It's your job to make them believe, sweetheart."

"But surely someone in the palace has met this princess before. It will be obvious I'm not her!" She couldn't bring herself to confess she had just met Prince Jaemin the day prior, and he wouldn't believe Alanna was a princess for a moment.

"No one in this queendom has met Princess Aliyabeth. She's a notorious recluse. When the queen sent a letter requesting her presence, everyone expected her to decline." Geeni stage-whispered, as if letting Alanna in on a joke. "She actually did decline. However, her polite letter of refusal was intercepted and swapped with a polite letter of acceptance." Geeni reached into her bag and pulled out an ashtray.

"But—"

"And you will pass as a princess of Naermore, thanks to this." Geeni dug deeper in her bag and retrieved a small oil lamp. She handed it to Alanna with a flourish.

Alanna held the strange gold lamp closer to the light. One side was marked with a curious symbol shimmering almost as if wet. The other side had three smaller symbols, glistening with their own light. "What in Qira's name is—"

"That is a clever piece of magic, so please treat it properly."

Alanna's fingers reflexively pulled away from the lamp, until she was holding the handle between her thumb and forefinger. Bibi hopped onto her shoulder to get a closer look.

Geeni rolled her eyes. "It's not going to bite you. In fact, I think once you see what it does, you'll fall in love with this little lamp."

"What does it do?" she whispered.

"It's the last piece of your costume. All you have to do is rub a tear onto one of the three small runes." She nodded at Alanna. "Try it."

"A tear?" Alanna stared at the odd markings in confusion.

"Yes, a tear. Hurry it up. We don't have much time." Geeni sighed dramatically. "I'd pinch you to speed up the process, but unfortunately the tear has to be authentic, and not from torture." She shrugged.

Alanna wasn't one to cry often, although the day before

44

she had cried multiple times. First, in relief from escaping the horrible theater director, and second, in bittersweet joy at hearing her mother say how much she loved her daughter. The emotions were still so close to the surface that the tears sprang naturally to her eyes.

Geeni grinned. "Perfect. Now rub it on the first small rune. Don't worry about the big rune. It's already active and working." At Alanna's hesitation, Geeni dropped her voice to a hypnotic whisper. "Aren't you just a little bit curious, dear? You've never seen magic like this before. Don't you want to know what it feels like?"

A tear traveled down Alanna's cheek, but she still hesitated.

"Come on, sweetie," whispered Geeni. "This is your chance for your wish to come true."

Alanna bit her lip, then before she could second-guess herself, swiped a thumb across her cheek and rubbed the tear into the first of the three small runes. She thought her tear would cause the rune to shine more, but instead, its glow faded until it looked like a regular carving.

She nearly dropped the lamp as a burning sensation sizzled across her skin. Bibi jumped off her shoulder with a squeak. Alanna squeezed her eyes shut and tried to breathe through the pain, but she could barely suck in a breath thanks to her corset. She rubbed her hands violently up and down her arms, trying to wipe away the prickle of sparks across her skin, when suddenly the sensation stopped, as if a heavy cloth had settled over her.

When she opened her eyes, she discovered a stranger in the mirror. Her sleek black hair was now strawberry blond, and her copper eyes, so much like her mother's, were a soft lavender. She touched her cheek, surprised when the pale hand in the mirror followed her movements. She blinked, trying to reconcile the new image with herself.

Geeni clapped her hands. "How perfect! I'm not sure if you look exactly like the actual princess, but since no one else knows what she looks like either, you'll be fine!" She laughed as she plucked a pair of silver slippers off a shelf and set them at Alanna's feet. "Step in. It's almost time for you to go."

"Time to go?" Alanna said the words, then clapped a hand to her throat, shocked at the difference in her voice.

Geeni pressed her ear against the closed door, and a smile lit up her face. "Your procession is on its way."

"My procession?" Alanna rubbed a hand over her perfectly smooth blond hair, then looked around frantically. "Where's Bibi?"

Geeni gave a cursory glance around the room while Alanna spun wildly. "Bibi! Where are you?" As she turned, a white cat stumbled out from under her dress. The cat shook her head and sat up on her haunches.

The white cat had a blue ribbon around her neck.

"Bibi?" whispered Alanna.

Geeni laughed in delight. "How unexpected! A cat is a much more appropriate pet for a princess, so well done, little one!"

Alanna bent to look at her transformed monkey, when the front door of the shop opened, and a young woman dressed as a high-class lady's maid rushed inside. "They're coming!" She tugged at her dress as if it was new, and smoothed her fingers across her windblown blond hair, tucking it neatly into place.

Alanna cocked her head, trying to remember how she knew the woman.

Geeni gripped the woman's shoulders, presenting her to Alanna. "Princess Aliyabeth of Naermore, here is the new lady's maid I hired for you."

The young woman appeared to be in her early twenties,

close to Alanna's age, and she sank into a lovely curtsy. "Princess Aliyabeth. It is my honor to serve you."

Alanna opened her mouth to reply, suddenly aware of how she knew the woman.

Geeni jumped in smoothly. "I found her at the local theater. I told her about the attack on your caravan and how you needed a new attendant so you wouldn't be disgraced showing up all alone."

Alanna shut her mouth, unsure what to say to that.

Geeni gave another of her loud secretive whispers. "Yes, I already gave her half the pay in advance, so there's no need to worry about her telling anyone she is an actress."

The young woman ducked her head and smiled. "My name is Hidalsa. It's an honor to meet a real princess. We have seven princes, but no princesses in the queendom."

Geeni ushered Hidalsa to the door. "Wait outside, dear, and be ready when it's time to go."

Hidalsa nodded and slipped outside. Before the door shut, the approaching thump of the bass drum and blaring trumpets rattled the shop. Alanna spun to discover Geeni at her back, holding up a pair of long gloves.

"Wear these at all times." Geeni's voice was stern. "This magic is just an illusion. It's like a bubble of light that can be popped with the softest touch. You must use your ability to charm, but without your usual ... physical methods. No one should touch a princess against her will anyway, so make sure you don't let any of those adorable princes woo you, do you understand?"

"Woo me?" she spluttered.

"Even though the queen has remained unmarried, it doesn't mean she intends for her sons to remain the same. There's a reason the queen summoned Princess Aliyabeth. She's one of the few eligible princesses in the world. But if one of those princes touches your skin ... Poof." She mimed an explosion. "It's back to Alanna, and your cover is blown. The lamp has two more small runes to change you back into the princess, but I don't recommend letting anyone see you use it."

Alanna's mouth dropped open as she hurriedly tugged on the gloves. "You didn't think to mention this earlier?"

The trumpets and drums were getting louder, along with the cheering of a crowd. Alanna dashed to the window and pulled aside the curtain. A parade marched down the center of the wide road leading to the palace.

In addition to two rows of trumpeters and a line of bass drums, gymnasts tumbled down the road and fire-breathers spouted flame. Jugglers darted across the street, tossing balls and pins and random objects they borrowed from the crowd. Five horse-drawn carriages sparkled gold in the morning sunlight, and the one closest to the shop opened its door as it progressed slowly down the thoroughfare.

"That's your ride." Geeni grabbed Alanna by the elbow, careful to avoid the small bit of skin showing on Alanna's upper arms. She opened the door and pushed Alanna toward Hidalsa, and the maid bustled Alanna and her monkey-cat into the carriage.

Before Hidalsa could close the door, Alanna leaned out and hissed at Geeni, "What is all this?"

Geeni's lip curled in a smug grin. "I'm granting your wish, darling. You are now truly unforgettable." She winked and snapped the carriage door shut.

8

Alanna sat unmoving, her unfamiliar skin barely holding her together. She considered jumping out of the carriage, popping the bubble of magic around her, then heading back to her regular life. Pretending to be a princess was ridiculous. If she could just grab Bibi and get away ...

Bibi perched awkwardly on the seat next to her. The strange monkey-cat seemed just as uncomfortable in her new skin as Alanna. Bibi tried to rest on her haunches like she did as a monkey but kept falling over with every bump in the road. The monkey needed to learn how to play the role of a cat, but not as badly as Alanna needed to figure out the role of princess.

Alanna twirled a strand of her now strawberry blond hair around her gloved finger. She had worn a lot of wigs in her life, but this didn't even compare.

"Your hair is beautiful, Princess," sighed Hidalsa.

Alanna looked up at the woman's bright blond hair. "So, are you originally from Naermore?" asked Alanna carefully.

Hidalsa laughed. "No, I was born here in Isandariyah. I

recently dyed my hair blond for a role, which is why Geeni picked me."

"Geeni is very clever." Alanna's finger twisted her hair into a knot.

"I'd like to play the maid as a country girl, if that's okay with you, Princess?"

"What are you talking about?"

"My character, the maid. I think she's originally from the country, which means I don't need to answer complicated questions about Naermore. My character is overwhelmed by the splendor of Isandariyah, obsessed with making you look beautiful because she gets to bask in your glory ... That's my image of the character. If you approve, of course, Princess."

Alanna grabbed hold of her words as if she were drowning. "Fascinating. And how would you play the role of a princess?"

"I actually did play the role of a princess before." Hidalsa's face lit up with the opportunity to share her knowledge of the craft, but she spoke hesitantly. "Of course, I'm sure all princesses are different, but my character was supremely regal—it was all about how she carried herself. As if she was completely comfortable with the power she held. If she didn't have something important to say, she didn't speak at all. Sometimes a haughty glance was more powerful than words. And she was confident. She expected everyone to fall in love with her, and they did."

Alanna closed her eyes and allowed the character to take shape in her mind. "I can do that," she breathed.

"What did you say, Princess?"

Alanna's eyes shot open, and she was suddenly the princess. "It sounds like you did your research. I'm sure you played the role well." She gave her lady's maid a benevolent nod.

Hidalsa ducked her head to hide her proud grin.

The carriage rolled to a stop as Alanna finished wrapping the character around her like armor. She allowed her maid to exit the carriage first as she smoothed down her dress and adjusted her gloves.

Bibi hopped out of the carriage unaided. Alanna wasn't sure what would happen if someone touched the monkey-cat. Would the magic around her pop like it would if someone touched Alanna? Luckily, cats had very strong rules regarding petting and consent, so hopefully Bibi could wander as she pleased.

A man in uniform held out a hand and helped Alanna descend the small step to the ground, as the other carriages pulled to a stop and began unloading trunks.

"Don't worry, Princess," whispered her maid. "The other carriages have the gifts from your kingdom and all your dresses." She gave Alanna a thoughtful glance. "I'm sure some things were lost when your caravan was attacked, but Miss Geeni said she accounted for everything you need."

Alanna wanted to mumble about Geeni, but instead, she said regally, "I'm sure she prepared everything."

Hidalsa took a step back, allowing Alanna to survey the palace. She craned her neck to stare at the towers soaring overhead and whispered to herself, "Palaces are completely normal places to live. Just a regular home." She gathered her skirts and walked up the wide stone steps leading inside.

As her foot landed on the top step, uniformed soldiers pushed open the heavy doors to the grand throne room. Alanna didn't swing her head from side to side to study the beautiful room, though she desperately wanted to. Massive columns lined the long corridor, framing stained glass windows. She couldn't make out the intricate artwork without turning her head, but the morning sunlight through the glass cast colorful patterns on the white marble floor. She kept her head lifted and stepped on the colors as if the marble were a common road beneath her feet.

A dozen courtiers studied her, and two dozen guards in ceremonial uniforms stood at attention, but Alanna focused on the three men on the dais. She recognized their faces from the silver coins pressed with their images.

Prince Jaemin was the oldest of all seven princes, though only three were in attendance today. He wore a navy blue uniform jacket with a white ceremonial sash across the front, a sword in a decorative scabbard at his waist. His dark hair curled in thick waves resting gently on his high collar, and his twilight eyes never wavered as she made her leisurely entrance through the throne room. He stood as if he were king, even though no one in the queendom would dare whisper that word.

The prince to his right wasn't in uniform, but wore a long sleek coat as was the fashion. The dark green fabric brought out his emerald green eyes, and his thick black hair was longer than his brother's, curling softly against his golden brown cheeks. His gaze also didn't waver, although his lips curled into a smirk as she approached.

The prince to Jaemin's left was obviously the youngest. Alanna remembered the celebration of his eighteenth birthday just a few months prior. A grand festival had been thrown celebrating the queen's youngest son coming of age, though there'd been a hint of unspoken concern running through the whole event: eighteen years had passed since the queen's last child was born, and none of those children were girls. Despite the shadow of an uncertain inheritance, the youngest prince looked as lively in person as he did on the banners flown throughout the city. His red hair was tousled just enough to be delightful, and his honey-colored eyes twinkled.

Alanna approached the foot of the dais, breathing in the

illusion of confidence she stole from the princes before her. She dipped her head in the smallest of curtsies, then met Prince Jaemin's eyes and froze.

He really was stunning. She couldn't believe she hadn't picked him out as a prince the moment she saw him in the marketplace. She should have seen it. Although, he'd looked completely different yesterday.

Yesterday, he'd actually smiled.

His eyes narrowed as he studied her, as if he was picking out her individual flaws. It was completely different from the way he'd looked at her the day before, and it set her immediately on edge. Who was he to judge her?

Oh yes … He was a prince.

But she was a princess. At least, on the surface she was. And she needed to make sure he believed it.

She spoke in a clear, ringing voice. "Thank you for your warm welcome, Your Highnesses."

Prince Jaemin's lips tightened a touch. Perhaps he realized he hadn't welcomed her at all yet. He recovered quickly, giving a small bow. "Welcome to Isandariyah, Princess Aliyabeth."

Her new name on his lips sent a shiver of panic down her legs, but she didn't let it show on her face. "This is a beautiful queendom. How disappointing the queen isn't here for me to tell her myself."

Prince Jaemin shifted uncomfortably. "The queen is attending to other matters today, but she asked me to welcome you and give you a tour of the palace."

Alanna blinked. "A tour? Already?" Could it be that easy? Would he let her into the family library today so she could grab Geeni's book and get out?

The emerald-eyed prince to his right smacked Jaemin casually on the arm. "She just got here, Brother Prince. Give her some time to get settled." He made his way down the steps, his movements that of a tiger stalking its prey. He bowed smoothly, taking her hand in his. His eyes flicked up to meet hers as his lips brushed gently across her gloved hand.

She raised an eyebrow in appreciation of his slick technique. Now this was the sort of man she knew how to work with.

He straightened, but didn't drop her hand. "I can show you to your room, if you'd like."

Her lips twitched, but she controlled her smile at his not-so-subtle invitation. This was exactly the type of opportunity she could use to her advantage. "Well, aren't you charming."

He gave her a rakish grin. "They say I'm the most charming prince, but you can call me Hawthorne."

"Noted," she said with a playful smile.

Jaemin cleared his throat. "Thank you for giving our guest such a warm welcome, brother. I'm sure—"

The youngest prince hopped down from the dais and gently took Alanna's hand away from Hawthorne. He also placed a kiss on her gloved hand, though it felt much less lascivious. "Welcome to Isandariyah. I'm Finn."

"A pleasure to meet you," she said lightly. "Anything I should know about you, Prince Finn?"

He grinned, and his honey eyes sparkled. "If you get overwhelmed with your princessly obligations, I'm the one who can show you all the hidden staircases so you can escape."

She disguised her shock with a ladylike cough. "Hidden staircases? How ... intriguing." She had imagined herself sneaking through secret passageways to find the family library on her own. How did she get so lucky meeting these two princes first?

Prince Jaemin sighed, then stepped down from the dais

to stand between his two brothers. He gave his brothers and the princess a disapproving look. "I'm sure you would like to get settled in your room, Princess Aliyabeth. I will have a servant direct you there."

She looked into his twilight eyes, finding no warmth in their depths. "You're different than I recall …"

His forehead crinkled in confusion. "We haven't met before, Princess."

She nearly choked. How had she let her character slip so easily? She laughed lightly. "I mean, different than I expected."

Jaemin narrowed his eyes, his long lashes unblinking. Alanna squashed the foolish fluttering of her heart over those twilight eyes. Perhaps the other princes were easier targets to get to her goal quickly.

"If you have more *important* things to do, Prince Jaemin, feel free to leave me in the capable hands of your brothers." She gave them both her most winning smile.

Jaemin smiled, but it didn't reach his eyes. "Don't tire yourself, Princess. There are still several more princes for you to pursue."

Hawthorne and Finn both looked at Jaemin with shocked expressions, but Alanna merely tilted her head like a serpent preparing to strike.

"I'm here at the invitation of the queen." Alanna straightened her shoulders and poured all the dignity she possessed into her words. "I traveled across half the world to get here, and now, you are trying to shuffle me off to my room so you can attend to more important matters."

Prince Jaemin lifted his hands. "I didn't mean—"

She enjoyed the powerful feeling of making a prince squirm, so she decided to play the role to the fullest. "If you had traveled the long road to my father's kingdom, I would have devoted all my time to making you feel welcome." She sighed dramatically. "I guess princes are a lot different from princesses."

As soon as the words left her mouth, she winced internally. She had taken the role too far. All three princes stiffened as if she had punched them. Princess Aliyabeth might not understand the complexities of matrilineal succession in a queendom with an aging queen who had only birthed princes, but Alanna had no excuse. She knew exactly what her words meant to them.

She opened her mouth, then shut it, unsure if princesses apologized. Jaemin's eyes hardened, and he stared at her, unwilling to break the awkward silence she'd caused.

Alanna wilted under his glare but covered it by brushing back a lock of her strawberry blond hair with an elegant gloved hand. "Perhaps I will retire to my room for a while."

Jaemin nodded once but didn't speak—merely summoning a servant with a raised hand. The servant hurried over and curtsied to Alanna before leading her out of the throne room. Alanna spared one last glance over her shoulder. Hawthorne and Finn gave her guarded smiles, but Jaemin's twilight eyes followed her like shadows on a gloomy night.

She blew out a sigh and whispered to herself, "I guess it could have gone worse."

9

I f Alanna had been alone, she might have spent the entire day inside. Carved mahogany lined three walls of her sitting room, with the other side an open balcony that overlooked the city. Her maid ran to the balcony, pointing at the theater in the distance. The princess nodded regally as if indulging her, but Alanna couldn't stop staring at the theater either. It had been the center of her world for most of her life, and from the height of a castle tower, it looked so small.

When she spotted the monastery where her mother lived, she stepped away from the balcony to hide her misty eyes. Her mother wouldn't miss her weekly visits, because the scholar didn't even know Alanna existed. If her mother missed anyone, it was seven-year-old Alanna, and there was no fixing that.

Alanna wanted to rifle through the trunks stacked neatly around the room to see what Geeni had sent along with her, but it didn't seem proper behavior for a princess to gawk over her own treasures. She nibbled daintily on sugared pineapple and sipped tangerine water from a gold-etched glass and pretended like that was normal. She reclined on a turquoise chaise lounge, wondering just what princesses did all day.

Her lady's maid looked at her as if she wondered the same thing. As an actress, she had no idea what royalty was like behind closed doors, which worked in Alanna's favor. But unfortunately, it also meant she was counting on Alanna to tell her what to do.

They stared at each other for several long moments, then Alanna stood abruptly. "I'm going to stroll through the palace."

The maid stepped forward eagerly. "Should I accompany you?"

"No!" Alanna took a little breath, trying to cover her jumpy response. "I don't require an escort. You may stay here and sort through the trunks. Hang up all the dresses and fluff them and ... whatever." She waved her hand casually as if she didn't care, but honestly, she knew how hard it was to get wrinkles out of satin.

Alanna hastened to the door, but her maid caught her with one last question. "You don't require anything else?"

Alanna reached into the pockets within her voluminous pink dress, her knuckles brushing against the little lamp inside. It was the only item she'd brought that held a clue to who she truly was. She looked onto the balcony, where Bibi relaxed in a patch of sunlight. Alanna was glad to see her finally exhibiting catlike behavior, though Bibi was sprawled in a strange way, even for a cat.

"I have all I need." She nodded regally, then slipped out the door.

Alanna strode confidently down the hall, glancing, but not gawking, at the beautiful tapestries and exquisite artwork. Servants bowed, then bustled out of her way. She should keep a peaceful, haughty expression, but she couldn't stop a little grin from curving her lips. Geeni's plan was insane, but Alanna had to admit it was exhilarating.

She had no real destination in mind, but the royal family drew her up short. Their family portrait was ten feet wide and surrounded by an ornate gold frame. The painting looked new—perhaps a celebration of the youngest prince's coming of age. The artist had captured how unique the princes looked: besides their individual clothing choices, their eyes, hair, and even skin covered an entire spectrum. Which made sense, considering they each had a different father from kingdoms far and near. The only trait they all had in common was an intensity to their eyes that they inherited from their mother.

Queen Illorienne sat on a throne in the center of the portrait, and her intense green eyes seemed to follow Alanna as she moved. The queen's reddish-brown hair twisted in elaborate curls atop her head and cascaded around her long golden brown neck. Nestled in her hair rested an intricate gold crown with a fat emerald right in the center.

The princes wore no crowns.

The queen was a direct descendant of the First Queen, Twice Blessed: the queen who'd won blessings from both Sister Goddesses, and then founded Isandariyah. The crown had been passed down from mother to daughter for over a thousand years.

The people of Isandariyah often made snide comments about kingdoms who passed their inheritance down to their sons. If the king was responsible for creating heirs, all it took was one unfaithful queen in the line, and the bloodline would be lost, and no one would even know. Isandariyans knew their queen was a direct descendant of the First Queen because it didn't matter who the father was if the new queen came from the former.

Previous queens had chosen to marry one man, but Queen Illorienne was ... unusual. When one consort failed to provide her with a female heir, she moved quickly on to the next. Her ability to spot handsome consorts had led to a diverse family of gorgeous princes, but ultimately, no princesses.

Despite the queen's magnetic presence, Alanna couldn't stop her eyes from traveling to Prince Jaemin. He was first-born and stood at the queen's right hand in the dark blue uniform of the Queen's Guard. Everything about him seemed precise—a perfect representation of discipline. His twilight eyes held the same intensity as the queen's, but Alanna had seen how gentle they could be. She brushed her fingers across the back of her hand as she remembered his soft kiss after they fled from the wizard.

"Princess Aliyabeth," said a deep voice behind her.

She spun, dropping her hands to her sides. As if she had conjured the wizard with a thought, he was there. She reflexively grabbed the lamp in her pocket to remind her of her new identity and felt a momentary disorientation as if putting the disguise back on. In her memory, she had been herself, and the wizard's presence jolted her back into her new body.

"Forgive me for startling you, Princess." He bowed his gray head in supplication, and as he straightened, he smoothed a hand down his long gray beard. "I am Drazen, the queen's advisor. I heard you were wandering alone, and I wanted to ensure you didn't get lost."

Drazen's dark brown hand shifted on his staff. What had looked like a smooth piece of wood from the top of the theater, up close was an intricately carved work of art. Flowers and vines and woodland creatures wound playfully around the dark wood staff, and it was topped with a rough-cut crystal. Alanna found the staff both beautiful and terrifying.

She rested a delicate hand against her chest and gave a tittering laugh she hoped sounded innocent. "I admit you did startle me. The castle is so beautiful that it's easy to get distracted."

His dark brown eyes studied her, and she was struck with a fear that if she met his gaze, he would see through her magical disguise. Did Geeni know the queen's advisor was a wizard? Perhaps the woman should have found someone who looked like the princess, instead of relying on magic.

"Would you like me to escort you back to your room, Princess? You seem … distressed." His cool eyes bored into her, and she felt as if he could see below her pale freckled skin to the golden brown skin below.

She swallowed, then gave another tittering laugh. "Perhaps that is best. It has been a long day."

He bowed his head and silently offered her his arm. With deliberate slowness, she forced herself to place her gloved hand on his arm.

Their walk back to her room was quiet other than the tap of his staff on the marble floors, and the soft swish of her dress and his black robes. Once he stopped at her door, she gently removed her gloved hand.

"Thank you for escorting me back," she said with extreme politeness.

"I'm sure we will see each other again soon." His dark eyes examined her, and his eyebrows drew together. "You are quite … puzzling."

She held her breath, afraid moving would shift her disguise.

"Enjoy your afternoon, Princess." He bowed and stepped

back, unashamedly waiting for her to go inside and close the door.

She squared her shoulders and bravely turned her back to him as she opened the door. Her full skirt was last to clear the door, then Alanna shut it with a *click* of relief.

She sagged against the door, trying to catch her breath. Her maid ran up to assist her, but Alanna stilled her with a raised hand. She closed her eyes and reformed her character around her before she opened her eyes. Hidalsa studied her while anxiously twisting her apron.

Alanna had barely devised an order to give her, when a knock sounded through the door at her back. She straightened quickly and waved the maid away. This time, she would meet Drazen with confidence. She yanked the door open, then stumbled, spoiling her composure.

It was Prince Jaemin.

His eyes widened, whether in surprise that she opened her own door, or from the strange expression on her face, she wasn't sure. Alanna looked both ways down the hall, surprised not to see black robes turning a corner. Jaemin blinked, then glanced left and right, following her movements.

She sucked in a breath, suddenly aware there was a prince on her doorstep, and she had left him waiting.

"I'm sorry, Prince Jaemin. I thought you were Drazen."

"Drazen? The queen's advisor?" Jaemin's wide eyes narrowed. "What business do you have with him?"

Alanna opened her mouth to reply she wanted nothing to do with a wizard, but Jaemin's look was so suspicious, she snapped her mouth shut. She feared any explanation she offered might sound even more suspicious to the prince, who had no reason to trust her.

She needed to flip the script to get back in control. "Did you need something, Prince Jaemin?" She took a line from her breathless character that distracted foolish men while she stole their coin. "I'm happy to assist with any of your ... needs." She fluttered her lashes as she looked up sweetly.

The words effectively threw him off his line of questioning, and he took a step back. "I ... um ... That's not—" He cleared his throat and tugged his uniform jacket as if getting himself under control. "I'm here to invite you to dine with me—to dine with *us*. My brothers will be there."

Usually, her targets jumped at that line, and it was up to her to escape before they took her up on it. However, the prince ducked his head and wouldn't meet her eyes. She swore she could detect a faint blush coloring his bronze cheeks.

She found him adorable.

As much as she would enjoy trying to make him blush again, she didn't think it was appropriate behavior for a princess.

"I would love to join you." She tried to keep her voice proper and not seductive, but she definitely had more practice at the latter. "I look forward to it."

He gave one precise nod, then turned on his heel and walked down the hallway. She watched him go with a raised eyebrow.

A smirk curled her lips as she whispered, "It's good to be princess."

10

———

Alanna swept into the family dining room, excited to see how dinner with the princes would play out. After the prince's invitation, she had sent her maid into a flurry of activity: picking out a new dress and shoes, testing out each of her perfumes, and searching the trunks for the perfect jewelry.

Alanna had forbidden Hidalsa from assisting in the bath, but the maid begged for permission to style Alanna's hair—a nice sign of the actress's devotion to the part. Alanna thought the young woman might accidentally touch her skin, but she permitted the hairstyling if Hidalsa wore gloves. She gave Alanna a look that said she really was an odd princess, but wore the gloves as told.

Hidalsa had done an excellent job. Princess Aliyabeth's blond hair twisted in curls held in place by tiny braids with jewel pins. She wore a glittering tiara studded with diamonds in the shape of shooting stars, and her blue-green satin dress shimmered to match the peacock feathers that hugged the top of her bodice. The princess had a slightly smaller chest than Alanna, but she had to admit, the feathers brought just the right amount of attention to her cleavage.

She approached the table of princes, ready for the game to begin. All three princes stood as she neared, but it was Prince Hawthorne who pulled out a chair for her at his side.

"Thank you for joining us for dinner, Princess Aliyabeth," he said with a sweeping bow.

She allowed him to take her hand and plant a kiss on her gloved knuckles. "You're too kind, Prince Hawthorne. I appreciate the invitation."

On the other side of the long wooden table, Prince Jaemin rolled his eyes, and Prince Finn hid his smile behind his hand.

Jaemin cleared his throat. "I was the one who offered the invitation, but Hawthorne does enjoy taking credit for my ideas."

Hawthorne chuckled quietly as he eased Alanna's seat in, and she fluffed her skirts prettily as the princes took their seats.

The table was long enough for their entire family, but aside from their four chairs, there was only one empty chair at the head of the table.

"Where are all your brothers?" she asked.

Hawthorne clasped his chest in mock agony. "Are we not enough for you, Princess?"

She giggled at Hawthorne, and Jaemin answered primly, "They are on diplomatic missions."

Alanna raised a brow. "*Diplomatic missions?* Is that a euphemism for spying or for cavorting with foreign ladies?"

Finn's golden eyes twinkled as he grinned. "It depends on the brother."

Jaemin shot Finn a warning glare.

She picked up her glass and said casually, "I'm no stranger to diplomatic missions myself."

Jaemin narrowed his eyes. "Of the spying or the cavorting variety?"

She held his eyes as she sipped her wine.

"Intriguing," purred Hawthorne. "Isn't she intriguing, brother?"

Jaemin gave him a flat look.

Alanna turned to the empty chair. "Will the queen be joining us for dinner?"

The princes stilled their movements and didn't meet her eyes. Why did her question cause the room to feel as if all the air had fled?

"I thought ... because her chair—" she stammered.

Finn gave her a sad smile. "We always keep a chair at the table for her. She joins us ... when she can."

Jaemin aimed another glare at Finn, but Alanna wasn't sure why.

Hawthorne waved the servers over with an excited grin. "Let's not worry about that. It's not every day we have guests at our table. Tell us what you think of the queendom so far."

"I haven't seen much yet." She drew her lips into a pout. "I've been trapped in a carriage for most of it. I'd love a tour of the palace. It's so big I got lost earlier!"

Hawthorne seemed ready to take her on a tour right then, but Jaemin leaned forward in his seat. "You found Drazen easily enough."

Her lips tightened into a thin line. Apparently, she hadn't rattled him enough to make him forget.

"You found Drazen?" asked Finn.

"He found *me*," she said haughtily. "I have no need to hunt down your family's servants."

Hawthorne nearly spit out his wine as he laughed. "Do *not* let Drazen hear you call him a servant, or he might turn you into a toad."

Her breath caught in her throat. "He could do that?"

Finn shrugged. "It's unlikely, but we have no idea what he can do. Drazen doesn't give explanations to princes. He only answers to the queen."

Jaemin shot Finn another warning glance, but Alanna kept her attention focused on the red-haired brother, who seemed the best at giving answers. "I didn't even know magic was real, Prince Finn." Which had been true until yesterday, when Drazen called a windstorm on a calm day. And of course, the magic lamp in her pocket. "How can magic be real, but no one believes it truly exists?"

Finn tilted his head as he considered the question, but Jaemin spoke first. "Perhaps others *do* know magic exists. Perhaps it's that you are just like us: trapped inside a palace, unable to see the magic being used in plain sight."

She wanted to retort that she had not spent her life trapped in a palace, and yet, before yesterday, she still hadn't seen proof magic was real. But his statement was the first sign of his treating her like an equal, so she followed the script.

"Why would someone hide magic from us?" she asked.

"Power," Jaemin said simply.

"You believe Drazen isn't the only one with magic?" Had they heard rumors of Geeni? It caused her to question Geeni in ways she should have done long before now. How long had she had access to the lamp? Did she have other magical items like that? And a question she'd buried since the first moment Alanna transformed into the princess: why would Geeni use the magic on Alanna instead of becoming the princess herself?

"I believe there are probably many others with magic. And I know for a fact some people have magic, but don't even realize what it is." He got a faraway look in his eyes. "If I could just be permitted to leave the palace to explore Isandine, I know I would learn more."

It finally clicked into place what she had rescued him from yesterday. He had snuck out of the palace, and it was Drazen's job to bring him back. Drazen must have caused the windstorm as a warning to make the prince relent and come home. She had seen Drazen's magic with her own eyes, but a secret society of magic users hidden just out of sight was too much to take in. She didn't want to believe it.

The princess laughed lightly and cut into the roast duck on her plate. "You've been trapped in the palace too long, Prince Jaemin. Your ideas are quite fantastical."

His eyes snapped to hers. "You can't make it untrue by laughing it away, Princess. You've been kept in the dark, the same as we have. The difference is I'm going to do something about it."

She looked down at her plate and speared a candied carrot to avoid the intensity of his eyes. "I've met Drazen, and I admit, there is something … unsettling about him. But as for a hidden world of magic, I can't believe it."

The other two princes continued eating their food in silence, trying to avoid their brother's angry glares. Alanna nibbled delicately on her carrots, waiting for Jaemin to respond.

His faraway look returned. "I've seen proof with my own eyes. A storm appeared on a sunny day and threatened to blow Drazen away. He's not the only one with magic."

Alanna blinked. A storm blowing Drazen away? That wasn't what had happened. She tilted her head. Was it?

Jaemin stared at a spot over her shoulder, lost in the memory. "I escaped into the city yesterday, looking for clues, but Drazen brought a retinue of soldiers to find me. A windstorm appeared, and Drazen could barely stand in the midst of it. The wind was powerful magic, meant to protect me." His lips curved in a small smile. "Alanna didn't even realize she's the one who caused it."

Her fork clattered loudly to her plate.

Jaemin's eyes refocused, and his attention shifted to the others around the table. He pursed his lips, as if he could call back his words, but Alanna had already heard. And so had the other princes.

Hawthorne jumped in first. "Alanna?" His eyebrows rose. "Who is this 'Alanna'?"

Jaemin dropped his gaze to his plate and began militantly chopping his duck. "No one. Forget I mentioned it."

Finn leaned in and whispered to Jaemin. "We will *not* forget, however, it's perhaps a conversation we should have in private."

All three princes stole a glance at her. So, they didn't want to discuss Alanna around the princess? Pride and jealousy swirled in a confusing mix in her heart. Was it possible to be jealous of herself?

Alanna wanted nothing more than to run away, but her only escape was through the princess. She straightened her shoulders and laughed lightly. "No need to hide your 'diplomatic missions' on my account, Prince. It's all part of the job." She lifted her glass in salute, then gulped it down in a very unprincessly manner. Alanna escaped into the recesses of her mind, while the princess continued her meal.

11

Alanna paced nervously in the cool morning air on her balcony. After her dinner with the princes, she had spent most of her night on the balcony, trying to coax a storm to appear. The idea that she had magic was crazy, but when she thought back to that moment on the roof, Jaemin's theory had a ring of truth. The storm had never attacked the two of them—it had been limited to the street where Drazen stood. But how had she done it? And why couldn't she make it happen again?

She continued pacing, twirling her fingers in little patterns in the attempt to stir the wind. Her maid followed her movements with anxious eyes. Despite Hidalsa's suggestion to eat breakfast, Alanna refused to leave the balcony. She couldn't focus on anything until she solved the question of her magic.

A knock at the door caused Hidalsa's face to light up as she ran to answer it. Alanna stopped her pacing at the polite tones of Jaemin's voice.

"Good morning. Is Princess Aliyabeth available for a tour of Isandine today?"

Alanna was still anxious to solve the mystery, but she

pulled on the character of the princess and approached the door. "Good morning, Prince Jaemin," she said lightly. "I would love to tour the city with you."

He nodded in formal acceptance, then his lips quirked into a little smile. "I will leave so you have time to prepare."

Only then did she realize she was still dressed in her silk pajamas. She smoothed a hand across the soft pink silk as regally as she could manage. "You're too kind, Prince. I will meet you shortly."

He bowed, hand on his sword hilt, then strode down the hall. As soon as the door clicked shut, Hidalsa scurried around the bedroom in a flurry of activity. She helped Alanna into a white linen dress with pale blue flowers circling the hem. Underlayers of crinoline puffed out the full skirt. The maid wore gloves to style Alanna's hair into a simple yet elegant braid laid carefully across her bare shoulders. Then she helped Alanna put on her delicate blue slippers and handed her a lacy white parasol to match.

The actress turned maid stepped back and studied Alanna with a proud smile. Alanna pulled on long white gloves and couldn't stop a smile from spreading across her own lips. She didn't have an answer about whether she had magic of her own, but she could still enjoy a pleasant day as a princess.

Guards opened the massive doors as she approached the exit. Morning sunlight streamed in, and she nearly tripped as she caught sight of the prince waiting beside the horse-drawn carriage. He stood with impeccable posture in his high-collared uniform, the blue and white highlighting his bronze skin. The carriage driver waited beside him, gesturing as if telling a humorous story, and Jaemin's genuine smile made her heart flutter.

When Jaemin's eyes met hers, she nearly tripped again.

Not because his eyes were gorgeous, though they were stunning. But because of what was absent in his eyes.

Desire.

She had seen herself in the mirror before she left her room and could objectively say she looked phenomenal. She wasn't being cocky—this body wasn't even her own. But the princess standing atop the staircase, morning sunlight striking her strawberry blond hair, pale shoulders bare with just the perfect amount of cleavage, was a sight the prince should be admiring much more than he appeared to be. She would have doubted her objectivity if the carriage driver's jaw hadn't dropped at the sight of her.

She disguised her little huff of indignation by opening her parasol before floating down the stairs. The carriage driver ducked a quick bow before hopping into the coach box, leaving the prince to hold the door for Alanna.

"I'm honored you would join me for a tour today, Princess Aliyabeth." He offered her a hand and helped her inside, his hands as chaste as if she were his grandmother.

He took a seat beside her, his motions stiff as he scooted close, but not too close. The carriage driver directed the horses into a calm walk through the large outer wall.

"What a lovely way to escape the castle, Prince." She rested her hands properly in her lap. "I'm glad I could provide you with a good excuse to get out."

A muscle flexed in the prince's jaw.

She'd guessed correctly.

He sank back into the carriage seat with a sigh; it was the first sign of imperfect posture she had seen from him. "We aren't exactly escaping unnoticed." He waved a hand toward the six soldiers in matching navy blue uniforms, riding on white horses at the carriage's side.

"I'm just teasing you." She grinned and patted his hand.

He flinched at her touch.

She jerked her hand back to her lap. Why were all her flirtatious moves failing her? "I apologize, Prince. I—"

"No, it's my fault." He studied the floor of the carriage. "I'm under an extreme amount of pressure right now." He inhaled deeply and met her eyes. "I apologize, Princess. I want nothing more than to have a pleasant day with you." He held out his hand.

She couldn't understand his strange reactions but took his hand with a sweet smile. He nodded as if she had made a good decision, then tugged his uniform jacket into place, perfect posture restored.

She studied their joined hands, both gloved and adorably chaste. "So, where are you taking me today, Prince? Somewhere romantic, perhaps?"

He looked down at his feet again. "Um ... no." Alanna struggled to contain her giggle at seeing such a regal man squirm uncomfortably. "I thought you might join me in an investigation."

She spun to face him, truly intrigued. "An investigation? How titillating!"

He cleared his throat. "Yes, well ... I thought you might be interested in investigating what we discussed last night."

She gasped with delight. An investigation into magic? Before she could respond, he nodded toward the carriage driver, signaling that Alanna should be careful how she responded.

Alanna gave him a conspiratorial grin. "That sounds fascinating. I'm honored you would invite me."

"Well, you guessed correctly that it's much easier for me to leave the palace with a good excuse."

She bent into a little bow. "I'm glad to be of service."

His mouth pulsed in the smallest appearance of a smile. "Plus, there are historical places I can take you as a visitor that look suspicious if I visit too often."

She leaned in closer and dropped her voice. "So, what are we looking for?"

He didn't recoil from her closeness, which pleased her. She tried to focus on his words, but his low whisper was distracting. "A locked room."

"How will we get in?" Her voice was breathless with excitement from the adventure and his nearness.

He shrugged. "We might not. But a locked door is meaningful in a place that is notorious for being open."

"What happens if we get caught? Will Drazen turn us into toads?" She asked the question with a twinkle in her eye, but Jaemin's gaze was serious.

"I don't know what he can do. Maybe he will make us forget everything we see."

She fluttered her lashes. "I could never forget you, Prince."

As the playful line left her mouth, she looked up to see where the prince had brought her, and a cold chill of dread slid down her backbone.

They had arrived at the monastery.

12

Alanna had visited the monastery once a week for years, though it hadn't been necessary in the beginning. When her mother was healthy, she visited young Alanna in the small aviary above the theater every day. Over the next few years, Alanna had noticed her mother growing forgetful and needing to be reminded of the simplest things. Then one day, her mother forgot to come at all.

Her mother remembered the next day and brought Alanna's favorite chocolate tarts to apologize. But after that day, she forgot more and more, until one day, she never came back.

Alanna knew where to find her, though she couldn't go often, since the scholars found it suspicious that an unaccompanied child would visit the monastery. For a while, Alanna avoided the monastery completely—she was too busy trying to steal enough money to eat. Adult Alanna could charm a meal off a man with barely a fluttered lash. As a child, though ...

She didn't like to think about those years.

As she walked into the monastery with Jaemin, she felt

oddly exposed. Usually she wore a disguise to hide how much she had grown to look like her mother, but today, she didn't have the comforting weight of a wig on her head. She looked nothing like herself but still felt underdressed as she stepped inside.

"Good afternoon, Sister Scholars," said the prince.

The two scholars standing in the vestibule curtsied and gave him a warm smile. "Welcome, Prince Jaemin."

"I've come to give a tour of the monastery to our guest, Princess Aliyabeth."

The elder scholar raised the flowing hood attached to her white robe. "Yes, Prince. I can give you a tour."

He raised a regal hand. "No need to disturb yourself, Sister. I can show her around myself." Before she could object, he ushered Alanna through the inner gate into the cloister.

Once inside, he held out his arm with a subtle grin. "Let's investigate, shall we?" he whispered.

Her only response was to loop her arm through his and give him a tentative smile.

He led her on a slow walk along the covered stone walkway around the perimeter of the central courtyard. "Have you heard the history of the monastery?"

Alanna's eyes kept darting to the bench under the mango tree where her mother usually sat. She answered his question with a vague "Hmm?"

"This monastery was built by my great-grandmother to honor the Twin Goddesses, Qira and Qara. Under her rule, the queendom flourished with scientific and medical advancements. It was a golden age of a queendom at peace with the world."

Alanna nodded as if listening, her eyes still searching the courtyard.

"When my great-grandmother died, the reign passed to

her only daughter. Historians say my grandmother was timid—the complete opposite of her mother before her. They say the only true rebellion my grandmother ever showed was to marry a man against her mother's wishes. As it turns out, she should have listened to her mother."

Alanna had never heard the history of Isandariyah laid out so clearly, but she struggled to listen, terrified her mother would appear at any moment.

"My grandfather was an ambitious man, not content to sit quietly at his wife's side while she ruled. During the first few years of her reign, the queendom stood poised on the brink of war because of her husband's ambitions, though the queen always managed to calm tensions at the last moment. Until the day she gave birth to a daughter." His voice dropped to a respectful whisper. "My grandmother died before my mother even took her first breath."

Alanna slowed her steps, turning toward him. "I never knew that."

He nodded sadly. "It was a tumultuous time. My grandfather became regent of the infant queen and used her as his right to lead. There were those who thought he might declare himself king." Jaemin had a faraway expression. "It might have been better if he had. He likely would have been executed during the resulting coup. It would have saved Isandariyah a lot of suffering."

Alanna blinked at the casual mention of his grandfather's execution.

Jaemin sighed wistfully, then continued, "Instead, he led the queendom into several years of war, with the child queen at his side at every battle."

"Your mother went to war as a child?" she whispered.

"Yes. She saw a lot of things she shouldn't have. It … affected her."

Memories of fleeing war-torn La Veridda with her

mother flashed through her mind, and she tried to imagine a father willingly bringing his daughter into a battle. They made it to the end of the walkway, and Jaemin turned the corner and led her along the far side of the courtyard.

"When the queen came of age at seventeen, my grandfather was killed by a wild animal."

Alanna knew that part of the story. "Yes," she said delicately. "I've heard he was not mourned."

"No." His voice was hard. "He was not." Jaemin took a deep breath, and his calmer voice returned. "When my mother became queen in her own right, she reestablished the monastery as a place of learning. She welcomed women scholars from throughout the world, and offered sanctuary to women refugees. She vowed she would never again be controlled by a man, and neither would her scholars."

Alanna gave a tight smile. She had heard that part of the story, too. That was why her mother had pretended she was unmarried and childless to be let into the monastery to continue her work as a scientist. A bitter response sat on the tip of her tongue, but there was no reason for Princess Aliyabeth to be bitter, so she choked down the words.

Prince Jaemin slowed and leaned a casual hand against a door handle to his left. It clicked open, and he peeked inside.

"A storeroom," he whispered.

Over the course of his story, Alanna had forgotten the point of their excursion.

"A locked door is suspicious?" she asked.

He nodded. "The monastery's founding principle is from one of the Twin Goddesses, Qara the Wise, who said, 'Knowledge is available to all.' A locked door is sacrilege." He peeked inside the next door they passed. "Classroom," he whispered.

"But what will a locked door prove other than

78

hypocrisy?" She already believed the queen was a hypocrite for raising her own children when Alanna's mother could not, so what was a locked door compared to that?

Jaemin studied her with a curious expression. Had too much of her own bitterness crept into the question? He peeked inside the next door. "Another classroom." He took several more steps before he answered her question. "There have been strange occurrences in the monastery."

"Strange in what way?"

He bit his lip, as if questioning whether he should tell her. Alanna suppressed a smirk. If he wanted to keep secrets from her, he should have started much earlier.

He sighed. "People have come here seeking medical attention, who returned home sooner than expected."

Alanna blinked, waiting for him to say more. "That's it?"

"These were serious injuries, Princess. People close to death, yet the next day they returned home to their families as if nothing had happened."

Her mouth dropped open. "And what do they say happened here?"

"They say they don't remember much. That it's all a blur. And they all say they are grateful to our merciful queen."

She stopped walking. "What does that mean?"

Jaemin merely stared at her.

She pulled him closer, her voice barely a whisper. "Are we investigating the queen?" Alanna wasn't fond of the queen and wasn't opposed to stealing from her, but treason?

"No, we aren't investigating the queen," he sighed. "The queen has been ... busy lately." Alanna raised an eyebrow. She wasn't sure why he continued being vague. "We are investigating her advisor." He led her to the next door and peeked inside.

"You think Drazen is responsible for magically healing

people?" She scoffed delicately. "If that's how he uses his magic, I think we should let him continue."

"Not just healing. There are reports of strange noises coming from the monastery. The sound of animals that don't exist in this queendom. The ground shaking in the surrounding area. Bright flashes of light at night. And in the midst of each strange incident, someone catches a glimpse of Drazen."

"Do you think he is practicing magic inside the monastery?"

"Perhaps. I'm just not sure why. What's his plan? Is he faithful to the queen or not?" He chewed on his cheek absently as he considered his own questions.

"Have you asked the queen?" she whispered.

His face went slack. "She's been busy."

She gave him a flat look. "Busy?"

He ignored her question and reached for the next door.

The handle didn't move.

They both stopped walking and stared at the door. It looked like all the other carved wooden doors, except this one was locked. Alanna had never added lockpicking to her skills, although it would have been suspicious if Princess Aliyabeth had been able to pick the lock on cue.

"Now what?" she whispered.

Jaemin's eyes turned fierce. "We savor the fact I was correct, and we make a new plan."

"We?" she asked with a small grin.

"Unless you'd rather stay inside the palace doing princessly things all day?" The edge of his lip curved in a smile.

"I like the sound of *we*." She playfully flipped her braid and spun to walk around the other end of the courtyard.

And collided with her mother.

Alanna recoiled in horror as her mother's books crashed

to the walkway. Her mother looked down at the books, then looked at Alanna with a dazed expression.

Jaemin stooped to pick up the books, and Alanna watched him, avoiding her mother's eyes. It was ridiculous to believe her mother would recognize her, but she couldn't stop imagining her mother calling her Alanna and ruining everything. She anxiously twirled the end of her blond braid, looking anywhere but at her mother.

"Here are your books, Sister Scholar," said Jaemin politely.

Alanna's mother studied him, and confusion spread over her face. "Do I know you?"

"I'm Prince Jaemin. I've been here before."

Her mother nodded slowly, like seeing a prince was normal. "Have you seen the crimson sunbirds?"

He blinked. "The sunbirds?"

Her mother pointed at the mango tree in the courtyard. "I study all the birds, but the crimson sunbirds are my favorite. Their feathers ..." Her voice trailed off, as if she'd forgotten what she had been saying.

"Ah ..." said Jaemin gently. "Sunbirds are very beautiful. Thank you for your work, Sister Scholar." He bowed and handed her the books.

Her mother clutched the books to her chest, giving one last lingering look at Alanna, before heading to her bench in the courtyard. Alanna's heart constricted, the force of her suppressed tears bearing down on her.

"She will be safe here," said Jaemin kindly.

Alanna flinched. A terror rose inside her chest that he could see the overwhelming love and sadness written on her face. "What do you mean?"

"You seemed concerned for her, but there is no need. There are many women like her being cared for here. The queen has a soft spot for anyone with illnesses of the mind. She watches over them."

Alanna turned slowly to face him, but he didn't notice. His lips were curved in a small smile as he watched her mother admiring the birds.

13

The prince and princess spent the rest of the day touring the city, but Alanna spent the time thinking about her mother. She giggled and smiled as the prince pointed out landmarks, even though her heart still wandered around the monastery. Her dream of owning a small farm played through her mind, and she imagined her mother on a porch, watching a flock of birds fly overhead, smiling with pride at Alanna, recognition clear on her face.

"Are you okay, Princess?" The prince gave her a worried look as their carriage rolled through the front gates of the palace. They rode between tall hedges of pristine greenery, and gardeners waved at them as they passed.

Alanna realized she had been staring off in a daze, so she pasted on a sunny smile. "I've had such a lovely day, Prince Jaemin. Thank you for making me feel so welcome."

"Speaking of welcoming you, I almost forgot to mention we are hosting a ball in your honor tomorrow night."

"A ball? How exciting!" Alanna required no false delight. A ball in the palace was truly beyond anything she had ever dreamed.

The prince smiled warmly. "I'm glad you're pleased. Perhaps we can discuss the event over tea?"

Alanna lounged against the seat, imagining a conversation about a ball while drinking tea with the prince. She was about to agree when she caught sight of a gardener by the hedges.

A gardener with pink hair.

She cleared her throat delicately to hide her gasp. "That sounds delightful, however, I'd like to walk through the gardens for a moment to stretch my legs."

"Would you like me to escort you?" His voice was as formal as usual, not even hinting at a secret tryst in the rose bushes.

She sighed. "No, that's quite all right. I'll be inside shortly."

He helped her out of the carriage, and she curtsied before strolling casually among the tall hedges.

"It looks like you are enjoying yourself, Princess." Geeni wore mint green coveralls like the other gardeners, but her intricately carved golden bracelets weren't part of the standard uniform. She leaned against a tree, one booted foot propped against the trunk as she smoked her pipe.

Alanna sat on the carved love seat beneath the tree and fluffed her skirts around her as she spoke in a haughty voice. "The queen must be very lenient to allow her gardeners to smoke while they tend to the gardens."

Geeni chuckled. "I knew you would be great in the role. So, what have you learned so far?"

Alanna considered the history lesson Jaemin had given her at the monastery, but she didn't think that was what Geeni was interested in. When Alanna took the job, she knew she was supposed to keep her ears open, meaning *spy*, but now that she thought about revealing what she'd learned to this odd woman, she had doubts. But since Geeni was the current source of her good fortune, she owed her something. "I think Drazen is a wizard."

Geeni waved her hand as if that knowledge was inconsequential. "Of course he is, dear. What else?"

"You already know? And you didn't think to warn me?"

Geeni shrugged. "He hasn't turned you into a toad yet, so you're fine."

"Can he really do that?" whispered Alanna.

Geeni ignored the question. "What else have you learned?"

Alanna's shoulders sagged. "I thought that was the big news. I haven't even met the queen yet. Jaemin keeps saying she's *busy*."

Geeni puffed thoughtfully on her pipe. "Interesting."

Alanna shook her head. Apparently, she had no idea what kind of intel a spy should actually gather. The only other information she had learned was about her own potential magic, but that wasn't any of Geeni's concern.

She asked the question that had been bothering her since the moment she became princess. "You know the kind of information you want, and you know what the book looks like ... Why didn't you use the lamp on yourself?"

Geeni smirked as she absently rubbed her hands on her engraved arm cuffs. "I'm not the best at disguises." She tossed her pink ponytail over her shoulder. "I'm too memorable."

Alanna narrowed her eyes. Having an employer was new to her, even though the task of charming treasures away from men was familiar. She found Geeni intriguing, but the mysterious woman clearly had plans she wasn't sharing.

Alanna stood. "I should get back inside to the prince."

Geeni's voice took on a warning tone. "I need you to get that book, Alanna. It's even more important than any gossip you gather."

Alanna ran an elegant hand over her strawberry blond hair, tucking a loose end under her tiara. "These things take time, dear."

Geeni closed the distance between them in three long strides. She dropped her voice to a husky whisper. "Do not forget this skin is not your own, child." The warm scent of tobacco filled Alanna's nose as Geeni leaned closer. Her golden bangles clicked as she lifted her hand, her fingers hovering beside Alanna's neck. "All it requires is a single touch ..."

Alanna froze as Geeni's finger trailed a lazy pattern above her pale shoulder. Geeni never touched her, but Alanna felt the path of Geeni's finger burning into her skin like a warning.

Geeni's hand lingered beside Alanna's bare upper arm, and her fingers flexed slightly. "Do you understand, dear?"

Alanna's whisper was barely more than an exhaled breath. "Yes."

Geeni's lips curled, and she stepped back, breaking the moment as if it had never happened. "I brought you something to assist with your task." She reached into her green coveralls and pulled out a small leather-bound book.

Alanna accepted the book, her fingers still shaking. "What is this?"

"This book and the one you are procuring for me are a matching set. You give that to the prince as a gift, convince him to let you into the library where he can keep it safe, then you grab the matching book." She examined Alanna as she breathed out a thin stream of smoke. "He'll end up with the same number of books, so you don't have to feel guilty about stealing."

Alanna smoothed her dress and didn't meet Geeni's eyes. "I don't feel guilty about stealing. I've learned to do what I must to survive."

Geeni raised an eyebrow and continued smoking her pipe.

Alanna cleared her throat. "If that is all—"

"You are careful with the lamp, aren't you? It's a very valuable tool. I don't need to remind you how much danger you would be in if it was discovered."

Alanna felt the lingering almost-touch of Geeni's finger against her skin. "Your previous reminder was enough."

Geeni's lips made the slightest twitch upward. "Good. Then get back inside and enjoy your time with the princes. Not everyone gets the chance to be a princess. You should enjoy it while you can."

The princess lifted her head and walked back to the palace with a purposeful stride, but Alanna felt the lamp in her pocket as a weight slowing her steps.

14

Alanna perched neatly on the edge of her chair as Hidalsa's gloved hands worked magic. Even though Alanna still found her new reflection disturbing, she loved to watch in the mirror as Hidalsa skillfully styled her strawberry blond curls into a work of art. When she pinned the last curl in place, she dipped a small brush into a jar of rose-tinted gloss and swept it across Alanna's lips.

"You look beautiful, Princess," said Hidalsa.

Alanna gazed at her reflection and rubbed a finger across the still-unfamiliar curve of her lips. "Maybe the prince will finally notice."

Despite Prince Jaemin's willingness to take her on a tour the day before, he remained stubbornly unwilling to appreciate the princess's stunning form. Even though it wasn't her own body, Alanna knew her wiggling and leaning and other strategic maneuvers should have had *some* effect on him by now, but he remained unfazed. He treated her with the same detached friendliness he might offer an elderly acquaintance.

Hidalsa grinned at her in the mirror. "The princes will fight each other for the chance to dance with you tonight."

"Dancing?" Alanna's mouth dropped open as she realized the problem with being a street rat invited to a royal ball. "I don't know any court dances."

Hidalsa patted her shoulder with a gloved hand. "I'm sure the Isandariyan dances aren't too different from the ones you are used to back home. Besides, I'm sure you can convince the princes to take turns teaching you."

Alanna tried not to panic about her lack of proper dance training as she considered dancing with each of the princes. She had noticed Finn's shy glances and Hawthorne's blatant ogling at dinner the night before, but it was Jaemin's attention she craved. Playing hard to get was a strategy she had employed many times, and she shook her head at herself. How could she fall for such a simple ploy? Her goal was to get into the library, retrieve Geeni's book, then get out. Any of the princes could let her in. She needed to stop focusing so much of her attention on Jaemin.

Hidalsa brought over a shimmering silk shift the color of the moon. Alanna stepped out of her robe and into the pale gray silk. It wasn't an undergarment, but a complete dress. The flowing silk hugged each curve and fell in a pool at her feet. The shape was almost indecent by Isandariyan standards, but the high collar and long sleeves gave it a formal air.

After Hidalsa fastened the last button, she looked at Alanna nervously. "I thought you might want to wear something more traditional of your own culture for the ball tonight. Did I choose correctly?"

"You chose perfectly, Hidalsa." Alanna ran her hand down the front of the smooth silk as her lips curled into a smirk. There was no way Jaemin could fail to notice she was a woman in this dress. He would lead her to the library or anywhere she wished. Jaemin would be eating out of the palm of her hand by the end of the night.

Or one of the other princes, of course. That would be fine, too.

Alanna admired herself in the mirror as Bibi sauntered into the room and sat on her back haunches. It wasn't until that moment that Alanna realized the problem with the dress.

It didn't have a pocket for the lamp.

Geeni had told her keeping the lamp safe was the highest priority, so Alanna kept it in her pocket anytime she left her room. In her room, she kept it in the pocket of her satin robe and slept with it under her pillow. Since carrying it with her would be impossible tonight, she would have to hide it somewhere safe.

When Hidalsa went to find earrings, Alanna grabbed the lamp out of the pocket of her robe and looked around the room. "Where can I hide it?" she whispered.

Bibi sprang onto the chair in front of the window and walked in tight circles. She had spent the morning dozing on the back of the cushioned chair.

"You're a genius, Bibi!" Alanna shoved the lamp between the cushions, then laid her satiny robe along the back. Bibi hopped onto the robe, used her claws to adjust the expensive fabric to her liking, then curled up on top. The partially retracted claws and sharp flick of her tail were so catlike, Alanna was sure anyone snooping around her room would think twice about disturbing Bibi's slumber.

"Thanks, girl." She picked up her gift for Jaemin and winked at the cat. "I'm off to seduce a prince."

The guards threw open the doors, and a small man with a loud voice announced, "Princess Aliyabeth of Naermore!"

The well-dressed crowd in the ballroom clapped politely as she entered. She sauntered across the floor, noting which nobles followed her movements with ravenous eyes. Not that she was planning on targeting any of them for an easy theft, but it was her habit to notice. The level of attention assured her that tonight Prince Jaemin would finally appreciate her as he should.

After crossing half the ballroom, she finally raised her eyes to look demurely at the prince standing at attention on the dais at the end of the room. And in his twilight eyes, she saw ...

Calm indifference.

If she hadn't been surrounded by a crowd of admirers, she would have cursed aloud. What more did he want? Was he not attracted to women? No, that couldn't be it. The day she had rescued him in the marketplace, he had been playful, even flirty. She hadn't even tried to seduce him that day. Why was he being so stubborn now?

Before she could approach the dais, the crowd surrounded her. Courtiers asked questions about Naermore's nobility, and wealthy merchants asked her about her country's exports. She giggled and avoided any true answers, but after a dozen questions, she started running out of clever ways to lie.

The princes rarely asked her any questions about her supposed native country, so she hadn't been prepared for the sudden onslaught of tests to her role as princess. Despite the open doors and cool marble, the ballroom was sweltering, and she wore silk from neck to ankle, with gloves under her long-sleeve dress. The crowd pressed in so tightly, she could only pull in little gasps of air. If she passed out, a simple pat on the cheek would be all it took to ruin her disguise. The thought spiked her heart rate.

Prince Jaemin appeared at her side, looping a gentle arm through hers. "Princess Aliyabeth, can I steal you away for a moment?" She couldn't speak, but sighed with relief as the crowd parted around him.

The guests had entered by the wide steps leading up to the ballroom on the second floor, but those doors were closed now that the ball had officially begun. Private balconies lined either side of the entrance, with doors thrown open to pull in fresh air. The prince led her to an unoccupied balcony, and they stepped out into the sultry moonlit night.

This was exactly the location she needed to do her job.

She dipped her head and looked up at him through her lashes. "Thank you for rescuing me, Prince Jaemin. Surrounded by all those people, I suddenly found it hard to breathe." She lifted a hand to her chest, hoping it would draw his eye to the way her curves glowed in the pale gray silk.

His eyes stubbornly remained on her face. "I realized you might not enjoy crowds. I've heard you prefer your solitude."

Alanna blinked at him, remembering how Geeni had said the princess was a notorious recluse. So, he hadn't brought her onto the secluded balcony for a tryst, but because he was truly kind. Her plans for seduction had failed once again, but her heart warmed at his compassion.

If she couldn't seduce her way into getting what she wanted, she would play her other card.

"I have a gift for you." She handed him the thin leather-bound book clutched in her hand. He looked confused by the offered gift, but as he flipped through the pages, his mouth dropped open.

"This is my great-grandmother's diary." He hungrily devoured each page, flipping faster than he could read. His eyes flicked up to meet hers. "Where did you get this?"

She had an answer prepared, but the sudden focus of his twilight eyes was nearly enough to make her forget. She cleared her throat and grinned. "A result of a favorable diplomatic mission." She bit her lip—how many diplomatic missions did the reclusive Princess Aliyabeth actually go on? Luckily, the prince's gaze had already dropped back to the pages of the diary.

"We have one of her diaries in the library, and I assumed there might be others, but I didn't think I'd ever find another one ..." He quieted while reading a passage. "This is from one of the battles with Verkeshe ... She talks about her strategies and how she led the people through a dark time." His voice dropped to a whisper, as if he had forgotten Alanna was there. "She was a truly great leader."

He flipped through the pages, reading entire passages without speaking to her. His hair had been neatly swept back, but a dark curl had slipped loose and brushed his cheekbone. She imagined removing her gloves and sliding the curl through her fingers before tucking it behind his ear. Her heart thudded wildly at the reckless thought, but she couldn't tear her eyes away from his face.

Jaemin's eyes rose to meet hers, then he smoothed back his hair self-consciously. "I apologize for my rudeness, Princess. You've given me a treasure more precious than you can imagine." His eyes drifted back to the diary, almost against his will. "My great-grandmother's wisdom ... It's invaluable for leading Isandariyah."

She studied him again as he read. Below his precisely styled hair, faint wrinkles marred his brow, earned before his time. He stood with a rigid posture and tension in his shoulders that never released. He carried a burden of leadership she couldn't imagine, and despite his regal appearance, in that moment she sensed the strain of responsibility on his soul.

She spoke as herself, without consideration of her role as princess. "For a prince who isn't allowed to lead, you do a lot of leading."

His eyes met hers again, and the sadness behind his twilight gaze was staggering. "Yes." The word escaped on a quiet exhale. His sorrowful eyes looked so vulnerable that her heart clenched in pain. The moment felt more intimate than any tryst she had imagined, and she held perfectly still, clinging to her disguise.

He looked into her eyes as if hoping to see his own burden echoed back. The real princess might have been able to relate, but Alanna didn't know what to say. She had never been so tongue-tied around a man, and a blush heated the princess's pale cheeks for her inadequacy.

The prince ducked his head, brushing his hair back. "I apologize for being so tedious, Princess. Serious topics like leadership have no place at a ball."

Her eyes widened. He thought his vulnerability embarrassed her. "No, it's not that—"

He straightened his uniform with a tug. "Let me get you something to drink. You deserve to enjoy yourself tonight instead of standing around while I read." He looked at the closed book in his hand. "Thank you again for her diary."

Opportunity slipping through her fingers, she reached out and grabbed his arm before he could flee through the open door. "Maybe you can take me to see the other diary? I'd love to understand why it's so special to you."

His eyes softened as the embarrassed tension between his brows melted away. He nodded once, then escaped into the ballroom.

She sagged against the stone balustrade with a sigh.

That wasn't how she'd planned for the night to go. She gently patted the sweat beading on her forehead as she considered her next move, when a loud voice from the ball-room startled her.

"Welcome Her Majesty, Queen Illorienne!"

15

Queen Illorienne strode to her throne with unhurried grace. Alanna remained on the balcony, peeking around the thick curtains surrounding the doorframe. This was the woman Alanna had secretly cursed from the day her mother said Alanna couldn't live at the monastery with her. Alanna needed some time to contain her bitterness, otherwise Princess Aliyabeth might cause an international incident.

The queen lowered herself onto the throne with perfect posture as Drazen took his place to her right, and the crowd straightened from their bows and curtsies. The queen's raised hand signaled the musicians to begin playing again, the gold rings on her fingers glittering like her crown, which was set with a massive emerald. The bodice of her dress shimmered with copper brocade, and her full skirt rippled like liquid gold as she settled herself back against the throne.

Alanna had to admit the woman was stunning. Her chestnut curls with red highlights spilled down her regal neck, and her warm brown skin had even fewer wrinkles than her eldest son. There was something about her that reminded Alanna of Jaemin, but she couldn't quite place it.

The queen studied the crowd with a possessive air, surveying each person in the same way Bibi would organize her trinkets. It made sense: everyone, including Alanna, technically *did* belong to the queen.

A soft breeze blew across Alanna's neck, tickling a tendril of blond hair against her cheek. She tucked it behind her ear and shifted to the other side of the doorway for a better view.

Queen Illorienne continued her possessive survey of the crowd, and as her eyes moved past Alanna's hiding spot, the queen blinked slowly. In that blink, Alanna recognized the similarity with Jaemin. Both had eyes with disguised sorrow. Jaemin had only briefly let her see his deep sadness, and she had only seen a hint of it in the queen's eyes. It was grief, quickly covered, held in check by rigid discipline.

The queen lifted her hand again, and suddenly Prince Jaemin was by her side. He handed off a glass of champagne to a server, and Alanna frowned—that was supposed to be *her* champagne. The prince bent his head toward his mother, who spoke with barely moving lips. He straightened and glanced at the balcony where Alanna stood.

The queen had commanded him to introduce the princess, but Alanna wasn't ready for that yet.

As the prince made his way through the crowd, Alanna slipped out of their balcony and escaped onto another balcony on the other side of the room. He would find her eventually, but at least she'd bought herself more time to observe.

She peeked out from behind the curtains again from a new angle. Why was the queen sad? Sure, the queen hadn't birthed a princess, and there was no solution to the problem of succession. But the queen had seven healthy sons whom she had watched grow up. She was beautiful, strong, and had a clear mind.

If only Alanna's mother had been so blessed.

A cool breeze floated across the balcony, and Alanna clutched her arms to her chest for warmth. Her mother's illness wasn't the queen's fault, but she *was* to blame for keeping Alanna from her mother for so many years. Alanna had missed her mother's last few moments of clarity, and perhaps if Alanna had been by her side through her decline, her mother might remember Alanna as an adult, not just a seven-year-old child. Now her mother had no idea who she was and never would.

Cold wind blew past Alanna, and she gasped, jolted into an awareness she had never experienced.

She *felt* the wind.

The current of air darted into the room, ruffling curls and fluttering skirts. The wind drew no attention other than coaxing shivers from the ladies with bare shoulders. To the crowd, it was just a simple breeze blowing through the many doors open to the night. But Alanna recognized it for what it was.

Magic.

Vision beyond sight opened to her, and she could see each air current floating around the room: Warm air blowing through the kitchen door every time the servers walked through. Cool air filtered by the trees of the queen's garden, sucked in through the clever ductwork in the palace. And the single cold gust Alanna had summoned—from where, she did not know.

She clutched the doorway as her vision clouded with the expanded sight. Each dancing couple swirled inside their own personal whirlwind, and each circle of friends laughed inside their own storm. Her own fluttering lashes stirred a breeze, and her head reeled with the dizziness caused by the enhanced view. Even when she closed her eyes, she could still see the outline of the ballroom, the boundaries marked by the trapped currents of air.

She took a steadying breath and observed the cold air she had drawn inside. She gasped. As it swirled through the room, it reacted to her. If she concentrated on a direction, the gust would flow that way. She held out her hand and focused on her palm, and the wind slid across her fingers. Her fingers snapped shut, but the wind slipped out of her grasp.

The cold gust spun through the otherwise warm room, mocking Alanna with its playfulness. She gave a prideful huff, then narrowed her aim as if the wind were one of her targets.

If she wanted to control the wind, she would need to seduce it first.

"Wind, come to me," she crooned softly. The wind stopped its lively spinning and began a slow curving path to her side, almost as if playing hard to get. Alanna's lip curved, and she beckoned the wind with a curling finger.

The cold wind headed in a straight line to her, and on its journey, it brushed the hem of the queen's golden dress.

The queen stood.

Alanna's double vision snapped, and her sight returned to normal. The queen's eyes roamed over the crowd, no longer in a calm, possessive way, but as a hunter searching for prey. Alanna ducked further into the shadow of the balcony and looked for a way to escape.

Jaemin exited the balcony he had shared with Alanna, confusion on his face. He glanced at the queen, her eyes still roving, and he began pushing his way through the crowd to her side. Drazen leaned down, holding his gray beard close to his chest to keep it from brushing against the queen's sleeve. Alanna couldn't read the queen's lips, but her expression was furious. His eyes widened as he listened, shaking his head. Her green eyes glittered, and she spun to face the wide central doors leading outside.

An icy tempest blasted the doors open.

The dancing crowd hadn't noticed the standing queen, but they noticed the sudden windstorm. They clutched each other, brushing their flying hair away from their faces, confused and shivering. Isandariyah's tropical climate meant cold air was unusual and icy wind nonexistent, and the crowd murmured anxiously at the bizarre occurrence.

Alanna tried to charm the frigid air, but it refused her control. Freezing tendrils of wind snaked through the room, chasing the balmy air out into the night. She grasped for a warm breeze, but it skipped across her fingers without stopping.

The queen's head snapped to Drazen with a sharp raised brow. His eyes unfocused for a moment, before he blinked rapidly, and dipped his head in a sheepish expression that looked odd on the intimidating wizard.

Then he pointed to the balcony where Alanna stood.

Alanna squeaked, shooting backward into the darkness. She peeked over the balustrade to find a thick bed of chrysanthemums. She had landed on worse things, though she wished she wore a dress with soft petticoats. The gray silk ripped as she pulled herself over the stone railing, lowering herself as far as she could before dropping.

She hit the chrysanthemums with an explosion of floating petals. As she followed the trajectory of the petals, her mouth dropped open. She had landed on a cushion of air that was now dissipating. Was that how she always managed to escape without injury? Had she always had the wind on her side?

A shout came from the ballroom, and she shook herself from her questions. She hugged the edge of the palace to avoid being sighted from above, then ran as fast as she could.

She had always been a fast runner. It had saved her life on numerous occasions. Her childhood would have been even worse if she hadn't been quick to escape danger. But only now could she sense the wind flowing around her. She couldn't bring back her strange double vision with the air currents overlaid on the world, but she could feel the wind wrapping around her. She had no control of it, at least not consciously, but now that she knew what to look for, she could feel how the wind sped her along and lightened her footsteps, which barely left any prints in the garden bed. Now it seemed so obvious.

Which was how she knew she was *not* the one who'd called the icy tempest through the front doors.

When that icy wind blew in, Alanna had wondered if she had called it by accident. But when she reached out to try to coax it toward her, she had clearly felt it under the control of someone else.

The queen.

16

Alanna expected to find guards lining the hallway outside her room, but everything was quiet. It wasn't smart to come back to her room, but she couldn't leave Bibi. If Bibi had still been a monkey, Alanna would have trusted her to escape on her own, but the monkey still hadn't adjusted to her cat body and was the clumsiest cat Alanna had ever seen. Even if a wizard was chasing her, Alanna couldn't abandon her friend.

She burst through her door, startling Hidalsa from her restful position on the couch. The maid jumped up ready to assist, but Alanna sped past her and slammed the bedroom door.

Bibi was still curled up on the satin robe on the back of the chair, but her ears had flattened at Alanna's abrupt entrance. "Time to leave, girl." The cat's eyes widened as Alanna threw open the wardrobe, pulling out a dark blue cloak. She ripped her silk dress even further, giving it a deeper slit so she could run faster. Then she picked up Bibi, shoved the lamp into the cloak pocket, and opened her bedroom door.

Hidalsa watched her with wide eyes. "Are you okay,

Princess? I didn't expect you back so soon."

She blew out a breath. "Neither did I. So, listen, I—"

A sharp knock came at the door, and Alanna froze. Hidalsa moved to answer it, but Alanna grabbed her arm and spoke in a barely audible whisper. "I'm not here, okay? I went to the ball and never returned." Hidalsa nodded slowly as Alanna clutched Bibi to her chest, pressing herself against the wall.

Hidalsa opened the door. Alanna couldn't see who it was, but she could guess based on the fear her maid swallowed down.

"Good evening. Is Prince Jaemin here?" Drazen's deep voice sounded calm, as if the evening were completely normal.

Hidalsa blinked three times without speaking. Then she shook her head as if shaking her thoughts into their proper order. "You're looking for the prince? No, he isn't here."

Drazen paused for a long moment. Alanna thought he might push into the room and find her pressed against the wall. Instead, he sighed, and said, "If you see him, will you let him know his mother is looking for him?"

"The queen? Is everything all right, my lord?"

Another long pause. "Just a little windy during the ball tonight. Everything is perfectly fine."

Hidalsa's blond brows rose, but she didn't respond other than to curtsy before closing the door.

Alanna puffed out her held breath and let Bibi jump out of her arms. Drazen had pointed at Alanna's location from across the crowded ballroom. Had he not realized who he pointed at? And could he not sense her in the same way now?

Another knock sounded at the door, and Alanna pressed herself back against the wall with Bibi huddling near her feet.

Hidalsa straightened her posture and opened the door again. Her shoulders relaxed slightly, and she bowed from the waist. "Good evening, Prince Jaemin. Princess Aliyabeth hasn't been here since she went to the ball."

Alanna considered staying hidden, but then dropped her cloak and stepped around the door. "Thank you, Hidalsa, but I will speak to Prince Jaemin privately."

Hidalsa's eyebrows rose, but she went into the bedroom and closed the door.

Prince Jaemin watched the door shut, leaving the two of them alone, then crossed his hands behind his back as if at parade rest. "There was a ... storm ..." His gaze drifted dreamily, then he cleared his throat and stared at the floor. "I couldn't find you." His eyes lingered at her feet but snagged on her ripped dress, which revealed her leg halfway up the thigh.

His attention snapped to her face. "Are you okay?"

She sighed at his once again kind, rather than lecherous, response. "I'm fine. I ripped my dress running away from the ... storm." She looked at him, waiting for his reaction. "Was that normal?"

"Normal? Um ..." He brushed back his dark hair, avoiding her eyes. "I've seen something like that before, but I wouldn't call it normal."

Did he mean the time she had unknowingly called the wind to attack Drazen and his soldiers?

He straightened his spine. "I'm sorry we didn't get to spend more time together. I had hoped to dance with you tonight, but ..." He smoothed a hand down the front of his uniform and gave her a precise bow. "Good night, Princess."

She caught hold of his arm, desperate to find a way for him to stay. "Wait! The queen is looking for you. Is everything okay?"

"The queen summoning me to her side is a better sign

than the times she doesn't." He frowned in thoughtful silence as Alanna tried to puzzle out what he meant. He sighed. "Unfortunately, I will have to disappoint her, because there is someone else I need to see first."

Alanna blinked. "Someone before the queen?"

He tugged the front of his uniform and cleared his throat. "I just need to track down someone who came to the ball in secret. After that, I'll have more answers about the strange storm tonight."

She blinked as the pieces fell into place. "You're seeking the person who called the storm."

A muscle in his jaw twitched. "Yes."

He thought Alanna had called the storm and was going to find her. Her heart fluttered at the thought of him scaling the theater to reach her rooftop aviary. But the idea of him finding her room empty brought her up short. "I don't think you should go. Let's just talk about it, then investigate together."

He shook his head and wouldn't meet her eyes. "I must go. I need to see ... this person."

She raised an eyebrow. Why was he acting so strange? He had already mentioned Alanna's name to the princess before, so why wasn't he being honest? She bit her lip as the last realization clicked into place: he didn't want to admit he was heading to see Alanna because he thought the princess might get jealous.

To be fair, if she really were the princess, she *would* be jealous to know the prince was sneaking out to see another woman. However, since his secret rendezvous was with herself, she found it delightful. But the princess couldn't risk sneaking out of the palace. She didn't want to raise needless suspicions on the night with the strange wind-storm at the ball. So, if the prince went to look for Alanna and found her missing ... Perhaps this was finally her chance to play hard to get with a prince who was exceedingly difficult to seduce.

She clasped his arm and smiled demurely. "I understand. You need to do as you must. But please be careful."

His lips tightened, but he nodded, then bowed himself out of her room.

Bibi rubbed around her legs until Alanna bent to pet her belly while she thought. The prince had no idea the queen had called the icy wind through the doors. He'd admitted to both Alanna and the princess that he believed Drazen was a wizard, but he'd said nothing about the queen.

Jaemin had no idea the queen possessed a Spark. He believed Alanna had snuck into the ball, called a storm, then left. What purpose could she possibly have for that? She guessed that was the question Jaemin planned to ask.

Another knock sounded at the door, and since Hidalsa was still waiting in the other room, Alanna opened it herself.

Prince Hawthorne stood outside her door in all his spectacular glory. She hadn't seen him at the ball, since all her time had been spent on the balconies. He wore a crisp white suit that set off his warm brown skin and highlighted his sparkling smile. He held out a hand, and Alanna gave him her gloved hand. He brushed his lips against her knuckles, sending tingles up her arm.

"Good evening, Princess. I can't express my sadness that I didn't get a chance to dance with you this evening." His twinkling eyes looked anything but sad.

"Perhaps we can dance another day, Prince Hawthorne."

He crossed his arms and leaned casually against the frame of her open door. "I heard you gave my brother a gift. Are you trying to make the rest of us jealous?"

She raised a coy eyebrow. "It was a diary of your great-grandmother's. I assumed that would be a gift for you all."

His lip curled into a smirk. "Just because we are princes, doesn't mean we like to share."

She bit her lip, amused at this prince with a personality so close to her own. His playful eyes examined the high slit in her dress with an appreciative expression, unconcerned with how she'd ripped it.

Hawthorne's eyes trailed all the way up to her face. "If you like books, Princess, I can take you to see the library." He gently wet his lips. "It's very private."

She stepped closer to him, and his eyebrows perked up. She straightened the lapel of his jacket, just for the excuse to touch him, and looked up at him under the princess's thick lashes. "Did you always steal your brother's toys as a child?"

His emerald eyes locked on hers. "Only the ones I wanted."

This prince offered everything she needed. An easy way into the library, along with flirty temptation up until the moment she ran away and collected her money from Geeni. His green eyes were filled with sunshine and laughter, unlike the queen's green eyes of hidden sadness.

And unlike Jaemin's twilight eyes, vulnerable and all alone.

Alanna closed her eyes, her foolish choice made.

She opened her eyes and tapped Hawthorne on the chest with a single finger, nudging him out her door. "We will play another day, Prince Hawthorne. Tonight, I'm taking a hot bath and going to bed." Alanna thought it polite to offer her rejection along with a subtle image of her bathing. Judging by the desire glowing in his eyes, perhaps it hadn't been subtle enough.

He bowed gracefully, his eyes tracing her body. "Good night, Princess."

She shut the door with a sigh, then put on her cloak, picked up Bibi, and jumped off her balcony.

17

Alanna ran through the city, faster than she had ever run before. She tried to focus on the wind and coax it to speed her up, but the more she concentrated on it, the slower she ran. With running, it worked best to just run and let the wind help her as it chose. But jumping off balconies ... She rubbed her sore backside. Perhaps she needed more practice on that one.

The theater came into view, and she hoped the wind, along with all the shortcuts she knew, let her arrive before Jaemin. She walked through the crowd leaving a performance. She pulled her hood further over her face and clutched Bibi to her chest under the blue cloak, then reached out a bare hand and brushed a woman as she walked past.

Alanna gasped as if doused with freezing water, and Bibi jumped out of her arms. She stumbled into an alley, trying to avoid drawing the attention of the passing theatergoers. The sensation slid over her skin like an icy gel dripping down her whole body. She shivered and rubbed her bare hands against the thin silk of her sleeves, then realized instead of the princess's pale hands, Alanna's hands were back to their golden brown. The sight was disorienting after so many days in the princess's skin, and she touched her face, trying to remember the contours of her own body.

Bibi hopped onto Alanna's shoulder, and the monkey shivered as her white fur settled into place.

"That was quite unpleasant." Alanna pushed back her hood and shook out her black hair. "We need to hustle to the roof, before Jaemin sees me in this dress."

Bibi jumped down, and Alanna followed her up the back of the building. Alanna exhaled a relieved sigh as she pulled herself over the ledge and found the roof empty. She ran inside the aviary and locked the door behind her. She lit a single candle, yanked off the cloak and the ripped silk dress and stuffed them both under her mattress. She put on a pair of worn cotton pants, the full legs gathered at the ankle, and shoved the lamp into her pocket. Her top had seen better days, and she frowned as she wrapped the ties around her waist, trying to cover up an old stain. She had worn her "good" outfit when she met Geeni and transformed into the princess, and now that outfit was gone. Alanna grumbled as she considered how much it cost to replace clothing.

Although Geeni had promised her enough money to never worry about the cost of clothing again. All she needed to do was to deliver the book to Geeni, and Alanna would be free. But for some reason, Alanna was back in her aviary, worrying about stained clothes, instead of stealing the diary as she should have been.

A polite knock sent a jolt through her veins, and her fluttering heart reminded her exactly why she had made this dumb decision.

Bibi bounded across the room to her shrine, playing with the silver coin from the prince. Alanna sauntered to the door and smoothed her hair away from her face with calm, deliberate movements. Then she unlocked the deadbolt and opened the door.

Prince Jaemin stood on her rooftop doorstep as if he were a guest stopping by for tea. She was grateful he wore the neatly pressed commoner's clothes he had worn the first day they met. Seeing him in full military regalia outside her door would have been too much. But in his starched white shirt, with his dark hair curling gently along his collar, he was perfect.

Her eyes met his, and she nearly staggered backward. She now saw what she had been longing to see from her first step inside the palace as the princess.

Desire.

He looked at her like a starving man who had stumbled upon a feast. His eyes devoured her as if she might disappear at any moment. Her new skin, which was her old skin, tingled with the footsteps of hundreds of butterflies alighting at once. Even in her stained clothes, she felt more beautiful than when she seduced men thanks to low-cut silk.

But in silk, she felt strong. Confident in her power. Like she was in control. In her worn cotton, she felt fragile. Exposed. As if he had seen into the very heart of her.

"Jaemin." His name fell from her lips on a shuddering sigh.

Her voice surprised them both, and the delicate moment scattered like petals on the wind.

She ducked into a curtsy, suddenly realizing what she had said. "Um ... Prince Jaemin, I mean, Your Highness. Forgive me."

He cleared his throat. "There's no need to curtsy, Alanna. And I should be the one to apologize for showing up unannounced."

She lifted her head and met his eyes. The look of desire

had fled, replaced with his familiar polite regard. And below the surface, something she had seen a few times as the princess.

Suspicion.

"Were you at the palace tonight?" His direct question startled her. Not that she hadn't been expecting it. She'd just thought he would be more subtle in his line of questioning.

"Of course not." The lie slipped easily from her lips. On the run home, she had wrestled with whether she should admit to calling the wind. Denying it would make him more suspicious of her, but if she took credit for it, he wouldn't consider someone else had magic. Someone like his mother.

She turned the questioning back on him to offset his suspicion. "What would I be doing at the palace?"

"Oh ..." He rubbed a hand through his dark curls. "I thought you might have come looking for me."

Her mouth dropped open, but she snapped it shut before he raised his head.

"Were you nearby?" His eyes scanned her face, seeking the truth. "I'm not upset with you, Alanna. I just need to understand what happened tonight."

His request was so earnest and his face so open, but she had no idea how to give him the answers he sought. "What happened?" she asked innocently.

His lips twisted into a frown, then he held out his hand. "Come with me."

She obeyed the command without thinking, but when his warm fingers slid around hers, a fiery panic shot through her arm. She had worn gloves every time she touched him as the princess, and his skin on hers felt like the threat of exposure. As he led her to the front of the theater's roof, she had to remind herself with each breath that she was herself.

He released her hand and stared down at the street in front of the theater. He looked at her, then whirled away. He opened and closed his mouth twice, then rubbed his bottom lip, unable to meet her eyes.

She tilted her head as he struggled with his words. The last time she saw someone this uncomfortable to discuss a topic was when she asked her mother where babies came from. A blush sprang up on her cheeks, even though the memory was also tinged with sadness. What was the prince struggling to say?

His eyes remained focused on the street below. "Alanna, do you remember how the wind acted strangely when Drazen came to find me?"

Her breath escaped in relief when she realized the source of his discomfort. "Yes, I remember. I thought Drazen called the wind to attack us."

He turned to her, and his twilight eyes bored into her. "Drazen isn't the one who called that storm."

She couldn't dissemble any longer, not while his eyes stared through her. "I know that ... now. I'm the one who called the wind."

His eyes lit up, and she glimpsed a lingering flicker of desire. "You figured it out? You can control the wind?"

The hint of restrained desire threatened to weaken her knees. She steadied her voice and said, "I wouldn't say I can control the wind. More like, we are acquaintances."

He took hold of both of her hands, and the contact startled her into a fresh wave of panic.

"Do you realize what this means?" he said. "There *is* a world of hidden magic, and you're the proof it's real."

He looked at her like she was the answer, the sign of something new. The sadness she had seen in his eyes had been eclipsed by a bright and shining hope. He believed that since she had magic, his life would change for the better.

But Alanna knew the truth about magic.

She had used magic to lie to him and pretend she was someone else. She'd used it to sneak into his home, planning to steal from him, in exchange for a comfortable life. And she planned to use her own magic to run away when she was done.

Guilt about conning a target was unusual for her. She had sworn to Geeni she could be professional, but she'd let herself get pulled into developing feelings for Jaemin like an amateur. She needed to snap out of it. And the only way she could do that was to get Jaemin off her roof.

"I'm sorry to disappoint you, Prince, but I'm nothing special. I'm just a girl struggling to survive. If you'll excuse me, I need to get some sleep—"

"Do you need money?" He dug in his pockets. "How much do you need?" He put a stack of coins in her hand, then rubbed a hand through his hair as he looked at her aviary home. "I don't know how much money it takes to survive, but I can get you more, if you need it."

Her fingers closed around the coins, but she was too stunned to speak.

"I need you, Alanna. There's more I need to discover, but I can't do it alone. Will you help me?"

Her hand full of coins sank to her side as she stared at him. She was in a dangerous position, and the best strategy was to get him off her roof as fast as possible.

But instead, she asked, "What do you need me to do?"

18

A lanna pulled the white robes over Jaemin's head, then tugged at the fabric stretched across his broad shoulders.

"Don't you think I'm a little tall to be a scholar?" he asked.

"Shh! Not so loud!" she whispered, while yanking downward on his sleeve, unsuccessfully trying to make it longer. "There are tall sisters. But we are limited on the costume sizes in stock."

She glanced again at the rack of scholars' robes in the dimly lit costume closet, but no larger costumes suddenly appeared. "Tuck your hands together in contemplation," she said quietly. He did as instructed, and she draped the sleeves together to mask how short they were. "You need to cover your hands anyway. They are a definite giveaway."

He untucked his hands and waved a hand in a circle around his face. "And this isn't?"

She stood on tiptoe to drape the silk hood over his hair. "You're a shy Sister Scholar. That's why you never speak."

He grinned. "Fair enough."

She pulled on her own better fitting robe over her

clothes and lifted the hood to cover her hair. "You'll need to duck to hide your boots. They aren't standard issue, and there aren't any in your size—"

A phlegmy cough and a wheezing breath headed down the hallway.

Alanna grabbed the prince and shoved him behind a rack of costumes. He gave a small huff of surprise, but otherwise let her guide him into place as she dove in next to him, then stilled the costumes with a shaking hand.

She held her breath and peeked through a narrow slit between the hangers. Leland examined the costume closet as the flickering candle cast his thin face into stark shadow. His wheezing breath shot panic through her body, and she grabbed Jaemin's arm to keep from keeling over.

Leland took a deep rattling breath to blow out the candle, plunging the closet into darkness. Then he began coughing as he shuffled away. She remained unmoving until Leland could no longer be heard, and then waited even longer.

"Alanna?" Jaemin's whisper startled her into awareness.

Her fingers were clawing into his arm, and she released him with a jerk. "Sorry."

"Why do I get the feeling that was about more than the risk of being discovered borrowing costumes?"

Did he know how personal his gentle question was? The costumes dampened the noise, absorbing even the soft hush of their breathing. The narrow space between racks was so cramped, their bodies pressed against one another, and though she couldn't see him, she sensed him looking for an answer more intimate than she was prepared to give.

She cleared her throat in a near silent cough. "We should go."

He moved with a quiet rustle, perhaps a nod, then slipped his hand into hers.

She bit her lip on a quiet curse at herself, then led him out of the theater and straight to the monastery.

∼

She had to shush him the entire way. He kept ducking to ask her questions: How did she plan to get them inside? Did she know how to pick a lock? Did she think they would be discovered?

But no matter how many times she told him to whisper, his voice still kept its low rumbling purr.

She sighed, resigned to the fact he would probably blow their cover. The only accomplice she had ever taken with her on a job was Bibi, who was remarkably quiet. Bibi currently loped noiselessly at her side, with the occasional swing from clotheslines overhead when someone passed by.

Bibi had wanted to follow them into the costume closet, but Alanna had ordered her to meet them outside. The monkey would have probably still followed were it not for Jaemin handing her a shimmery blue feather. The prince didn't seem frivolous enough to carry feathers without a cause, which meant he had purposefully brought it to give to Bibi.

Alanna ground her teeth at how much that delighted her.

They approached the entrance of the monastery, and she hissed, "Absolutely no talking from now on. Got it?"

Jaemin folded his arms into his sleeves and gave her a slow, contemplative bow.

She lifted the edge of her dress, and Bibi scampered underneath as Alanna studied the single sister who waited inside the vestibule, reading a book. Two sisters might normally walk through the open front gate without a word, but she didn't know for sure. What she needed was a distraction.

Usually Bibi could provide a distraction, but Alanna thought the monkey would be useful later, so she needed to find the solution on her own. She closed her eyes and tried to remember what it had felt like to see the wind in the ballroom.

The strange double vision of "seeing" the wind didn't return, but she did sense a playful breeze she thought she could convince to do her bidding. She held out her palm and whispered, "Come."

Jaemin's hooded head twisted around, but he wouldn't be able to see the breeze tickling her fingers. She imagined the breeze scattering the pages on the desk in front of the sister, blowing her long gray hair and spilling the book from her hands. Alanna hoped that would be enough of a distraction for the two of them to sneak by.

She wiggled her fingers, softly caressing the breeze that swirled across her hand. She raised her palm to her lips and whispered, "Go." Then she exhaled a gentle breath to send the air on its way.

The wind reacted more enthusiastically than she'd expected. The soft breeze from her hand gathered the surrounding breezes and swarmed the poor sister. Papers flew off the desk in a whirlwind, and her book bounced out of her hand and slid across the narrow room. The sister's hair nearly blinded her, and the loose hood blew across her eyes. The iron front gates rattled, but luckily stayed open.

Jaemin's wide eyes blinked at her from underneath his white hood. She pulled the hood further over his face and grabbed his hand, dragging him inside.

They made it past the woman, then halfway down the cloister around the courtyard, before they slowed their hurrying steps. A backward glance through the arching stone columns told them the wind had settled down and the sister was gathering the scattered papers with a confused expression.

"I can't believe you did that," said Jaemin, his low voice distinctly *not* a whisper.

"She's not injured," whispered Alanna guiltily.

"It was amazing," he breathed.

Deep within his hood, his twilight eyes glowed. He looked at her like she was the most remarkable woman he had ever met. And while she wanted to bask in that wonder all night, they had a job to do. She tucked her hood around her cheeks to hide her blush, then started walking to the locked room.

He took a few hurried steps to catch her. "How do you know where we are going?"

Her confident steps faltered—she had discovered the locked door with him while she had been the princess. She covered her awkward steps by raising her skirt to let Bibi out. "I don't. But we shouldn't stand around in one place, drawing attention to ourselves."

He nodded serenely, his hands still hidden inside his sleeves. "Very wise, Sister Scholar. The room you seek is on the far side of the courtyard, the third door from the end."

Alanna made a show of looking through the arches and across the courtyard to see the door. She couldn't help looking at her mother's favorite bench, even though it was past midnight and her mother had probably gone to bed long ago. The courtyard was still—even her mother's favorite sunbirds were fast asleep.

A warm wind wrapped around her, and Alanna closed her eyes and savored its embrace. She sensed Jaemin had stopped walking and Bibi hopped around his feet, but her focus remained on the wind. It wound its way through her hair and traced a loving breeze across her shoulder blades, down her arms, then swirled around her wrist. She opened her eyes and could see it with her enhanced sight. The warm breeze unwound itself from her wrist, then floated to her face, dropping a kiss on her forehead, before flowing out into the courtyard.

It spun around the mango tree with her mother's sleeping birds, then skipped across the grass. It floated up the arches, across the roof of the covered walkway, then slid inside a grate directly above the locked room.

Alanna turned to Jaemin, who watched her with a question in his eyes. She was grateful he was too polite to ask, because she didn't have the words to explain. She held her arm out, and Bibi sprang onto her shoulder. They closed the distance to the locked room, then Alanna pointed at the arch leading to the covered grate.

She gave Bibi a firm look. "If you can't open it, come back out the same way." She could swear the monkey rolled her eyes.

Bibi scampered up the column and leaped onto the roof. She fiddled with the grate the breeze had entered, the metal clanking unbearably loudly in the quiet courtyard. Then with a click, Bibi removed the grate and slid inside.

Jaemin hadn't spoken since before the breeze's warm embrace, but he stared at her with fascinated confusion. He flinched at the clicking lock of the door, but Alanna merely raised her eyebrow as the door swung inward with Bibi hanging from the door handle.

Jaemin's mouth dropped open, and Bibi gave him a smug look as she jumped onto Alanna's shoulder.

Alanna shrugged, despite the weight of the monkey on her shoulder. "She's a clever girl. Now let's go see what's so important the scholars would risk heresy to hide it."

19

Alanna stepped inside the monastery's only locked room. It looked like a simple laboratory. She had seen the inside of her mother's laboratory back in La Veridda, before they had to flee to Isandariyah, and this room felt very similar. Bookshelves lining the walls. Workspaces for the scholars to spread out their books and notes. A few devices Alanna vaguely remembered as tools to measure temperature and density. A chalkboard with complex equations.

Overall, it looked pretty dull.

Jaemin spun in a slow circle, as if he had entered the most beautiful room in the world. "I can't believe we made it inside." He lowered his hood, taking in the lab. He stepped closer to the board with math equations and laid his hand on the frame as his eyes skimmed the numbers and letters written in neat lines. "This is it. This is where they study magic."

Alanna scoffed. "I don't know how you can tell based on that gibberish, but for some reason, I believe you."

He turned back to her, eyes shining with wonder. "I knew you would understand. That's why I had to come find you. Of everyone I've ever met, I knew you were the one person who would understand."

His impassioned faith in her stirred her lingering guilt. She ducked her head, moved to one of the workstations, and opened a random book, just to avoid his eyes.

He moved to the other side of the workstation, pulling a book of his own off the stack. He fell into a thoughtful silence, flipping through pages quickly, then grabbing another book.

Her eyes dropped to her book. It was a ledger with dates, names, and various illnesses and injuries. The book seemed like something one might find in a doctor's office: a record to track treatments.

Except in this case, instead of listing a treatment, each line ended with one of two people's names: Melora or Ethelwin.

Broken Leg:
Melora - Successful

Sprained Ankle:
Ethelwin - Successful

Tumorous Growth:
Melora - Unsuccessful
Ethelwin - Unsuccessful

Concussion:
Ethelwin - Successful

Night Terrors:
Melora - Unsuccessful
Ethelwin - Unsuccessful

Broken Ribs:
Melora - Successful

Fear of Open Spaces:
Melora - Unsuccessful
Ethelwin - Unsuccessful

Jaemin had told the princess there were rumors of people entering the monastery injured, and then returning home healed when they shouldn't have survived. Was this proof of that? The names of each patient were laid out with such cold efficiency, it gave her a shiver of unease. If this Melora and Ethelwin had the ability to heal in the same way she could summon the wind, shouldn't more people know about it?

Although judging from their success rate, perhaps it was better if they practiced more.

Jaemin slapped his hand down on the book in front of him, causing Alanna to flinch. He looked up at her with wide eyes, and whispered, "A Spark."

She gave him a weak smile, waiting for him to continue.

He jumped up from his stool at the workstation. "That's what it's called. A Spark." He grabbed her hand. "You have a Spark, Alanna."

She didn't find the name as much of a revelation as he did, but she nodded encouragingly.

He started pacing behind her. "There's a name for this magic. There are books written about the different types of Sparks that have been discovered. Scientists are studying it. And yet, they are still keeping magic a secret. Why?" He continued pacing, and Alanna's eyes dropped back to her book.

And landed on her mother's name.

Sunah. Her mother. Alanna flipped through the book

and found her mother's name listed on almost every page. Her symptoms were noted in dizzying detail: misplaces objects, forgets names, easily distressed, remembers scientific principles but forgets the year ... Each record alternated between Melora or Ethelwin, but always ended the same way.

Unsuccessful.

They'd tried to heal her over and over for more than a decade, and each time they'd been unsuccessful. While someone might be grateful for the determination, Alanna saw this ledger and their work for what it was.

Experimentation.

They were experimenting on her mother.

Her hands trembled as she imagined them measuring her mother's symptoms, seeing if Sunah had suddenly remembered something forgotten. Her mother got distressed when she realized there was something she was forgetting. Melora and Ethelwin surely distressed her mother each time they tried to heal her, then they kept careful notes about it, sending Sunah off to watch her birds until the next experiment. And Alanna knew exactly who had ordered these experiments.

The queen.

The scholars were easy targets for the queen's experiments. By her decree, they could have no family. They had no one to protect them. Alanna's mother had been trapped inside the monastery for over a decade, subjected to these experiments, with no one to rescue her.

But Sunah wasn't truly alone. Alanna would rescue her.

Alanna didn't notice the whirlwind until Jaemin grabbed her hand.

"Alanna! Can you hear me? What's wrong?" His dark curls floated in the swirling wind, and the books fluttered their pages like anxious birds.

Alanna took a deep breath and said, "Stop."

The warm wind stopped its wild spinning, then trickled upward, calmly coiling against the ceiling.

Jaemin's twilight eyes looked deep into hers. "What happened? I called your name, but you couldn't hear me."

Though the wind had settled, a whirlwind still raged in her mind. She had to get her mother out of the monastery, but couldn't bring her to the aviary atop the theater. Her mother needed a safe place to watch the birds and live in peace. And for that, Alanna needed money. Jaemin had offered her money, but would he be so willing if he knew the truth about her?

Bibi scampered from the doorway, leaping onto the workstation with frantic but silent hops. Then Alanna heard the footsteps herself.

She shot a terrified look at Jaemin, then they both ran to the back of the laboratory, looking for a way out. She jerked open a door that turned out to be a closet. He found a small washroom. The next door opened to stairs leading up, though she didn't know where to.

The key clicked in the lock, and they darted up the stairs.

They ran up two flights that ended in a balcony over-looking a private garden filled with unusual plants. She didn't feel like flinging herself from another balcony, plus she didn't see any way out of the enclosed garden. She scrambled onto the gently sloped tile roof, and looked down at Jaemin, who was removing his white robes so his arms could bend enough to climb up.

"Jaemin, you are the prince." She made her voice firm. "You can walk into that room right now and demand answers, and you'd get them. But I'm a nobody. I can't be found here. Hand me your robe and go back in and play your role as prince."

He wrapped the robe around his waist. "I'm not leaving you." His voice rang with finality and was the exact tone she'd wanted him to use inside.

He pulled himself onto the roof beside her, and she sighed. "Fine. Don't fall off."

She couldn't see it, but she felt the wind holding her tight, keeping her feet steady as she ran across the sloped tiles. She hoped the wind was as friendly to the prince following her. They made it to the edge of the upper roof and crawled onto one of the shorter outbuildings. This roof was less sloped, but they would be visible to anyone in the courtyard below. She saw nothing that would help them climb down, so they only had one option.

She held out her hand. "Do you trust me to get you off this roof?"

He looked at her hand with awe. "Can you fly?" he whispered. He took her hand before she answered.

"Not quite." She yanked him off the roof.

They landed with a bone-rattling thump, painful but not bone-breaking. They leaned against the outer wall of the monastery, gasping for breath while Bibi hopped down gracefully, a pitying expression on her monkey face.

"That's not what I expected," wheezed Jaemin.

She shrugged as she choked out, "I need more practice."

"Practice ... jumping off roofs." His laugh mingled with his gasping coughs.

His amusement brought a smile to her lips, before the knowledge of what she'd discovered caused it to fade.

"What is it, Alanna?" They still leaned against the monastery wall, but he turned to face her. "What did you find back there?"

She had too many thoughts racing through her head, and she longed for someone to talk them over with, but since her angry thoughts were about his mother, she didn't think he'd appreciate her accusations.

She also didn't want to mention her own mother's name. The thought of her mother being experimented on for years sent a fury through her body that could not be contained. Her mother was weak, and they had preyed on her. Alanna would not reveal her mother's name and put her even more at risk.

But Jaemin believed magic, these Sparks, were the answer. She had to let him know the cold reality.

"They are experimenting on them, Jaemin."

He stood. "What do you mean?"

"Taking notes. Tracking their symptoms. Trying to heal them, some of them over and over again."

His brow furrowed. "That sounds like regular medical procedure."

"Not if they haven't given permission!" she hissed.

"Um ... Did the notes say they didn't ask permission?"

"She couldn't give permission!" Alanna snapped her jaw shut, then took a deep breath through her nose. "I mean ... I can tell from the symptoms. The patients couldn't give permission."

He rubbed a hand through his hair, which was still messy from the whirlwind. "Sometimes that happens with doctors as well. They have to treat them without permission if the person is unconscious."

"She's not—" She clenched her fists, then spoke again. "It's clear from their notes, they are experimenting on them. Treating them over and over. For over a decade. It's not right. I don't care if you don't believe me. But it's the truth."

He exhaled a long breath. "I believe you, Alanna. If you say it's clear, then it is. The notes I read were detailed enough. Over a decade of experiments isn't hard for me to believe."

She sagged against the wall. Even though she'd said she didn't care, she did want him to believe her. "Thank you for believing me. I thought you might not believe your mother could be involved in something like that."

"My mother? She's not involved in this. It's Drazen."

She gave a bitter huff of laughter. "Of course she's involved! She has a—" She bit her tongue to keep from saying the word. The princess was the one who'd discovered the queen had a Spark, not Alanna. She wasn't sure how she could extricate herself from the lie about not being at the ball to reveal the truth.

Jaemin just shook his head. "It's Drazen. He's the one doing this. The queen would have told me if she knew about magic. Besides, she's too … busy."

Alanna rubbed her fingers through her thick hair, nearly pulling it out in frustration. "Busy? Yes, perhaps she's 'busy' doing experiments on sick people without their consent!"

A muscle in Jaemin's jaw twitched, but he didn't respond.

She held out her hand. "Give me the robe, then head back to the palace. I'm sure you're just as 'busy' as the queen."

Pain flashed behind his eyes, but he quickly hid it, ducking his head to untie the robe from around his waist. "I'll walk you home."

"There's no need, Prince. I can take care of myself." She snatched the robe from his hand. "I always have."

20

The princess buttered her toast savagely. Alanna tried to hold the knife with delicate fingers as a princess should, but she kept squeezing the handle like a dagger every time she glanced across the table at Prince Jaemin.

He had barely spoken two words to her since they sat down for breakfast. The food on his plate remained uneaten, and he drained his second cup of black coffee without even looking up. He had dark circles under his eyes, proof he had been out too late breaking into the monastery. If Alanna hadn't been able to transform back into the perfect appearance of the princess, her eyes would look just as bad, considering she'd stayed out even later than him.

She pried her fingers off the butter knife and took a dainty bite of toast.

Jaemin had walked straight back to the castle after she left him—she made Bibi follow him to be sure of it. But Alanna climbed back up to her aviary room and patched up a seam the prince had split on the scholar's robe, before returning both robes to the costume closet. Then she grabbed her dark blue cloak and met Bibi back at the palace.

She didn't think it wise to use the lamp before going inside, since discovering the princess outside the palace walls would raise a lot of questions. Causing a distraction with the wind could get her in, but after the storm at the ball, she thought the guards would be even more suspicious about a sudden gust of wind. So instead, she used more conventional means to get what she wanted. And since she wasn't burdened with the princess's inability to touch people, she could flirt with a guard and distract him enough to sneak in.

After that she snuck into the garden and used the lamp to transform back into the princess. She needed a tear to activate the rune carved into the side, but after thinking about her mother being experimented on with no one to protect her, the tears came easily enough. The burning illusion settling onto her skin hurt just as bad as before, but the princess pulled her cloak around her as she and her clumsy cat walked proudly into the castle as if they had just taken their morning walk in the garden.

She found Hidalsa pacing in her rooms. After privately changing out of her worn clothes, Alanna gave her maid a vague answer about her whereabouts. Based on Hidalsa's raised eyebrows, she suspected the princess had spent the night with the prince. Alanna felt no need to defend the princess's reputation, so she offered no further explanation.

If Hidalsa saw Prince Jaemin this morning, she would realize no seduction had happened last night. He didn't notice as the server refilled his coffee cup, but merely stared blindly into the distance over Alanna's shoulder.

"Brother, if you are going to so thoroughly disappoint Princess Aliyabeth, please give me leave to entertain her instead."

Jaemin's eyes shot to Prince Hawthorne's face, and Alanna turned in her chair to study the flirty prince. She had ignored him and Prince Finn when they sat down, so intent was her glaring at Jaemin.

Hawthorne leaned back against his high-backed chair. "I'm not sure what you are fighting about, but the princess deserves to enjoy a pleasant time in Isandariyah." His eyes twinkled mischievously as he said to her, "I can make sure you are quite pleased."

Prince Finn covered his snorting laugh behind his coffee cup, but Jaemin wasn't amused. "The princess and I are not in a fight, brother. We have nothing to fight about."

The princess had no reason to be angry, but Alanna surely did. She took a sip of tea to hide her glare.

Hawthorne chuckled. "Well, you did leave the princess all alone last night with nothing to do." He gave the princess a sly glance. "Nothing except a very lonely hot bath."

Prince Jaemin blinked as his head swiveled between Alanna and Hawthorne, aware he'd missed something, but not sure what.

Alanna set down her teacup and spoke to Jaemin in a pleasant voice, as if ignoring the whole conversation. "How did your evening go? Did your mysterious contact give you any information about the strange storm last night?"

Jaemin's mouth dropped open, then snapped shut. Prince Finn twisted in his chair to give Jaemin an excited grin, and Hawthorne raised his brows, scenting the possible cause of the argument.

"I ... um ..." Jaemin sighed. "No."

Of course, he didn't know who had caused the storm. Even if Alanna told him, he wouldn't believe her, because he was too stubborn to admit the queen could be involved.

"Who is your contact?" asked Finn. "Is it that Alanna girl?"

Jaemin glared at him, and Hawthorne laughed out loud. "Thanks for clearing up the mystery of your argument, brother. At least we all know what you did wrong now. Traipsing off to see strange girls when you have a beautiful princess here under your own roof."

Prince Jaemin flicked his gaze toward Alanna, finally aware the princess might have cause to be angry with him. "It's not like that. I—"

She picked up her teacup with elegant fingers. "There's no need to explain to me, Prince Jaemin. I've already said you are free to go on as many 'diplomatic missions' as you choose."

"A diplomatic ...? It wasn't— I didn't—"

Hawthorne and Finn both laughed while Jaemin sputtered a very unconvincing response.

The princess picked up her fork and scooped up a tiny portion of her fluffy eggs. "So, you learned nothing from this girl? I thought a prince would be more effective at tempting a lady to reveal her secrets." She took a bite of the eggs, her eyes locked on him as she slowly pulled the fork out of her mouth.

She expected him to continue squirming, but instead he sat up taller, tugging on his uniform with military precision. "I did not ask Alanna to *reveal* anything to me last night."

Hawthorne and Finn exchanged a look that said they didn't quite believe their brother, and the princess's eyes widened. Jaemin was defending the honor of a common street rat. The thought sent a jolt of warmth through her belly, but she shoved it down beneath the princess's facade.

Jaemin huffed. "It was nothing like that. Our interaction was strictly professional."

The princess set down her fork and folded her hands in front of her plate. "Professional? What exactly is her profession?"

They had never spoken of Alanna's profession, but her interactions with the prince flashed across his face, the answer pretty clear. It was a reckless conversation, even though she never planned on seeing the prince again in her own body. But watching him think about her felt like a piece of Alanna was still close to him. And she wanted to see if he would admit what kind of person he'd spent the night with.

He raised his head, and answered in a clear voice. "She's a fighter, who wears many masks in order to survive."

Alanna's breath caught in her throat, and her current mask threatened to slip. She picked up her teacup with two hands, taking a steadying breath through her nose as she pretended to sip. She cursed herself for a fool. Why hadn't she shut down the conversation when she had the chance?

"I'm sorry, Princess."

Jaemin's polite voice shook her out of her self-condemnation. She set down her teacup, unable to answer, and merely waited for him to continue.

He straightened in his chair, the epitome of a dutiful prince. "I have done a poor job making you feel welcome. I promise I will be a more gracious host." He shot Hawthorne a sharp scowl. "I will fulfill my obligations."

Hawthorne leaned back in his chair and raised an eyebrow.

Jaemin looked back at Alanna with warm politeness. "I have a training scheduled with the Queen's Guard, but after that, I'd love to spend time with you. Perhaps we can have dinner together, then visit the library, like we discussed?"

She tried to convince herself that her racing heartbeat was because of the possibility of completing her mission, not because the library had the reputation of being "private."

The princess gave him a small yet regal bow. "That

sounds delightful, Prince Jaemin. I look forward to being entertained by you."

His lips tightened, and he gave a single sharp nod, before eating his cold breakfast.

21

Alanna walked through the palace's gardens in a much better mood after her nap. She was still irritated at Jaemin's unwillingness to admit the queen had any part to play in what happened at the monastery, but since he planned to take her to the library after dinner, it didn't matter. Alanna would get the book for Geeni, and use the money to buy a small farm where she could give her mother the peace she deserved.

After that, she would never see Prince Jaemin again.

She shoved down the uncomfortable sadness and tossed her blond braid over her shoulder, letting the princess's sensations wash over her. The sun shone in a bright blue sky. The scent of jasmine floated on the breeze. The grunts of men intrigued her.

She passed through the garden's decorative gate and found the outdoor training space of the Queen's Guard. Men and women in rough training leathers gathered around the low fence, watching a guard spar with Prince Jaemin.

The prince's leather pants fit him with an exactness only achieved by a clever tailor and proper care after each use.

He lunged at the guard, revealing his muscular form. The brown leather pants looked buttery soft and well-worn.

She bit her lip. Definitely well-worn.

His white shirt was tucked in but unbuttoned halfway down his chest. She had only seen him in his uniform or the starched white commoner's shirt buttoned all the way to the top. The sight of him so undone entranced her.

She had no understanding of the intricacies of their sparring match, but she saw plenty of things clear enough: Jaemin's windblown hair, sunlight sparkling on the sweat trickling down his neck, his strong grip when he helped his opponent to his feet, his smile as the others patted his muscular back.

When another match began, he moved to the side of the barracks and gulped down a cup of water. Then he removed his shirt and poured a cup of water over his head, running long fingers through his hair. Water and sweat trickled down his light bronze skin, and he slumped against the barracks with a contented sigh.

"You should close your mouth, dear," said Geeni. "If the prince sees you drooling over him, he'll know he's got you hooked."

Alanna's jaw snapped shut with a click. She hadn't been drooling. Had she?

Geeni leaned against the garden gate, shaking her head at Alanna. She wore similar brown leathers to the Queen's Guard, but the pink hair wasn't strictly dress code.

"I thought I was dealing with a professional." Geeni clicked her tongue. "I guess even the strongest among us can fall to a dreamy prince's charms."

Alanna smoothed a hand across her blond hair, trying to regain some of her dignity. "I have not fallen for the prince's charms. I was merely enjoying the sparring match."

"Oh, you were definitely enjoying it." Geeni smirked as she raised her pipe to her lips.

Alanna cleared her throat. "Yes, well, the prince has offered to take me to the library tonight, so don't worry. I'll finish the job and be out of here before I'm distracted any further."

Geeni grinned. "Good. You can meet me here tomorrow morning, and I'll take the book off your hands."

"And my money?" There was no way Alanna was handing over the book without a hefty payout.

"When I have the book, I'll give you the money and a letter in the princess's handwriting saying she got called away suddenly, and you can escape the palace in your real body."

The plan sounded easy enough, but a pit of unease churned in her stomach. She hid it with the princess's easy smile. "Perfect. I will see you then."

Geeni grabbed her gloved hand before she turned away. "What else have you learned?"

Alanna had learned so many things, many of them so personal she didn't want to discuss them with Geeni: her Spark, the experimentation on her mother, Drazen pointing at her from across a crowded room ... She had to reveal something, so she aimed for the target highest on her list.

The queen.

"During the ball, a strange storm blew open the doors."

Geeni chuckled. "Yes, I heard. I assumed you got mad and caused it."

Alanna's planned script suddenly flew away. "You assumed *I* caused it?"

Geeni blew out a thin curl of smoke. "Are we still going to pretend you don't have a Spark?"

Alanna opened her mouth, then closed it.

Geeni flicked her hand as if brushing away Alanna's

impending denials. "I saw you summon a breeze on the first day we met. You should be glad I did, otherwise I wouldn't have noticed before you stepped in front of that carriage."

Alanna recalled the day they'd met. She had just left her mother in the monastery and had walked without seeing through a small storm of floating leaves and flower petals. Geeni had rescued her before she stepped in front of an approaching carriage.

Her eyes widened with understanding. "You offered me a job because I have a Spark."

"I hoped it would give you an edge."

"But I didn't even know I had it!"

Geeni shrugged. "Most of the time, people don't. They think they just have a knack for something, a natural talent. It's rare that people realize what they have been given and do something about it."

She stared at the woman. Geeni was the person Jaemin longed to find, but Alanna could never introduce them. Geeni had answers about magic. She understood magic so well, she had given Alanna a lamp with carved runes that let her use magic not her own. Alanna examined Geeni's layered necklaces and the gold bangles on her wrists.

Her jewelry was covered with runes.

The gold chains around the woman's neck sparkled with charms, each with a different-shaped rune, and her thick bracelets had neat runes running the full perimeter. Geeni was practically dripping with potential magic ... What power did the woman have at her command?

Alanna whispered, "Making runes ... Is that your Spark?"

Geeni merely grinned and puffed on her pipe.

Alanna blew out a breath. Her world had once again shifted, and she needed to find a way to bring it back under control, so she lashed out at her prime target. "I'm not the one who called the wind. It was the queen."

She thought the statement would elicit a calmly raised brow followed by the word "Interesting." Instead, Geeni gripped Alanna with both hands, her fingers digging into Alanna's arms.

"Where is the lamp?" she hissed.

Alanna's heart skipped in panic as she considered the possible scope of Geeni's magic. She wiggled one of her arms enough to pull the lamp out of her pocket. "It's here."

Geeni released her, grabbing the lamp from Alanna and turning it over in her hands. Alanna rubbed her gloved hands along her arms to soothe the pain from Geeni's sharp nails. She was glad she always wore long sleeves, or Geeni would have pierced her disguise without a second thought.

Geeni rubbed a finger across the large rune, which still glistened with a soft glow. Of the three smaller runes, only one retained its shimmer, since Alanna had already transformed into the princess twice. Geeni growled. "This is exactly why I avoid that Spark-thieving queen. I won't let her add my Spark to her arsenal."

Alanna's eyes widened. The queen stole Sparks?

It couldn't technically be "theft" since Alanna still possessed her own Spark, but somehow the queen had gained Alanna's magic for herself. That was how she'd known Alanna was in the room—she'd suddenly gained Alanna's Spark, then wanted to hunt down the owner.

Geeni handed the lamp back to her. "But the large rune on the lamp should have protected you from the queen's Spark and from being detected by Drazen. Why didn't it work?"

Alanna put the lamp back into her pocket and stayed silent. Geeni had said to keep the lamp safe, so Alanna had thought safe in her room would suffice. Geeni hadn't said to carry it at all times or else she would be detected by the queen and her wizard! Plus, Geeni was the one who'd given her the skintight dress with no pockets.

But perhaps Alanna would keep all that information to herself, in addition to never letting the lamp out of her possession again.

Geeni's head snapped up, and Alanna smoothed her face into a neutral expression. "Does Drazen know it was you? I'm guessing not, otherwise you wouldn't be freely walking around the garden."

"I don't know if he knows." She huffed out a frustrated breath. "I have no idea how any of this works!" She crossed her arms, then slowly processed Geeni's words. "What do you mean about me not walking freely?"

Geeni snorted. "Why do you think more people don't know about the existence of magic? It's because Drazen and the queen keep those with Sparks all to themselves—most of them are no better than slaves, using their Spark tirelessly in service of the queen." She raised her pipe to her lips as she looked Alanna up and down. "If Drazen knew you could control the wind, he'd have chained you to a windmill for the rest of your days."

Alanna's arms slipped to her sides as she imagined a queendom full of people with Sparks living as slaves to the queen. Even Melora and Ethelwin, the two who had experimented on her mother, were just using their Spark at the queen's command.

"She has to be stopped," whispered Alanna.

Geeni breathed out a smooth stream of smoke. "Get me that book, and I'll see what I can do."

22

Alanna tapped her lip as she considered the dresses Hidalsa had laid out on the bed. The dress had to be perfect for her trip to the library with the prince. Not because of any planned seduction, but because she couldn't let her mask slip again. She needed to be firmly committed to her role as princess, get the diary, and get out.

"Your Highness, Prince Jaemin is here," said Hidalsa.

Alanna hadn't even heard the knock. She pointed at the delicate lace dress the color of marigolds. "That one. I'll tell the prince he must wait for me to be ready."

Alanna sauntered into the sitting room. The prince stood on her balcony with the same stiff posture as the Queen's Guards. "Prince Jaemin, you should have warned me you would stop by so early. I'm not even dressed."

Jaemin's eyes widened, and a faint blush crept over his cheeks, even though she still wore the same fluffy pink dress from breakfast.

"You *are* dressed ..." He looked her up and down, then his eyes shot to her face, as if concerned his statement might be incorrect.

She bit her lip on a giggle. "Yes, Prince, I am dressed. Perhaps by having only brothers, you never learned that ladies like to wear something special for dinner, especially when that dinner is with an attractive prince."

He ducked his head. "Ah yes, about that."

Alanna frowned and crossed her arms. Was he backing out of their trip to the library?

"I wondered if you might join me on an excursion to Ylara instead?" She blinked in surprise, but he pressed on, blurting out the words. "It's a settlement at the base of Mount Qara. Since it's a long trip by carriage, we'd need to leave soon and stay the night."

"Oh ... stay the night ..." Alanna had told Geeni she would get the diary tonight, then deliver it in the morning. What would she do if the princess left on a sightseeing trip all the way to Mount Qara?

"Your maid will accompany us, of course!" Jaemin looked as nervous as when she made one of her flirty comments. "You will have your own room. It will be very proper."

She knew by now not to expect any dalliances with the prince, but she still found his high regard for propriety adorable.

"It's not that ... I'm just not sure about a long trip ..." She didn't know how to get out of it. Sudden illness? That would prevent her from having a date in the palace with him as well. Traveling sickness? The princess had arrived looking healthy enough after a long voyage from Naermore. She chewed on her lip as she considered other excuses.

He stepped closer and lowered his voice, pausing all her thoughts midexcuse. "I have another reason for proposing this trip, but I don't want to speak of it until we are on the way."

After that, the princess's decision was easily made.

Hidalsa packed enough of the princess's dresses for a week-long excursion, despite the whole trip lasting only slightly more than a full day, then helped Alanna into a more comfortable dress for traveling. Within an hour, the princess and her cat rode in a carriage with the prince, while Hidalsa rode in a separate carriage packed with Alanna's dresses, with a host of the Queen's Guard riding along on horseback.

Alanna made a nest in her skirts for Bibi and studied the prince, seated opposite her. "So, what is this mysterious excursion all about? Not that I mind being whisked away by you, but this is so spontaneous, and you always seem so ..."

"Methodical? Rigid? Boring?" His lips curled in a sardonic grin. "Believe me, my brothers tell me that often enough."

She carefully folded her hands above the sleeping cat on her lap. "I was going to say 'strategic.' I assume there is some tactical reason we are making this trip."

He looked pleased she understood him. Still no hint of desire, but Alanna thought he might actually consider the princess a friend. "I appreciate your shrewd assessment, Princess. I'm sure growing up around politics has forced you to be as pragmatic as I am."

"Yes ... politics, of course." A blush warmed her cheeks at the compliment, despite his false assumption.

He leaned forward. "Drazen is headed to Ylara today. I think he is hunting someone with a Spark—with magic."

She dumped Bibi off her lap and plopped next to him. "We're following Drazen?" she breathed. Bibi scowled at Alanna's rudeness, then curled up in the center of the seat, claiming it as her own.

The prince tried to scoot away from her, but there was nowhere for him to go. "Yes, I heard he had prepped a carriage for a trip to Ylara, so I thought we would follow to see what he does."

She grinned. "And I'm once again a useful excuse to go on a sightseeing adventure?"

He rubbed a hand through his hair, still pressing against the carriage wall. "Well, yes ... I've been to Ylara many times but have no specific reason to go today."

She snuggled against the seat and closer to his arm. "I knew there was a strategy behind it." She tapped her lip as she considered. "You think he's hunting someone with magic? What does that even mean?"

"I'm not sure," Jaemin admitted. "But I think he has some way to locate people with magic, then bring them back to the monastery. Beyond that, I don't know."

The princess found the idea of magic and a strategic trip to the base of the volcano thrilling. But Alanna needed to know the answer for herself. How did Drazen identify people with a Spark? Was his Spark the ability to detect others? Geeni had said the large rune on the lamp would protect her from being detected by Drazen. Would Alanna need to carry the lamp for her whole life to avoid him? She had to find a way to keep the lamp when she was done with the job.

Alanna woke with her head propped on the prince's shoulder. She sat up with a jerk, realizing where she was. She flung her hands in front of her face, terrified they'd be the warm brown of Alanna, but she wore gloves and couldn't tell.

"Sorry if I startled you awake, Princess." Jaemin spoke quietly, bending to look at her. "I just needed to adjust my arm. I didn't mean to scare you."

She rubbed her chin, both checking for drool and to feel the comforting mask of the princess's face. Bibi, still a cat curled up on her side of the carriage, opened one sleepy eye, then closed it again. "No, I'm sorry for falling asleep on you. I haven't been a very good traveling companion."

He smiled kindly. "Honestly, I dozed a little myself. Apparently we both needed naps."

Considering they had both spent the night before breaking into the monastery, that made sense. Had the prince lowered his head onto hers as he slept? She frowned as she patted her mussed hair and began pushing the stray bits back into her braid.

"Luckily, you slept through the boring farmland that surrounds Isandine. We're officially in the jungle proper."

Alanna scooted away from him and looked out the window with an open mouth. They traveled on a narrow road flanked by trees and vines and strange flowers. She raised a gloved hand to her mouth and whispered, "I've never been this far."

"I assumed you hadn't."

She'd spoken as Alanna. She mentally grasped for the princess's identity, but Jaemin continued on, unconcerned.

"You came in through the main port, correct? There is enough city built up around the port and the roads leading to Isandine that you wouldn't ever travel through a dense jungle like this."

"Yes, that's exactly it." His words were true enough. Even though she hadn't arrived at the port as the princess, that was where she had arrived with her mother after fleeing La Veridda. And the truth was, once she'd entered Isandine as a girl, she had never been outside its walls again. Street rats didn't have money to travel.

He leaned in and gave a conspiratorial whisper. "Even though our sightseeing is tactical, it doesn't mean we can't still enjoy it."

The jungle surrounded her on both sides, pulling her

further and further away from Isandine. Away from her life of the last fourteen years.

Away from her mother.

Alanna pictured a map of Isandariyah and an imaginary line connecting her to her mother. She was further away from her than she had ever been in her life. And the further the carriage rolled, the longer the line between them grew.

Panic strangled her heart, and she considered jumping out of the moving carriage. What if her mother wandered out of the monastery? What if she made her way to the aviary and Alanna was gone? Alanna continued to pay Leland's unreasonable rent because she wanted to be there if her mother went looking for seven-year-old Alanna. She had subjected herself to years of his inappropriate advances, but now she'd willingly left her mother behind for the chance to go on an excursion with the prince.

Guilt and dread warred within her. Just a few days ago, she had believed her mother safe in the monastery, but now Alanna knew the queen's scholars were experimenting on her. What if the experiments distressed her mother so much that the birds couldn't soothe her anymore? What if the rest of her life was spent in an unconsolable terror? What if her mother even lost the memory of seven-year-old Alanna?

"Are you okay?"

His voice was so gentle, she couldn't help but answer as Alanna. "I miss my mother." The words came out as a strangled whisper, and a tear trickled down her cheek.

Jaemin pulled a handkerchief out of his pocket and handed it to her. "I'm so sorry. I heard about the queen's passing several years ago. I'm sure you miss her very much."

Alanna took the handkerchief and tried to write the words that had accidentally fallen from her lips into the princess's script. "Yes, the queen died. Seeing new places like this makes me think about her." Alanna looked out the window. A bird with bright green and purple feathers perched on a nearby branch. "She would have loved to visit the jungle. She would have found the birds fascinating."

"They are stunning, aren't they?" Jaemin sighed. "I don't often get out this far, and when I do, I rarely take the time to pay attention to how beautiful it is."

"My mother always took time to find the beauty in the world. From the curve of a feather to the shapes of the clouds, she believed it all a miracle of science."

He hummed in agreement. "Sounds like your mother loved discovery, but allowed space for mystery. She would have fit in well with the Sister Scholars."

She didn't know whether to laugh or cry, so she just nodded and used the handkerchief to hide how hard she squeezed her lips together.

"And your father? What is he like? They say he is a good king."

Alanna knew what they said of the King of Naermore. That he was good, but weak for allowing Verkeshe to control his country's ports. But that was the extent of her political knowledge. However, she did remember her own father.

"Yes, my father is a good king and a great man. But even to me, he's more legend than real." It was hard to speak about him as if he were alive, considering he'd been dead for almost fifteen years, but her memories were crystal clear. "He's strong and powerful, a little terrifying, but always gentle with me. I remember measuring my hand against his as a child and thinking he was the strongest man in the world." Her laugh held a hint of sadness. "I still believe it."

"I can't imagine what it must feel like for you to be so far away from him and the rest of your family. You are so brave to travel all this way on your own."

She gave a rough laugh. "Brave? I'm riding in a comfortable carriage through a beautiful jungle with a handsome prince, and I'm crying for my mother, who has been gone for years. I'm not what I'd consider brave."

"Yes, but you made the journey. Some people never do."

She could take very little credit for the actual journey she'd taken with her mother so many years ago. Her father had died in the war when Verkeshe invaded La Veridda. Alanna never saw her mother cry for him, though her mother's smothered sobs filled many dark nights. During the day, her mother's face showed a cold resolve, a determination to get Alanna and herself out of the country before it collapsed. She packed a few important journals, clothes, and all the travel rations she could fit in their backpacks, then snuck them both out of the occupied capital.

Alanna was only seven years old, with no concept of what it meant to suddenly be a refugee. She only knew it meant walking, endless walking. She watched her mother's face every day, and tried to copy her cold resolve and determination with every step they took. They would stop occasionally, and her mom would take up work in one of the small occupied towns along the coastline, but always her mom pushed them onward to Isandariyah.

Her mother told her that Isandariyah had a queen with scholars controlled by no man, especially not King Ruzgar of Verkeshe. Alanna's mother would become one of the queen's scholars, and finally, they would be able to rest.

They had traveled for almost a year when her mother came to her and said she had found a boat that would take them the rest of the way to Isandariyah. Alanna wasn't sure what her mother had to do to earn passage for the two of them on that boat, yet her mother's face shone with the hope of their freedom.

Her mother stood on the prow of the boat and held Alanna to her side as Isandariyah came into view. The beautiful capital city—Isandine—perched high above the docks, framed by the twin volcanoes rising proudly into the dazzling blue sky. The land around the city bloomed in a patchwork of farms interspersed with bright patches of green. And beyond, a jungle grew wild and free for as far as the eye could see.

"We made it, Alanna," her mother had said as they pulled into the port. "We finally made it home."

Tears streamed down Alanna's face as she remembered her mother's eyes that day. So brilliant and clear. Alanna hadn't seen those eyes for years.

Her voice was no more than the softest trickle of air. "I made the journey, but I'm not sure I survived it."

Jaemin looked at her like he wanted her to explain what she meant, but instead, he took her hand and allowed her to cry.

23

Alanna's tears had dried by the time they reached Ylara. She pulled herself together enough to look like a proper princess as the prince helped her out of the carriage, though the effect was spoiled by the look of open-mouthed wonder upon her face.

Ylara was nothing like the city where she lived. The capital of Isandariyah—Isandine—was open to the blue skies and sea. Isandine's stone towers and tree-lined streets possessed a regal beauty, with a style both elegant and orderly.

But Ylara's beauty was wild and barely contained. Dark teakwood buildings nestled beneath the trees, with the jungle coming right to the doors. Jasmine twisted around every surface, the scent almost overwhelming. She couldn't tell if someone had planted the jasmine intentionally, or if the vines had just been allowed to grow where they wished. A chorus of birds called out to her, and cicadas buzzed so loudly the air pulsed with their song.

The riotous sights and sounds and smells sent her staggering back a step, and she gripped the carriage as she tried to take it all in.

"Sorry, I forgot to warn you ... it's a little overwhelming the first time." The prince offered her his arm. "How about I show you to your room before we do any exploring?" His look implied different words: before they hunted down Drazen.

She allowed him to lead her inside the inn. The interior was larger than she'd expected—judging the inn's true size from the outside was hard since it was surrounded by jungle. She walked through the open common room straight to the back wall of the inn, to a wall of windows looking out into the jungle itself. A lime green iguana watched her with a bored expression, and a yellow bird fluffed its feathers, perched on a sunlit branch. Sunshine filtered through the tall trees, dappling the inn's polished floors with gently changing light.

Jaemin approached her, his arms clasped behind his back. "I asked the innkeeper to provide you with clothing more suitable to the jungle. I want to make sure you are comfortable as we ... explore."

She looked up at him, studying his twilight eyes. No playful hint that he'd like to get her out of her current clothes—just his usual kindness. "You are a very considerate man, Prince Jaemin."

He ducked his head and shyly led the way to her room.

The jungle had been pushed further back around the windows of her room, allowing more sunlight to shine through. An ivory comforter and puffy pillows lightened the severity of the dark wood trim, and someone had left a vase with a huge arrangement of orchids and lilies on the table in front of the windows. The breeze from the open windows fluttered the sheer white curtains and the finely woven mesh hanging from the points of the four-poster bed. The netting had been tied back, and a neatly pressed set of clothes lay on her bed.

"Thank you for bringing me with you to such a magical place, Prince Jaemin." Alanna thought the princess would be equally entranced by such beauty. "I will meet you after I change my clothes." She looked up at him with a mischievous grin. "Unless you'd like to assist?"

He choked, but tried to hide it by clearing his throat and tugging at his uniform jacket. "I'm sure you are up to the task, Princess." He dipped into a shallow bow and left the room.

Hidalsa entered, followed by porters carrying a large trunk between them. Bibi rode on the trunk, giving Alanna a regal stare as if the porters were her very own servants. When the porters lowered the trunk, Bibi hopped onto the bed, curling up into a sleek white coil right in the middle of the fluffy comforter. Alanna had to admit Bibi had done a better job adjusting to her new form than Alanna had.

"You enjoy teasing the prince mercilessly," said Hidalsa, the words floating somewhere between statement and admonishment.

The princess put her hands on her hips. "What do you mean by that?"

Hidalsa began unpacking the trunk and shook her head without meeting Alanna's eyes. "He blushes more than any man I've ever met."

Alanna's mischievous grin returned. "I think it's adorable."

Hidalsa did meet her eyes then. "Yes, but did you ever wonder *why* he blushes so?"

Alanna's eyebrows pinched as she frowned. "Because he's ..." The prince's self-description came to mind: methodical, rigid, boring. But none of those were right. "He's ... shy."

Hidalsa raised a cool eyebrow, but didn't respond.

When she had finished unpacking, Alanna sent Hidalsa off to her room and changed into her new clothes by herself.

The loose pants were like the simple pair she owned, but these shimmered purplish-blue in the sunlight, with a gold ribbon gathering the fabric around her ankles. She spoke a prayer of thanks to Qira the Trickster for the tailor who had designed pockets large enough to fit her lamp. Apparently even fancy ladies needed pockets.

The pale blue top wrapped around her waist, and embroidered gardenias wove their way along the neckline. She was grateful for the long sleeves gathered with more gold ribbon at her wrists, but she didn't know what to do about her gloves. Even the most casual pair looked ridiculous with her outfit, but the thought of someone piercing her disguise terrified her. She disregarded fashion with a sigh and pulled on a pair of white gloves.

She found the prince waiting for her in the common room. He had changed out of his uniform into a lightweight tunic and pants like the men in the city wore, yet his were very finely made and showed off his form in exquisite detail. The sleeveless tunic revealed his muscular arms, which she had only seen the time she had watched him strip off his shirt after sparring. She quickly buried that memory before it led to more drooling. His light bronze chest revealed by the gold-trimmed cream tunic was enough to cause drooling on its own. The matching pants flowed enough to be cool, but were thin enough to reveal hints of his muscular legs.

A thousand flirty lines sprang to her mind, but her tongue stuck to the roof of her mouth as she considered Hidalsa's reprimand.

Her pause gave him time to speak first. "You look lovely, Princess. I asked the innkeeper if they had anything in your size with long sleeves. I've noticed you like to keep your arms covered."

Her flirty remarks dissipated. He had once again surprised her with his thoughtfulness, which helped her grasp a helpful explanation. "My pale skin isn't used to the tropical sun. Best to keep it covered." She rubbed a hand down her arm all the way to her fingers, including her gloves in the explanation.

He nodded graciously as if her explanation was perfectly reasonable, then offered his arm and led her outside. Her fingers warmed inside her gloves at the strength of his arm. Even though she had held his bare hand as Alanna, as the princess she usually had two layers of fabric between them. She found the single layer of fabric titillating in a way that flaunting her bare skin was not.

They followed the tree-lined road from the inn until it opened onto a long thoroughfare, with rows of shops restraining the encroaching jungle. The market was a mixture of old and new: pristine teakwood stalls huddled against ancient stone taverns and storehouses.

"The outposts of Ylira and Ylara are even older than Isandariyah itself," said Jaemin. He pointed at the peaks of Mount Qira and Mount Qara, closer than Alanna had ever seen before. "Even before the founding of the queendom, people have always been drawn to the volcanoes."

The wind blowing off the volcano stirred her hair, sizzling with energy. "Of course. The volcanoes contain the power of the Goddesses."

He blinked at her, surprised. Her response was that of a follower of Isandariyan religion.

She tightened her lips primly. "I studied your beliefs before my arrival. To avoid an accidental offense."

She ducked her head, focusing on the crunching gravel beneath their feet. Pebbles of black volcanic rock blanketed the wide road between the buildings, but an occasional sprout of green shot through the rocks.

"It takes a whole team of landscapers to maintain these

roads," he said. "The jungle is relentless. It's quite a job to carve out enough space for people to survive here."

"So, plants grow well in the jungle? Is farming here easier than in other places?" She had never even cared for a single plant before, but to escape life as a slave to the queen, a secluded farm still seemed like her best shot.

Jaemin laughed. "I don't think farming is easy anywhere. But here the job isn't so much about the struggle to get something to grow—it's killing off everything else so what you want to grow actually has room. The battle never ends."

She sighed internally. Maybe Geeni would pay her enough money to hire several farmhands.

As they walked into the covered portion of a shop, two men followed them at a distance, their clothing too nondescript.

"I take it we won't be exploring Ylara alone." She casually glanced behind her. "Assuming those are your men. If not, we have a problem."

He chuckled. "You have a sharp eye."

She tried on a wide-brimmed hat and turned her head in a regal fashion. "It's always good to be aware of your surroundings, Prince. There are a lot of unscrupulous people who would find a prince and princess a tempting target."

"That's true," he said with a thoughtful nod. "Luckily, I'm less recognizable here than in Isandine, so I'm allowed to travel more casually than with the full guard required in the city."

Her eyes flicked around the store, then she held out a hand. "Do you have any of those coins with your face on them, Prince?" She fluttered her hand. "Or any of the other princes. I'm not picky."

She'd meant it as a playful jest, but he reacted as if the words stung. Hidalsa's scolding came back to her, but she pushed it away as he placed a stack of silver coins into her hand.

"Are you looking for a souvenir?" His tone rang with forced cheer.

She passed a coin to the shopkeeper in exchange for her purchase, then she nudged the prince to the other side of a wall made of sturdy parasols. She handed him a pair of gray coveralls worn by the landscapers who battled the aggressive jungle. "Put this on."

He obeyed her firm command but gave her a questioning look as she stepped into coveralls over her own clothes. She peeked around the wall of parasols. Their nondescript guardians waited casually outside the shop.

She plopped the wide-brimmed straw hat onto his head and tucked his curls underneath it with her gloved hands. "If they look closely, they will spot your handsome face, so let's hope they don't look too close before we get away."

She pulled on her own hat, hiding her blond braid inside her coveralls, and he watched her with a curious expression. "Do you often wear disguises, Princess?"

His question startled her, but then she grinned smugly. "I like to keep an eye on what's happening in my country without guards swarming me. Have you never done the same?"

At least he was honest enough to look guilty.

She tilted her straw hat to a jaunty angle. "The landscapers don't often walk arm in arm, Prince, but if you lead on to where we might find Drazen, I will happily join you."

He grinned as he pushed his hat further back on his head and led her down the street to look for Drazen.

24

Alanna ducked into a shadow at the jungle's edge and wiped the sweat off her brow before replacing her hat. After an hour of fruitless searching, she had to admit it was impossible to spy on someone when she didn't know where the person might be headed.

"I think we need to admit defeat, Prince. Your best strategy would be to walk up to a guard post and demand they tell you if Drazen has been here. I'm sure they would tell you."

Jaemin ripped off his hat and rubbed his fingers through his sweaty hair. "I don't want Drazen to think I am suspicious of him. Plus, I have no proof of wrongdoing on his part, only suspicions. He might not be involved."

Based on Drazen's pinpointing of Alanna's location and his lack of surprise at the queen's Spark, Alanna knew he was involved. But the prince didn't know any of that. And neither did the princess. "From my first day in the palace, I've found him suspicious. There's a reason, but I don't think we will find it here."

The prince slammed his hat back on his head and

growled quietly. The fierce sound from the usually stoic prince brought a smile to the princess's face. She looped her arm through his. "Come on, Prince. Use some more of your coins to buy me a drink."

If the sight of two landscapers walking arm in arm into the tavern was unusual, no one said anything. The tavern was an ancient building—rough granite floors worn smooth by centuries of patrons. They stepped up to the bar and removed their straw hats, and Alanna savored the breeze blowing through the unshuttered windows. Jaemin dropped a coin onto the bar, and the bartender poured them each a tall glass of beer.

Alanna unbuttoned the top of her coveralls and drank half the beer before resting the cool glass against her neck. As she raised the glass to drink the rest, she caught Jaemin staring at her. "What?"

His lips curved in a grin, but he quickly hid it behind his glass and took a sip. "Nothing."

She fanned herself with her hat. "I know it was my idea to wear two layers of clothing in a jungle, but you can feel free to stop me from making foolish decisions like that in the future."

His back straightened, and he swallowed. "Understood, Princess."

She looked at him, trying to understand his strange expression, when the tavern door opened and the two nondescript men walked in. She sighed. "Looks like our playdate is at an end, Prince. Our minders have spotted us." She pulled a coin out of her pocket, leftover from her purchase of the hats and coveralls. She slid it to the bartender and tipped her head toward the guards. "Those two could use a drink. They were given quite the runaround while just trying to do their job."

The prince raised an eyebrow. "You made me buy the drinks when you still had money leftover?"

"Are you complaining about buying a lady a drink?" She crossed her arms with a playful huff. "What kind of a grand excursion is this?"

"An unsuccessful one, I'm afraid." He finished his beer and stared into his glass morosely.

"Now, Prince, don't be so down! I'm sure you'll catch your wizard doing something dreadful at some point. What's the rush?" She tapped a gloved finger on the bar, and the bartender brought them two more drinks.

"There's just so much I don't know. About ..." He silently mouthed the word "magic" while scanning the bar for eavesdroppers. "I need to find some answers, and I think it will be easiest to do that here in Isandariyah before I leave."

She blinked. "Before you leave Isandariyah?"

Her question brought him up short. His mouth opened slightly, and a faint blush rose to his cheeks. He swiveled in his chair and downed his entire beer. "We should go." He put another coin on the counter with a nod to the bartender and picked up his hat. He saluted the two guards before heading outside.

Alanna had to scurry to catch up to him. "Are we heading back to the inn?"

He shrugged. "Sure. I don't know where else to look."

"Before we walk back, I am stripping off one layer of clothes." She wiggled out of the coveralls, but kept the straw hat. The prince didn't pay attention to her strategic wiggling, but she was pleased that at least a few bystanders appreciated her effort.

He was so lost in his thoughts, she had to shake him when a carriage started down the thoroughfare. A carriage bearing the insignia of the queen. She pulled him to her side. "Is that our carriage?"

His wide eyes answered her.

She pulled his hat down further on his head, then angled his body so she could stand behind him. "Is it him?" she whispered.

His glance into the carriage was more obvious than she preferred, but everyone on the thoroughfare had stopped to watch the royal carriage roll past, so he wasn't alone.

As it passed in front of them, Alanna risked a peek inside. Drazen sat on one side of the large carriage, his face as severe as always. Alanna clutched the lamp in her pocket and stopped breathing. She couldn't tear her eyes away from him, because she was convinced his eyes would suddenly dart up and fix on her. She clung to the lamp, hoping Geeni's rune held strong.

The carriage continued its slow progression down the road, and Alanna finally let her focus switch to Drazen's passengers. A man and woman sat close on the other bench, a tired look on their faces. And right before the carriage rolled out of view, two little heads popped up in the window.

"He took children?" she whispered.

Jaemin watched the carriage until it dipped out of sight, a sick look on his face. Alanna still couldn't breathe, but Jaemin turned to a shopkeeper and asked, "Do you know who that man was?"

"The queen's man?" He shrugged. "I think he's been here before, but I haven't met him."

"Who were the people riding with him?"

The shopkeeper eyed Jaemin's coveralls, probably trying to decide if he really was a local. "That was Magistrate Leston and his family."

Jaemin tipped his head to the man and looped Alanna's arm through his.

"He took children, Jaemin." A chill shivered through

Alanna despite the heat. She allowed Jaemin to lead her as they walked back to the inn. "What does he want them for?"

He shook his head. "I'm not sure."

"You believe he has magic?"

"Yes. I think he can sense magic ... a magic 'sniffer' if you will ... That's why he's gone so often. He comes to places like this and gathers up the ones with Sparks."

Alanna believed the same, but she hadn't realized Jaemin had put together the pieces. The princess asked innocently, "Does the queen know?"

"I don't know."

She had expected him to outright deny it, but his slumped shoulders made it difficult to celebrate the victory. She gave his arm a comforting squeeze. "You'll find the answers. Maybe you can just ask her and see what she says."

His head drooped further. "If she does know, she has kept it a secret from me, possibly for my entire life. But if she doesn't know, and I reveal Drazen's secrets to her ... reveal to her a world of hidden magic ... I have no idea what she'll do." He whispered, "I honestly don't know which option is worse."

She studied him, his solemn face dappled by the sunlight through the trees of the shaded drive. She asked her question gently, so as not to put him on edge. "Are you afraid of her, Jaemin?"

He shook his head sadly. "No. I'm afraid *for* her." He bit his lip and walked the rest of the way to the inn in silence.

25

Alanna tied the lamp to her thigh. The dress Hidalsa had laid out for dinner didn't have pockets, but Alanna refused to leave her room without the lamp, even though she had watched Drazen head back to Isandine.

The jasmine-scented bath had cooled her off after her romp around the jungle outpost in two layers of clothes. Her airy dinner dress hugged her body with clever folds of draped fabric, though she had to adjust a fold to hide the outline of the lamp strapped to her thigh. The white dress did have long sleeves, but a slit ran from her shoulder to the gathered wrists, exposing her arm every time she bent her elbow.

In addition to the exposed skin on her arms, there was no way she could reasonably wear gloves. The sun had already set, and her dinner with the prince wouldn't be in the palace's formal ballroom. She had to trust in the prince's continued kind formality and assume he wouldn't suddenly try to woo her with a gentle caress.

The thought of the prince running his fingers up her

bare arm sent a shiver of terror and delight racing across her borrowed skin.

A knock at the door startled her out of her dangerous daydream. She pulled the edges of her sleeves together, the protection more mental than physical, and opened the door.

The prince looked stunning in a lightweight tunic and pants in navy blue with silver scrolling trim. He offered his arm with a courteous smile. His tunic had long sleeves, and Alanna realized the difficulty if he had still been in his sleeveless tunic from earlier. As she rested her bare hand in the crook of his arm, she took a deep breath to calm herself.

His clean scent filled her nose. He smelled of warm spices with hints of coconut, and she savored the comforting scent with half-lidded eyes. "I guess you also took a refreshing bath after our sweaty outing?"

The prince stumbled a step but said calmly, "Yes, Princess."

She hadn't been imagining him in the bath, but now she was. She cleared her throat delicately. "Where are you taking me, Prince?"

He had led her through the inn's common room and down the hallway opposite her room. He stopped at a door carved with flowering trees and released her hand.

"It's not like our dinners at the palace, but I hope you'll enjoy it." He threw open the door and ushered her outside.

She staggered down three steps onto the mossy ground, her mouth open wide. A candlelit table for two sat at the center of the outdoor dining "room." Flowering trees with orange blossoms made up the walls, fitted close enough to hold back the encroaching jungle. Branches with emerald leaves arched overhead, depositing orange petals onto a moss floor as soft as a rug. Stars twinkled through the canopy of leaves, brighter than she had ever seen.

He pulled out her seat at the table. "I take it you approve?"

She closed her gaping jaw with a laugh. "Yes, I approve! You are full of surprises, Prince."

He took a seat across from her as the husband and wife innkeepers deposited a plate in front of each of them. Alanna breathed in the scent of warm curry and rice with a hint of citrus. Jaemin thanked them both before they ducked back inside, and Alanna grabbed her fork and took a bite.

Jaemin lifted a hand. "I should warn you—"

The spicy curry sent a rush of heat across her cheeks and all the way down to her belly. The meat was well seasoned and cooked to perfection. She closed her eyes as she savored the warmth and intricate flavors.

Jaemin still watched her as she opened her eyes. She gave him an arch look. "I enjoy spicy food, Prince. No need to warn me."

He bit his lip. "Um ... it's not that. I wanted to warn you that the meat is iguana."

She blinked at him. Just how should a princess respond to this news? Alanna herself had eaten iguana many times in the city. She loved nothing more than a spicy iguana meat pie, however, a princess ...

If she reacted poorly, she wouldn't get to finish the curry, and there was no way she would send it back to the kitchen. She gave a light laugh as she scooped up another bite. "In Naermore, we eat delicacies you'd find even more unusual. You should try them all someday." She took a sip of white wine, the smooth oaky taste setting off the spice.

He ducked his head, suddenly very interested in his curry. She frowned, unsure what she'd said wrong. Without the other princes around, it was up to her to keep the dinner conversation moving, but she couldn't figure out why she occasionally drove it to a halt.

She picked up a new topic. "So, are we headed back to Isandine tomorrow?"

His gaze left his curry, and he sighed. "Yes, unfortunately we are. I'd love to spend more time here. It's so restful." He stared at the canopy of trees and the starlit night. "Back in Isandine I have the Queen's Guard waiting for me to train new members, a meeting with the city guild leaders, and whatever else piled up while I was gone." He looked back at her with a sad smile. "There's so much to do, and I can't hide in the jungle forever."

He did so much for the city, often acting as king in all but name only. He carried responsibilities that should be carried by the queen, who was always mysteriously "busy." Just because Jaemin had been born a man, he couldn't rule Isandariyah. He was responsible and thoughtful and cared deeply for his people. If anyone was made to be a king, it was him.

"It's not fair," she sighed. "You should be king."

His eyes shot up to hers, and Alanna scooted back in her chair at the intensity of his twilight gaze. He spoke in a brittle tone. "It's fortunate you aren't a citizen of Isandariyah. Otherwise, I'd have to execute you for treason."

Her breath froze in her lungs. She wasn't sure if he was serious. She hadn't heard of anyone being executed for just suggesting a king, but perhaps that was because she was the only one foolish enough to say it out loud.

"I'm sorry, Prince," she whispered. "I shouldn't have said—"

"It's forgiven." He sipped his wine without looking at her. "You're from Naermore. Your ways are different."

"Yes, that's it, of course." She watched as he poked at his curry, moving it around without eating.

This was it. The cause of the sadness and vulnerability in his eyes. It was because of the burden he carried.

The burden he carried alone.

It wasn't right of her to ask him to share the burden with her, not when she hoped to steal from him and escape as soon as she got paid. She should leave him be and hope he found someone worthy to share his burdens. Yet, she couldn't bear to see the sadness in his eyes.

"If the queen doesn't give birth to a daughter ... " She spoke gently, unsure if her words would hurt him. "What will happen to Isandariyah?"

The night air stilled like an indrawn breath, waiting for his answer.

"I don't know," he whispered. "I wish I had an answer, but I don't." His shoulders bowed under the weight of the admission, but the burden shouldn't have been his to bear.

"Has the queen given any indication of what she plans to do?"

"The queen is ..."

Alanna thought he would say "busy," but he paused, biting his lip. He studied the princess with intense eyes, before closing them and whispering, "The queen is unwell."

Alanna blinked, trying to understand what he meant. She had just seen the queen at the ball. Queen Illorienne had looked powerful and strong, even if sadness lurked behind her eyes.

He opened his eyes, and his words flowed out, as if they had been pent up for a long time. "She has been unwell for many years, but she pulls herself together for occasional public appearances. We barely speak about matters of state anymore ... She trusts me to handle it." He drew in a shaking breath. "We never speak of succession."

He leaned forward in his chair, his voice barely more than a whisper. "She's just so tired. I fear one day ... one day she will give up and name me king." He shook his head as if he could shake the thought away. "The country won't survive that ... *She* won't survive that."

Alanna longed to reach across the table to take his hand but couldn't. She had forced him to unburden himself, yet there was nothing she could do.

"Oh, Jaemin ... I'm so sorry. I wish there were some way for me to help."

He looked up at her with bright eyes, then shifted them back to his plate. "It's best if I leave ... If I'm here, playacting as king, one day in a weak moment, she'll renounce the throne, and it will all fall apart."

She tried to understand why he spoke again about leaving but couldn't figure out what she was missing.

He gave her a small smile, though it was still tinged with sadness. "Thank you for listening, Princess Aliyabeth. It's nice to talk with someone who understands the challenges of royal bloodlines." The muscles in his jaw worked as he swallowed. "I feel like we could become good friends. For people like us, that's often the best we can hope for."

Something in his eyes set off warning bells in Alanna's mind. He perched on the edge of his chair, as if waiting for something ... as if waiting for her. She didn't know what was supposed to come next, and couldn't find the next line of her script.

The princess's skin felt stretched taut, like Alanna was right below the surface waiting to break out. The night air rushed through the trees, rippling the candlelight and dropping orange petals onto their uneaten food and into their wineglasses. The cicadas' song vibrated in waves that thrummed across the soft moss. Birds flapped their wings, creating gusts of wind that fluttered the princess's dress and ruffled the prince's hair.

The prince blinked and suddenly stood.

She gasped and shot to her feet, looking at her hands, sure they would belong to Alanna, but finding the princess's pale skin. Her panicked breathing spun into a whirlwind flying around their small table, blowing out all the candles and spilling their wine.

She tried to gasp out a denial, but couldn't pull any air into her lungs, not with it swirling around her. She looked at the prince, expecting to find betrayal in his eyes, but instead he stared into the trees. His eyes darted between the branches, reckless longing written on his face.

He was searching for Alanna.

Jealousy flared in her chest that he would so quickly forget the princess before him for a street rat roaming the shadows. But then her true heart stuttered with the knowledge: he completely disregarded the princess for *her.*

The wind spun fiercer, until orange petals rushed by at dizzying speed. Birds squawked as their restful perches swayed in the strange wind, and the cicadas' buzzing hit a fevered pitch.

The prince reached across the table to take her hand. She jerked back, knocking her chair over.

The whirlwind stopped, and the petals rained softly onto the mossy ground.

"I'm sorry, Princess. I'm so sorry." He covered his mouth with his hand, and his eyes no longer studied the trees.

He had taken the abrupt withdrawal of her hand as anger. As if she were a jealous princess who knew her prince had been dreaming of another.

She used her momentary flash of jealousy as a shield to protect her true heart. "We're merely friends, Prince. You can search out your mystery woman with no objections from me."

Her sweeping exit provided the perfect excuse to escape his eyes—beautiful yet sick with guilt.

26

It was Alanna, not the princess, who found him at the bar. He wore the landscaper's coveralls again, yet he looked too clean to be mistaken for the other landscapers, who had been working all day. Although, his wavy hair was still windblown from her storm, and he hadn't taken the time to straighten it.

She sat beside him and slid a coin to the bartender, signaling for two drinks. Jaemin drained the beer in his hand without looking at her. She didn't see any undercover guards in the room but didn't know if he had outsmarted them or simply commanded them to leave him alone.

The bartender brought them two drinks, then handed the change to Alanna. She drank beside the prince in silence, unsure what to say, fairly confident she shouldn't have come at all.

She hadn't planned on coming. After she made it back to her room, breathless with desire and jealousy and fear, she'd sworn she would go right to bed, avoiding the prince until her awkward return to the palace as the princess the next morning. Hidalsa had taken one look at her, said that her nightclothes were in the top drawer, then walked out without another word.

The "nightclothes" in the top drawer had been Alanna's clothes, not the princess's. She wasn't sure how much Hidalsa suspected, but Alanna had put on the clothes without thinking too hard, then snuck out to find him.

"Where's Bibi?" he asked.

She hadn't known what his first words to her would be, but that wouldn't have been her guess. "She heard noises in the jungle that sounded like 'friends.' I hope she doesn't get into trouble."

His eyes stayed fixed on his drink. "You followed me."

She couldn't tell if his assumption brought him joy or not. "I heard there might be things to learn in Ylara."

He shrugged. "Drazen took Magistrate Leston, along with his whole family, but I don't know why."

Alanna drained the rest of her beer and waved down the bartender again. As she handed him money for another glass, she asked him, "I heard a queen's man took the magistrate with him. Any idea why?"

The bartender shrugged. "No idea. It's a shame, though. He was a good magistrate. He had a real knack for knowing if people were telling the truth." He slid her the drink, then moved on to other customers.

Jaemin finally turned to look at her. Some of his misery fled in light of this news. "A 'knack' for spotting the truth? That's a helpful skill."

Alanna took a drink to hide her face. Along with the queen and Drazen, Magistrate Leston now stood at the top of her list of people to avoid.

From the corner of the tavern erupted a screech that resolved itself into an out of tune melody. The man playing the screechy violin tapped his foot in time to the melody, then began a well-known song with bawdy lyrics.

Alanna expected the prince to blush as he did when the princess said something provocative, but he just looked mildly disinterested. When the other customers joined the chorus, he sighed. "I'm not in the mood for sing-alongs tonight. I'll just wait outside."

Alanna stood to follow him, but the barkeep pulled her back with a warning glance. "I hate to be the one to break this to you, sweetheart, but he was in here earlier with another woman."

She took his meddling as a kindness, and said, "Thanks for the warning, but he's just a ... colleague."

He raised an eyebrow and silently polished a glass.

She cleared her throat. "I appreciate the concern, though. And thank you again for the information about the magistrate."

He studied the clean glass with a little frown. "I hope he's not in trouble. He's had a rough time lately. His young daughter was almost trampled by a horse, but luckily an odd pink-haired lady rescued the girl."

Alanna disguised her shock with a careful voice. "I'm sure the magistrate is just fine. Good night, sir."

She shuffled out of the bar, reluctant to see Jaemin until she composed herself. Geeni had been in Ylara looking for the man with a Spark to spot the truth. What was she up to?

Alanna found Jaemin sitting on an ancient stone bench behind the tavern, his eyes fixed on the jungle just a few feet away. He didn't move as she sat at his side.

"I'm not normally so brooding, just so you know." He stared into the jungle, although the moonlight only struck the very edge of the trees. "I'm giving myself a single night of wallowing before I stop being so dramatic."

Her lips curved in a gentle smile. "That sounds lovely. My life is full of drama, but I rarely take a full evening to enjoy it."

He huffed out a small laugh. "Well, I'm usually the responsible one. The one who does the right thing, no matter how painful. Yet every choice before me is painful, and none of them feel right." He ran his fingers through his windswept hair, tousling it even more. "Tomorrow I will apologize to the princess, and hopefully she will still want to marry me."

Alanna's mouth dropped open as she thought through all their conversations. Had she somehow missed a proposal? "I didn't realize you were engaged to the princess."

He slumped back in his seat. "No, we aren't officially engaged yet. Though I've tried to make it clear that I would say yes if she asked."

A gale-force wind slammed into her mind, though the night air remained still. The princess was supposed to propose to the prince. He'd arranged a romantic dinner for the two of them, talked to her about friendship, and waited for her to propose. Instead, Alanna had caused a whirlwind that spiraled the night out of control.

"Oh ..." She drew out the sound, trying to buy time to think. "Maybe she still will?" The princess would do no such thing. Alanna would not add a broken proposal to the list of her sins against him.

He studied his hands clasped in his lap. "She teases me with no regard for my precarious position." He swallowed, a muscle in his jaw flexing. "I will go to her bed, because it's my duty, but she seems to enjoy flaunting her power over me."

Guilt threatened to consume her. Hidalsa had asked *why* the prince blushed, but Alanna hadn't truly considered it. Prince Jaemin was a strong, proud man who should have been king, yet he was dependent on a foreign princess to offer him a proposal. A marriage of bloodlines and convenience, with friendship the best-case scenario.

And the princess treated him like a piece of meat without offering a pledge of marriage.

She chewed on her lips as she considered her flippant words. "The princess has treated you unfairly."

He finally turned to look at her, and Alanna realized how close they sat. A poorly played ballad drifted out of the tavern, and the firelight shining through the open windows lit his twilight eyes with a muted intensity.

"Would you dance with me, Alanna?"

The question caught her off guard. "I ... I don't know how to dance." The answer wasn't completely a lie. She didn't know how to do any proper dancing. The only moves she knew involved strategic wiggling designed to distract from her fingers lightly lifting a man's purse.

He stood and offered his hand. "I'll keep it simple enough. I'm not looking for intricate court dances."

Putting her bare hand in his required an intentional reminder that she wore her own skin. His skin on hers wouldn't pierce her disguise. She would be safe.

Yet when he pulled her close, she felt anything but safe.

The worn cotton of her shirt offered no protection against the warmth of his strong hand on her back, while his other hand clasped hers with such a steady grip, she could feel each callus on his palm pressing against her soft skin.

She bit her lip, then looked up at him. "Are you sure this isn't further proof that you're being too dramatic?"

"Perhaps. But I gave myself one night to enjoy it." He spun her in one quick turn to distract her, then they settled into a slow step, more swaying than dancing.

"I'm going to ask the queen about magic," he said.

He held her so close that she couldn't look into his face without pulling away. And Goddesses help her, she didn't want to pull away.

She answered quietly. "Are you worried about how she will react?" He had confessed the queen's illness to the princess, not Alanna, so she left him to interpret the question as he wished.

"I can't imagine a good outcome for the conversation." His muscular chest pressed against her, rising and falling in a sigh. "But I need to know. My brothers need to know. Even if this confrontation brings about the end of the queendom."

He worried that the queen would surrender to her illness and name him king. The tension forever lurking in his rigid posture tightened his shoulder beneath Alanna's hand. He stood as an unyielding fortress in the midst of a storm, but deep weariness lay below the surface. She had no answers to offer, no more than the princess did, but this time she could be intentional with her Spark.

The violinist had started another lewd song, his notes quick and sloppy. Alanna lured the breeze carrying his song closer and took hold of the notes, smoothing the sharp edges and pulling the song into a gentle rhythm in time with their swaying steps. The prince tilted his head as if confused by the change in the music, but his grip on Alanna never faltered.

Alanna gathered up the distracting buzz of cicadas and pushed the pulsing air to the ground. The grass trembled and sent vibrations through the soles of Alanna's thin slippers, but the air near their ears quieted to allow other sounds to filter through.

She diverted the chatter of the people in the tavern and on the street beyond, but allowed the soft coo of sleepy birds inside the bubble of air surrounding her and the prince. He had stopped swaying, which was for the best, since she needed to focus on creating the rest of her song.

Her voice had never been spectacular, but she was adept

at whistling. She closed her eyes and whistled a children's tune, melancholy yet oddly soothing. She tied the melody's breeze into a neat bow, letting it spin around them in a tranquil loop. The violinist's drone threatened to veer off course, but she nudged it back into place with a raised finger against the prince's shoulder.

His shuddering indrawn breath tightened all his muscles, then he relaxed against her, his body melting into hers. Her eyes popped open, but he held her so close, all she could see was his broad shoulder.

A strong shoulder now at peace.

The illusion of dancing had fled, leaving only an embrace behind. The prince's body rose and fell with steady, even breaths, but Alanna barely breathed at all. She blamed her struggling breath on the magic she wove around them, but the truth was, she could have held the song in place all night.

Holding her soul in place was another matter.

When she took the job from Geeni, she had never imagined falling in love with the prince, but she could no longer deny that was what had happened. She had fallen for him as both Alanna and the princess, and every other identity she had worn. Alanna the street rat had fallen in love with the prince, and she wanted him more than she had ever wanted anything in her entire life.

Except for one thing.

She had to get her mother out of the monastery. Alanna had traveled so far away, leaving her mother all alone in Isandine at the mercy of Drazen and the scholars. Even now she imagined Drazen testing the magistrate against her mother, checking to see if the man's truth-detecting Spark worked on someone whose mind struggled to understand reality. Despite Jaemin's strong arms around her, she felt her mother's need pulling her back to Isandine.

She leaned against his chest and briefly considered confessing it all to him. He knew magic existed, so perhaps he would believe the wild tale of Geeni and the lamp, and could forgive Alanna enough to not execute her for treason. But she would still have no money to buy a farm to let her mother escape the monastery. And when she thought about how he would react if she confessed, stoically taking in all her lies, the tension in his shoulders returning, his eyes hardening as he found proof he truly was alone ... She couldn't do that to him. Better for him to wake up one day finding Alanna and the princess had mysteriously disappeared. She would leave him before revealing her betrayal.

"I know it was wrong of me to ask you for a dance." His low voice resonated against her chest more than floated in the air. "I'm a prince of the queendom. I should be strong enough to handle a dark night without the solace of a woman's arms around me. Yet, I can't bring myself to feel guilty for enjoying the comfort of your magic ... the comfort of *you*."

His strong physique rippled with muscles, yet his body yielded to her touch, melding against her with a formidable gentleness. His steady heartbeat pulsed against her chest. How could she ever bear to let him go?

"Thank you, Alanna." His words fell softly inside their bubble of air, only for her. "I'm ready to face what must be done. And when I leave Isandariyah, I'll treasure this moment always."

His words shattered her quiet contemplation. She leaned back to finally look him in the eyes. "You're leaving Isandariyah?" He had mentioned leaving to the princess and had blushed when she didn't understand.

Jaemin blinked, as if confused he needed to explain. "When I marry the princess, we will travel back to Naermore to live there."

Her hand dropped from his shoulder, but he didn't surrender his hold on her other hand. "Why would you do that? The queendom needs you."

He shook his head sadly, adjusting his grip on her hand to hold it between them. "I can't marry a princess and continue to live here. Imagine if we had a daughter ... some might conveniently forget she wasn't a direct descendant of the queen."

"Maybe they *should* forget! That would fix a lot of things."

His face hardened, but he didn't drop her hand. "I wouldn't forget, Alanna. The bloodline is sacred to the Goddesses, and passed down from queen to female heir. What if the princess was unfaithful to me? The bloodline would be lost, and we wouldn't even know."

Alanna wanted to vouch for the princess's faithfulness, but she had firsthand knowledge that the princess lied exceedingly well. A gentle rain began to fall, and the water droplets sliced paths through her woven song, sending the notes spinning off in discordant waves.

She tried to calm her racing heart, knowing the prince would not go to Naermore because *she* would not be proposing anytime soon. She looked up at him, rain trickling into her eyes. "And what if the princess doesn't propose?"

He pulled himself taller, some of the tension returning to his shoulders. "I will find another strategic match to benefit the queendom and follow my bride back to her home."

A dissonant note fluttered past her ear, and she batted it away. "But what about Isandariyah? You know how fragile the queendom is without a succession plan. How can you just leave us?"

Her real question floated on the last remaining thread of

her song. "How can you just leave *me*?"

The question was unfair, considering how she planned to abandon him without an explanation, fleeing the city to live in secret on a farm, yet still, the question burned in the air between them.

His fingers brushed against her cheek, wiping away raindrops and tears alike. He tilted her face to his until all she saw were the raindrops balanced on the edge of his lashes. All traces of her song had been borne to the ground by the falling rain, so his soft voice cut through the silent air.

"Isandariyah will fall, Alanna. There is no stopping it. And I can't bear to watch it happen."

He pressed his lips against hers, and the illusion of her control shattered. She wrapped her arms around him, clutching the fabric of his coveralls as if he might flee at any moment. His hand slipped from her cheek into her hair, tangling in her waves flattened by the rain, while his other hand wrapped around her waist, heat searing through her wet cotton blouse at his touch.

His lips met hers with the ferocity of a hurricane unleashed, and he kissed her as if this kiss was their last. Alanna feared that was exactly what it was, and her salty tears mixed with the rain pouring down their cheeks.

He pulled away, his hand sliding from her hair to curl gently behind her neck. Raindrops scattered from his lashes with each slow blink, and alongside the sadness, his twilight eyes held a resolve that could not be swayed.

Her hands sprang loose from his coveralls, and she staggered back a step, guessing his next words.

"Goodbye, Alanna." His voice rang with finality.

Her breath caught on a sob, but he made no move to reach out to her.

She turned and fled, her escape barely stirring the lifeless wind.

27

The prince and princess sat on opposite sides of the carriage, unspeaking. Alanna didn't trust herself to speak. She didn't know whose words would spill from her mouth—hers or the princess's. Her conversations with the prince blended in her mind, and she could no longer recall what he had told to whom. The only thing that mattered was he believed the queendom stood poised to fall, and he didn't want to watch.

It must be nice to have the luxury to leave and avoid the calamity of a coup or revolution or anarchy or however the queendom would come to an end. He could watch from the comfort of a neighboring kingdom in the arms of a willing princess eager to have a former prince in her bed.

Wait ... was she that princess?

No ... she was a street rat, not a princess. Her identity distorted around her, and she couldn't place her heart within the right body. She shook her head, trying to get her thoughts to line up as they should. Bibi glanced up with her judgy cat face, before returning to the job of licking herself, which she had done nonstop since she had returned from the jungle sopping wet the night before.

Alanna risked a glance at Jaemin, who hadn't moved from his position the entire trip, staring out the window with a morose expression. He had said he would allow himself only a single night to wallow in his misery, but it appeared he continued his wallowing this morning.

But he'd said that to Alanna, so the princess remained silent.

The princess fumed for different reasons. He had run away from their romantic evening, an evening when the princess probably would have proposed, to drink in a bar with a common thief. He knew what the strange girl was, and yet, he'd asked her for a dance in the moonlight. And then he'd kissed that street rat as if his heart was breaking, as if he would never kiss anyone like that again.

She brushed a gloved hand across the stranger's lips she wore. Alanna had felt the prince's lips imprinted on hers all the way back to the inn, but after she rubbed one of her bountiful tears onto the lamp's final small rune, his kiss had faded along with Alanna's skin. She wondered if, when her true skin returned, so would the feel of his lips, or if even the memory of his kiss was lost to her.

Their eyes met briefly, and she abruptly dropped her hand into her lap. The princess looked at him, waiting to see if he would apologize for running off on her. If he would swear his devotion to her. If he would deny falling in love with a street rat.

He looked at her and, very clearly, said nothing at all.

His focus returned to the window. She leaned her head against the seat and fell asleep.

She awoke as they passed through the gates of Isandine. The stiff pain in her neck reminded her how she had fallen asleep in the carriage on the way to Ylara with her head resting comfortably on the prince's shoulder. Now the prince wore his uniform, and his shoulders were as rigid and immovable as they had ever been. She would find no comfort there.

The carriage pulled to a stop outside the gates of the palace but didn't roll inside. The prince looked out the window, and a Queen's Guard explained that a vine had wound its way into the gears controlling the gate. Unusual, considering how many times a day they opened the gate, but since the vine had natural causes, they'd ruled out sabotage. Jaemin stepped out of the carriage, then turned back to the princess, speaking for the first time the entire trip. "Wait here."

The princess didn't like being bossed around any more than Alanna did, so she stepped out of the carriage, happy to stretch her legs. As two more Queen's Guards followed him into the gatehouse, Alanna waited for her reprimand with held breath.

A hooded scholar approached.

"Good afternoon, Sister Scholar," said the princess with a bow.

Geeni raised her bowed head. "You're late."

"We were called away—"

Geeni placed her hand a breath away from the princess's cheek, an apparent sign of blessing, which Alanna experienced as the threat it was. "You will bring the diary to me in the garden at midnight, or I will pop the illusion myself and have you replaced." She tucked her hands back into her robes, the appearance of a serene sister. "Do you understand?"

"I understand." Alanna bowed her head, not looking up until Geeni had walked away. Then she stepped back into the carriage and waited for Jaemin to return.

He entered the carriage, still silent. Would he explain? Was the vine a random natural occurrence? Or did he think it had been caused by someone with a Spark? He said nothing. If they were to proceed, she would have to make the first move.

"I will have dinner in my room tonight," she said.

The prince nodded absently.

"After dinner, I would have you escort me to the library."

He studied her, trying to interpret her two seemingly contradicting statements, yet her reasoning made complete sense. She couldn't eat a meal across from him, knowing what she planned to do.

"I will try to accommodate, Princess, but I've been gone for almost two days, and I have—"

"I heard the library is very private," said the princess calmly.

"Um ... yes ... only family members have keys and—"

"I'd like to ask you a question. In private."

The words hung in the dead air inside the carriage. The prince looked at her with a mixture of dread and relief—the same expression a convicted man might give to the executioner the moment before the axe falls. She wished she could draw the words back. She had sworn she wouldn't add a broken engagement to her list of sins, but she had to make sure the prince took her to the library tonight. This was her last chance to finish the job and escape.

Yet, if she was honest, there was another reason, so complicated she tried to deny it. Geeni had threatened to put someone else in her place. She imagined someone else in the princess's skin, sitting at Jaemin's side, eating dinner with him, and jealousy flared inside her chest. Even though the new fake princess would be just as unable to touch him, the thought of him going on excursions with someone else filled her with as much jealousy as when he jilted her to chase after that street rat.

Wait ... *she* was the street rat ...

She squeezed the confusing mix of jealousy and guilt

below the surface and clung to the princess's identity. "Will you take me to the library tonight, Prince?"

He held his posture so rigidly, Alanna thought he might crack. A muscle in his jaw flexed, and he said, "Yes, Princess. I would be happy to."

The solemn look on his face contradicted his words, but the princess allowed him the lie. "Thank you, Prince. I look forward to you taking me."

She hadn't intended the words to torment him, but he blushed just the same.

28

Alanna had no appetite, so instead of dinner, she changed her clothes a dozen times. Her first outfit of stiff silk looked too imperious, as if she relished her position of dominance over him. Her second outfit with delicate lace suggested she would be a meek wife, allowing him to seek out other women whenever he desired. The low-cut dress said she planned a seduction for their rendezvous in the library. She tossed away dresses that said submission or conquest, and dresses without pockets weren't even a consideration.

She finally chose a grayish-blue dress with a square neckline and a skirt just full enough to hide the outline of the lamp in her pocket. She studied the princess's now familiar face in her bedroom mirror, and had almost talked herself into changing again, when a knock came from the other room.

Hidalsa bowed her way into the bedroom. "The prince is here for you, Your Highness."

The princess took a deep breath and swept into the sitting room.

And found Prince Hawthorne at her door.

"Good evening, Princess. I missed seeing you at dinner." Despite her plain dress, Hawthorne still ogled her from head to toe.

"Do you need something, Prince?" she asked politely.

"I heard my brother is taking you to the library tonight." He leaned forward so his sultry tone worked to its full effect. "But if he's not here in the next five minutes, I will take you myself."

She had to appreciate Hawthorne's skill. If the queendom did fall, and he lost his position as prince, he could have a lucrative career seducing women out of their money.

The princess crossed her arms and looked him up and down. "And have you ever known your brother to shirk his obligations?"

His lips curved in a grin. "No. But he's never known me to stop flirting until a woman is officially engaged."

She held out her hand. "Good night, Prince Hawthorne. It's been a pleasure flirting with you."

He kissed her gloved fingers. "The pleasure's been all mine." He winked before walking away.

She closed the door and blew out her breath.

"Are you proposing to the prince tonight, Your Highness?" Hidalsa cleared Alanna's uneaten dinner off the table without glancing up.

"I'm not sure." She bit her lip and sank against the closed door.

"Are you going to break the prince's heart?"

Alanna turned to Hidalsa, who stared at her with hard eyes. The princess wanted to reprimand her maid for being impertinent, but Alanna felt too guilty to fake it. "I'm afraid I will do that no matter what happens."

A knock vibrated the door against her back, and she

straightened with a sigh. Her maid continued clearing the dishes, so the princess opened the door herself.

"Good evening, Princess," said Prince Jaemin formally. "I'm ready to escort you to the library."

His face once again resembled that of a condemned man, though he stood with an unbowed back, as proud and regal as ever. She looped her arm through his and allowed him to lead her to the library. Jaemin took her down a long hallway with candlelit alcoves between each tall door and stopped at the door at the end of the hall. He picked up a candlestick from one of the alcoves and pulled a thin key out of his pocket. He gritted his teeth and unlocked the door.

The prince's candlelight only reached a few feet inside the dark room, so all she could see were the ten-foot-tall bookcases standing on either side of the door. She followed him inside, and he locked the door behind them.

She could reach out and touch both sets of bookshelves, and less than a dozen feet in front of her, a bookshelf appeared to block them in. She would have assumed the bookcases enclosed them in a small room if she hadn't looked up.

A domed ceiling of glass soared high above, giving Alanna some scope of the library's size. Prince Jaemin's candlelight only fell upon the books directly around them, but faint moonlight shone on the books further away, casting the room in a soft silver light.

He waited until she had stopped staring open-mouthed at the massive ceiling before he began walking. Where the bookshelves seemed to end, an opening emerged to their right, leading to another set of shelves that curved in a circle around the edge of the domed ceiling. An opening appeared on their left, but the prince passed it by, turning at the next opening instead.

"It's a labyrinth," he explained. "You can find books along every dead end, but there's only one path all the way through."

Alanna glanced at the book titles as they passed. Without the prince's guidance, she would never find the book she wanted. Geeni had truly needed someone who could convince the prince to lead her to the treasure, and not just a common thief.

He took two turns to the left, before following another long curving path around the outside.

"A single candle seems like a poor way to read all these books."

"Most scholarly activity happens during the day, while the sun lights the entire room. But since there are no wall sconces, for obvious reasons, it's quite dark at night. Hence its reputation for being 'private.'" He cleared his throat, then continued. "There are more candles in the seating area at the center of the labyrinth. I thought we could go there."

She couldn't stop staring at the starlight sparkling through the dome stretching overhead. "I had no idea this was in the palace. It's truly stunning."

Prince Jaemin's voice relaxed as he took on the tone of a tour guide. "The queen who built this library was my seventh great-grandmother. She designed it as a gift for her husband, a scholar of some renown."

Alanna glimpsed fine scrollwork between the panels of glass. The dome would be stunning in the daylight. "She must have loved him very much."

"Yes," he said stiffly. "Sometimes royalty is lucky enough to marry for love."

She had no hopeful response to offer.

They moved closer to the center, before turning away again, arcing in a wide circle on the other side of the room. She could only keep track of her position by the moon through the dome's glass, but that wouldn't be a reliable source as the night continued.

"How do you find your way around in here? Do you ever get lost?"

He shrugged. "I've come here since I was a child. I've become familiar with its secrets."

She gave him a saucy look. "I thought Qara the Wise said knowledge was available to all?"

He laughed bitterly. "That's what the scholars believe, but queens make their own rules."

The weight of her impending betrayal pressed down on her. She recognized this moment as the heartbeat before she slid her fingers into a rich man's pockets. In that heartbeat, she had the choice to steal from him or to leave him be. Yet truly, the choice was always made long before she ever laid eyes on him.

"And where would you look for a book like the one I gave you?" she said lightly. "You said you had its match?" Her heart thudded heavily, counting down the moments until her escape.

"It's just up ahead—close to the center of the labyrinth." He seemed eager to show her.

She covered her self-hatred with a tranquil smile.

He'd said they were almost to the center, but their path took them close to where they'd started, and she could almost sense the entrance a few bookshelves to her right. He stopped in front of a bookcase that looked the same as the rest.

He took a leather-bound journal off the shelf and put it right into her hands.

She tried to hide her trembling by casually flipping through the journal. "And these are truly special books?"

"I don't know if everyone would find them special. My great-grandmother wrote about everyday things that some might find tedious. But I value her wisdom. Anyone looking to be a great leader would be wise to study her words." He held the candlestick carefully while removing the matching diary from his pocket. He looked at it with longing, before placing it on the shelf where the other diary had stood.

She pretended to study the book, though her eyes rose to watch him. He laid a hand against the diary's spine. "I've decided to leave both diaries here. They should remain inside the queen's library where they belong. I won't need them after I go."

Her fingers tightened on the book, the remembrance of her false pretenses settling over her. She had all but promised to propose to him tonight, then take him away to live out the rest of his days in Naermore. Would it be kinder to propose, then disappear, or to reject him outright? Both options seemed terrible, but now that she held the book in her hand, the decision was finally here.

She cleared her throat. "Prince Jaemin ..." Her weak voice didn't travel far, yet he turned to her, careful of the candle he held between them, and watched her with unquiet eyes.

A key rattled in the lock.

They both spun in the direction of the door, so close, yet an entire maze away.

"It's probably Hawthorne," said the prince. "I assume he brought a 'friend.'"

Since Hawthorne knew where Jaemin had planned to bring the princess, the library wouldn't be as private as Alanna thought he preferred. The key could belong to Finn or one of the other princes returned home without her knowledge. But Alanna sensed that was not the case.

The lock clicked, and Alanna blew out the candle.

29

Light spilled across the edge of the dome closest to the entrance, accompanied by soft footsteps, shuffling fabric and the clicking lock. Alanna could barely see Jaemin in the sudden darkness, but he opened his mouth—whether to speak to her or the newcomer, she didn't know. She shifted the diary into one hand and put her other gloved hand over his mouth. His eyes widened in surprise and a little bit of outrage.

"Did you retrieve the magistrate?" The queen's clear voice stopped any words Jaemin might say. His posture shifted as he folded in on himself, and she pulled her hand away. His question had finally been answered: the queen had been keeping secrets.

"Yes, Your Majesty." Drazen spoke smoothly, as if a clandestine meeting in the dark with the queen was commonplace. "His family is enjoying their vacation in Isandine. I told him they could all return home once he identifies the spy inside the monastery."

Alanna clutched the lamp in her pocket so hard that the large rune felt imprinted against her palm. Even though

Geeni hadn't admitted she created the runes, Alanna prayed the woman was a master.

"I have a lead on someone else with a Spark. He owns a music shop near Qira's shrine. I'm going to look for him tonight."

"Another healer?" The queen's voice trembled.

A gentle sigh. "No, Your Majesty. There are rumors he can transform into an animal." He paused, then spoke gently. "I will keep looking."

"I feel it, Drazen ... The illness ... It's creeping in. I—"

"Everything will be fine, Your Majesty." Drazen's normally calm voice held a rising note of anxiety. "We will find a healer, then make a plan to solve everything."

"She's here, Drazen," the queen whispered.

Alanna clutched the lamp tighter, thinking the queen had finally spotted her.

"She's snatching up those with Sparks before we can find them. I'm sure she's the one who broke into the monastery. She's responsible for the spy." The queen pulled in a shuddering breath. "I feel her. So close, yet just beyond my reach."

Did the queen mean Geeni or Alanna? Maybe she believed they were one and the same.

"We will find her, Your Majesty. This is not the end."

A pause. Then a key rattling in a lock. A door opening and closing, before the lock rattled until it clicked. Then silence.

"I have to warn her," Jaemin whispered.

Alanna turned to him but could barely make out his face in the dark. "Who?"

"The queen knows. I must warn Alanna."

Alanna shook her head, but it was the princess's head that shook. She had lost track of her identity in the dark.

"I'm sure the girl knows to be careful, Jaemin," said the princess. "Unless she's an idiot?"

She felt him bristle, but he merely said, "We need to go." He spun on his heel, headed back the way they had come.

"Wait!" Alanna had to hurry before losing sight of him. If he left her alone in the labyrinth, she'd have to climb the tall bookcases to find her way out.

"I'm sorry, Princess. I will show you the center of the labyrinth another day." He practically sprinted through the twisting passageways, and Alanna had no idea how he could remember the way.

The princess huffed, angry that he didn't even glance behind him to make sure she followed. The princess didn't want Jaemin running off to find Alanna, but neither did Alanna. Unless she ran straight to the theater, he would arrive there first and find her missing.

But she couldn't run straight there. She had to deliver the book to Geeni.

She still held the book. She stuck it in her pocket alongside the lamp and wiped her sweaty hands on her dress. Jaemin had sped up again, and she sprinted to catch him. She lifted her skirts to keep from tripping, and ran cautiously, trying to not awaken the wind.

The princess called out, "Jaemin, just think about it! They said *she* is gathering up people with a Spark before Drazen can find them. Do you honestly believe your girl is doing something like that?"

He slowed again, and Alanna could sense his thoughts racing: Of course that wasn't Alanna. But in the case of the monastery, it *was* her. That bit of conflicting information did not sway him.

They had almost made it back to the entrance. Without a lit candle in his hand or dread slowing his steps, they had sped back through the maze at a much quicker pace. She tried to think of any excuse to keep Jaemin away from Alanna, but her mind came up blank.

He slid to a stop in front of the door, key already in hand. He had the courtesy to wait for the princess to exit instead of slamming the door in her face. She smoothed back her hair, trying to catch her breath, before she stepped into the hall, which was brightly lit by comparison.

He calmly locked the door behind her, then turned to walk away.

"Prince Jaemin!" called the princess.

He jerked to a halt and waited for her slow approach. "I'm sorry, Princess. I must—"

"Is this how every night will end, Prince? With you running off to find another woman?" The princess watched his face carefully, wanting to make sure he knew what he would sacrifice if he ran off now.

He knew the cost of his words. "You have made no pledge to me, Princess Aliyabeth, nor I to you. I'm sorry if it causes you pain, but I must go."

Cold realization seeped into her heart. The princess could not command him to stay with her, and even if she could, by the next morning, the princess would be gone. Tonight he would climb the theater to Alanna's aviary home, but she would not be there and would never return. The result would be the same if he went tonight or tomorrow morning or a week from now.

This was the last moment between them, and she couldn't even kiss him goodbye.

She looked at him in his formal uniform, a king in all but name, the very picture of duty and responsibility, and yet, throwing it away for a thief. Even though she would never see him again, Alanna's heart soared knowing that, in the end, the prince chose *her*.

"Do as you must, Jaemin," said the princess. Alanna

swallowed the lump in her throat, and whispered, "I love you."

The prince blinked, confused by her out of character proclamation. She knew he couldn't rightfully say it back and was pleased he didn't speak a lie. He simply gave her a respectful bow and left to find Alanna.

30

The princess walked with head held high all the way to her room, but once inside, Alanna ran to her bedroom, barking, "Hidalsa, follow me."

The maid jumped off the couch, surprised by the princess's sudden entrance, but she scampered after her. "Is everything okay, Your Highness?"

"No," said Alanna. "It most definitely is not." She opened one of the trunks and handed Hidalsa all the money in her possession, plus one of her simpler necklaces and two pairs of earrings. "I would give you more jewels, but if you are found with them, I'm afraid people will think the worst."

"What's happening?" Hidalsa stared at the jewels in her hand and didn't move.

The princess took one of the fine cloaks out of the closet and wrapped it around her maid. "I need you to walk calmly out of the castle, and if anyone asks, you are running an errand in the city for your silly princess." She straightened the hood around Hidalsa's face and gave her a stern look. "If you see a gray-haired man named Leston, say nothing. Not a word. Just get away as fast as you can. Do you understand me?"

Hidalsa nodded slowly, tucking the jewels down the front of her dress. "Who are you?" she whispered.

Alanna dug through the wardrobe until she found her own clothes and stripped off the princess's dress. "My name is Alanna, and if I somehow survive the night, I will pay you what you are due."

Hidalsa watched her remove the diary and lamp from the princess's dress and stuff them in the pockets of Alanna's pants. The actress spoke carefully. "Has someone been assassinated?"

Alanna's hands stilled while tying her top in place. She took a deep breath and gave the woman a calm look, trying not to distress her further. "No one is dead, but many people will be upset that I deceived them, and if I'm caught, I'd prefer not to bring you down along with me. You've been very good to me, Hidalsa. I appreciate your friendship."

Alanna pulled her dark blue cloak out of the closet and fastened it around her own neck. "You should go now. Remember what I said about the gray-haired man."

Hidalsa headed for the door, then spun back around. "Am I safe to return to the theater? Will someone come looking for me?"

"I don't think so, but if they do, tell them everything you know. You owe me no further loyalty."

Hidalsa nodded, then scurried out the door.

Bibi sat on the floor, following Alanna's movements with the watchful eyes of a cat. Alanna sighed, "Yes, Bibi. It's time to go." Her hand skimmed across the drawer full of jewels, and she whimpered in frustration at being forced to leave them behind. Though she still wore the face of the princess, if someone pierced her disguise, she had no runes left to transform back. Alanna would have a hard time explaining not only why she had the princess's jewels, but where she'd hidden the princess's body.

She patted the pockets with the lamp and diary, picked up her cat, and jumped off the balcony.

Alanna paced in the garden, waiting for Geeni to appear. As she walked to one side of the garden, she imagined racing to find the prince, then running back to the palace to deliver the book to Geeni at midnight. Then as she walked to the other side of the garden, she cursed herself for a fool the entire way. Bibi lounged on the stone lap of a statue, her eyes following Alanna as she paced back and forth, dreaming then cursing.

"Anxious to be gone from the palace, dear?" Geeni wore the same clothes as the day they met: blue leather pants and a tight vest along with gold chains and bangles that shimmered in the moonlight. "Do you have the book?"

Alanna pulled the diary out of her pocket. "Do you have the money?"

Geeni grinned and lifted a large jingling purse.

They walked toward each other warily, then exchanged their items with slow movements, before stepping away to examine their rewards.

Geeni's eyes hungrily scanned the diary, though Alanna doubted she could read it in the dark. Alanna kept one eye on Geeni while pulling open the purse. Judging by the weight, it seemed to be enough silver for her needs, but she wanted to be sure. She tilted the contents inside to look closer, and her mouth fell open. The face of the queen was stamped on each coin.

"This is all gold!" A bag full of gold was much more than Alanna had expected. It was enough to buy several farms, and still have a fortune left over. She couldn't fathom such wealth. Her eyes narrowed, and she took a step back. "Why did you give me so much?"

Geeni laughed merrily. "Child, you have no idea what you have given me. Compared to this, gold means nothing. Run off now, and enjoy it."

"You're just letting me go?"

"I'm very pleased with the results of this business transaction. Why aren't you?" She tilted her head, inspecting Alanna up and down. "Is this about the lamp? Keep it. I have several copies of that rune, plus the concealment rune may be faulty anyway." Geeni ran a tender hand across the front of the book. "You made me nervous there at the end, but it was a pleasure working with you. Perhaps we'll work together again someday." She tipped her head to Alanna and turned to walk away.

"Wait!" Alanna called out to her, feeling like there should be more to their interaction. "Why is that book so important to you?"

"I told you on the first day we met, dear. It's a family heirloom."

Alanna shook her head. "No, it's a diary that belonged to the queen's grandmother ..." Alanna trailed off, and she stared at the pink-haired woman as a slow smile spread on her lips.

"Yes, child. A diary belonging to her grandmother and mine. I had her other diary for some time, but this is the one I needed: the one that mentions her second child. My mother was born as the result of an affair, so my grandmother hid her away, out of courtesy to her husband. But as the current queen could tell you, fathers are quite irrelevant when it comes to tracking the royal bloodline."

Alanna's hand floated to her mouth as she realized what she had done. She had handed tangible proof of the royal bloodline to a contender to the throne while the current queen suffered from a mysterious illness with no plan for succession.

Alanna might be responsible for overthrowing a queen.

"But what about the princes?" she gasped. "What will happen to them?"

Geeni held still for one moment, before bursting out in laughter. "You really *did* fall for one of them, didn't you? How disappointing. I thought I had uncovered a true professional."

Alanna shook her head. "I can't do this. I can't take this money. I—"

"Yes, you can, dear. You will take the money and run off, spending it on everything you've ever dreamed. Do you know why?" She stalked closer to Alanna, her smooth voice that of a predator bearing down on its prey. "Because you are a con artist and a thief. A spectacular one who managed to con a prince out of his family's birthright. I imagine that even with all that gold, without the need to ever work again a day in your life, you'll still choose to steal again. It's who you are."

Alanna staggered back a step, clutching the bag of gold to her chest. "No, I—"

Geeni made a shooing gesture. "Time to run off now." She chuckled, looking into the dark shadow of Alanna's hooded cloak. "That's the other thing you are good at, isn't it, dear? Running away."

Alanna inhaled a shaking sob, gathered the wind around herself, and ran off into the night.

31

The moment the sun rose, Alanna went to the monastery. She had wandered the streets the entire night, unable to enter the monastery without looking suspicious until sunrise. Her mother wouldn't wake until morning, and it would confuse her mother to wake up to a stranger trying to steal her out of the city.

During her restless walk, Alanna had considered touching someone to pop her disguise and return to her own face, but she couldn't bring herself to do it yet. Between her two identities, Alanna was the one she was the most angry with. Alanna was the one who'd made a deal with a contender for the throne. It didn't matter that the princess had stolen the diary and handed it over to Geeni. Alanna had made the deal, and she was the one to blame.

And Alanna was the one who had kissed the prince, then betrayed him.

She sat on her mother's usual bench underneath the mango tree where the birds gathered. The birds sang their morning songs in peace, since Bibi the cat roamed around *outside* the monastery.

Alanna planned the distraction to sneak her mother out of the monastery. It needed to be big—the wind whipping violently to distract the scholars, birds fluttering their wings, feathers floating down, her mother watching in terror, unable to understand what was happening ...

Alanna shook her head. She had to get her mother out of the city, even if the process disturbed her mother deeply. After they made it out of Isandine, her mother would be happy ... Although they would still have a long and confusing trip ahead of them.

After they traveled far enough from the city, her mother would be happy ...

After Alanna bought a farm, her mother would be happy ...

After Alanna learned how to farm and how to cook and how to care for her mother and how to survive the look of confusion on her mother's face every day for the rest of her life without a single soul who recognized Alanna for who she truly was ...

She dropped her head into her hands and sobbed quietly to not disturb her mother's birds.

"Are you hurt, child?" said a kind voice.

Alanna looked up, wiping her tears. Her gloves were filthy after a night crying while roaming the city, so she hid them inside her cloak. A scholar with long, thick gray hair looked down at her, checking her face and body for noticeable injuries.

"I'm fine," said Alanna, trying to drag a smile onto her face. "I've had a long night."

The scholar took a seat next to Alanna on the bench. "Long nights do happen from time to time. If you need to talk, I'm here." She held out her hand. "My name's Ethelwin."

Alanna stared at the scholar's hand as if it were a viper. "Ethelwin? You have a Spark!"

Ethelwin glanced around the courtyard, but no bystanders had heard Alanna's exclamation. "Yes, I do. I don't remember you, so you must be a family member of someone I've healed."

Alanna's face hardened as she recalled how many times the ledger recorded this woman had experimented on her mother using her Spark.

"Ahh ..." said Ethelwin slowly. "A family member of someone I *failed* to heal."

"You tried to heal her over and over, and even though you failed, you continue to experiment on her, tracking your results like she's a laboratory test subject."

Ethelwin studied her, but she wouldn't be able to guess her identity while she wore the princess's face. Ethelwin breathed out a sigh, and said, "Our attempts to heal are not perfect, child. Melora and I can heal different parts of the body, but neither of us can fix everything. And yes, we keep detailed notes each time we use our Spark. There is too much at stake to do otherwise."

Alanna remembered the desperation in the queen's voice when she asked if Drazen had found another healer. "You're looking for a way to heal the queen."

Ethelwin sucked in a quick breath, then leaned forward and whispered, "Who are you?"

Alanna refused to shrink from her piercing glare. "I'm someone who won't let you continue experimenting on innocent people who can't defend themselves."

Ethelwin rested her hand on Alanna's shoulder as if comforting a child. "My Spark doesn't hurt anyone. The worst I can do is be ineffective. I'm sorry I failed your family member, but I can prove to you it doesn't hurt, child."

A bright warmth radiated from the scholar's hand and flooded Alanna's veins. Her heart thrummed with a renewed energy, and her gut no longer churned with acid from her uneaten dinner. She closed her eyes, savoring the well-being, before she remembered she didn't deserve well-being. Alanna was a con artist and thief living in a stolen identity.

Her eyes popped open, and she raised gloved hands to her cheekbones to see if Ethelwin had popped her disguise. She felt the familiar lines of the princess, yet Ethelwin stared at her like something about her didn't fit. The scholar lifted the princess's braid, running the blond hair through her fingers with a confused expression.

Alanna jumped up and drifted backward. "I should go." She would return with Alanna's face and sneak her mother out later.

Her mother entered the courtyard and sat on the bench next to Ethelwin. She opened her notebook in her lap, then raised her eyes to the birds.

Ethelwin's piercing gaze shifted from Alanna, and softened as she focused on the woman next to her. "Good morning, Sunah. I'm glad to see you looking so well."

Her mother shifted toward Ethelwin with a smile, then turned back to her birds. Her mother's smile filled Alanna with dread. Would she have to drag her terrified mother out of the monastery? Despite her mother's mental decline, her body still appeared strong and healthy, and Alanna didn't know if she would be able to physically restrain her. The thought of wrestling her scared mother sickened her.

Ethelwin had focused back on Alanna, watching her with keen eyes boring straight into her heart. The scholar lifted her hand and slowly placed it on Sunah's shoulder, never breaking eye contact with Alanna.

Alanna took a single step forward, before stopping. Her mother closed her eyes and lifted her face to the sun, breathing in what Alanna knew to be a general sense of well-being. After several deep breaths, she opened her eyes and blinked at Ethelwin, as if confused to see her. Ethelwin removed her hand from Sunah's shoulder and gave her a serene smile that said everything was okay. Alanna's mother blinked once, then returned to studying the birds with a peaceful smile.

Her eyes remained fixed on her mother, even as Ethelwin stood and walked slowly to Alanna's side. "She's cared for, child," said the scholar. "She isn't healed, but she's okay."

Alanna bit her lip, trying to hold back her tears.

Ethelwin regarded the woman on the bench, a proud expression on her face. "Sunah was a brilliant scholar. Her ideas contributed to many scientific discoveries, which informed other scholars, who discovered even more. She's a part of this community, and always will be."

Alanna studied her mother with the princess's eyes, and not those of her daughter. Sunah lived in a community of her peers who loved and accepted her for who she was. She was cared for and physically healthy and allowed to spend her days doing activities that soothed her anxious mind.

Despite the princess's reasoned thoughts, Alanna's shoulders trembled with the realization: this was her mother's home, and Alanna couldn't rip her away from it.

A red bird hopped onto a low branch, and Sunah raised her hand to her mouth with a look of happy surprise. Ethelwin spoke gently. "Her grasp of reason may have slipped away, but she's never lost her sense of wonder."

Alanna rubbed her dirty gloves across her eyes and whispered, "She called their wings a miracle of science."

Ethelwin smiled. "She has the heart of a true Sister Scholar."

Jaemin had said much the same thing, and her chest

clenched at the thought of him. "I should go." She choked out the words as a means of escape, but she had no idea where she would go. She couldn't go to the aviary on the chance Jaemin was there. She couldn't leave the city as she had planned now that she realized this was her mother's home. If her mother stayed in Isandine, then so would Alanna. She had no friends other than Bibi, and though that had been true for years, only now did she realize how lonely she was.

Ethelwin must have sensed her loneliness, because she placed a gentle hand on Alanna's shoulder. "You are welcome here anytime, child. Come back without your disguise, and I will provide what little help I can while you talk with her." She bowed, then walked to Sunah's bench and sat beside her in a comfortable silence.

Alanna staggered out of the sunny courtyard into the covered walkway and leaned against one of the arches, gasping for breath. Ethelwin knew she wore a disguise and had invited her to come back as her true self. Alanna laughed bitterly. Who was her true self?

She tipped her head back against the cool stone and rested her eyes. After roaming the city all night, what she needed most was to find somewhere to rest. With the giant bag of gold in her pocket, she could afford to buy an entire inn, or a whole city block. But the thought of spending even a single gold coin made her stomach churn with guilt. Instead, she would continue to roam the streets until she eventually passed out. Then perhaps someone would steal the gold, and she could feel a measure of relief.

"Is Drazen here?" asked Jaemin.

Alanna's eyes shot open. The prince's voice had come from inside the vestibule and sounded uncharacteristically frantic. She edged closer to the inner gate and listened to the Sister Scholar's response.

"No, Your Highness. Drazen is—"

"You must tell me the truth! I know he has a secret laboratory here. But he's missing today ... even the queen says so. I must find him."

Alanna leaned closer to listen. Where had Drazen gone? He had told the queen he was headed to find someone with a Spark ... Had something gone wrong?

"It's not just him," said Jaemin, his voice rising. "The princess has disappeared, along with her servant. And so has ... someone else ... Drazen might be able to find her, though. If he's here, you must tell me."

Alanna covered her mouth with her filthy glove. Four people in Jaemin's life had disappeared overnight. He must believe their disappearances were all related, which was mostly correct, except for Drazen. Hopefully Drazen would turn up soon, and the prince could forget all about Alanna and the princess. Jaemin could marry a foreign princess and get out of the queendom before Geeni made a play for the throne and spiraled the country into a civil war.

"I'm sorry, Prince Jaemin. He is not here."

Alanna couldn't see the woman, but she thought the scholar told the truth.

"Oh ... okay. If you do see him, please tell him to return to the palace immediately."

She waited for the scholar's reply, then peeked carefully into the vestibule. Finding him gone, Alanna raised her hood and followed him outside.

He strode away from the monastery, his shoulders tense and steps hurried. He didn't wear his uniform, just a simple shirt and leather pants like he wore to train, and a sword strapped to his waist. Alanna let him get a block ahead of her, then fell into step behind him.

Bibi slid through an opening in a low grate, her body

shifting like liquid as cats could do. She fell into step beside Alanna with a glance at the prince.

"Yes, I know it's a bad idea, Bibi. I just want to see where he's heading."

The cat trotted forward, not meeting Alanna's eye.

Alanna scanned the road, trying to determine if she was the only one following the prince. She hadn't seen anyone who appeared to be in the Queen's Guard, but as her jaw cracked with a yawn, she realized she might miss the usual signs.

The prince came to an intersection and paused. Alanna casually bent to pet Bibi. She peeked at him out of the corner of her eye, and spoke to Bibi. "If he goes right, he's likely headed back to the palace, probably to wait for Drazen's return. If he goes left ... well, he could be going anywhere, really."

Obviously, Bibi did not fall for her pretense. If he headed left, there was a chance he was headed to the aviary to find her. He knew she was missing, which meant he had already been to the aviary once, but a left turn could mean he headed there again, just in case Alanna showed up.

Jaemin rubbed a hand roughly through his hair, then turned right, toward the palace.

Alanna patted Bibi on the head, though the cat gave her a cranky look for the fake performance. "Well, if he's headed to the palace, I guess now is our chance to head to the aviary to make sure we left nothing behind. Then we can escape before he comes back ... if he ever does."

Bibi very pointedly said nothing in response, and they both headed home for the last time.

32

The aviary looked the same as it had the night she'd broken into the monastery with Jaemin. She didn't own many things, but she gathered her fake earrings and the items from Bibi's shrine and put them into her bag with the gold. She wandered out of the little aviary onto the roof and watched the sun continue its slow climb above Mount Qira and Mount Qara.

As a gentle breeze floated by, she wondered if she had always loved her rooftop home because of her affinity to the wind. She savored the gusts that flowed over the volcanoes down into Isandine and the gales that flowed in from the sea. She breathed it in one last time, then pulled the hood of her cloak around her face. "Come on, Bibi. Time to go."

The cat had been curled up on the floor while Alanna packed, and at her call, Bibi stretched and rolled on her back, revealing the slip of paper she had been sleeping on.

Alanna growled at the cat and snatched up the paper. "It's time you become a monkey again. You're entirely too good at being a cat." Only one person would leave her a note, yet she still found his words a surprise.

Someone is after you. It isn't safe for you to come find me. Wait here, and I will help you escape. Please be careful. - J

He offered to help her escape. Even when he knew Drazen and the queen searched for people with Sparks, he thought she was innocent and deserved to escape. Even though he might be worried about her, he still believed in her. She clutched the letter to her chest, grateful she'd left him with an unsullied illusion.

"Alanna!" The prince hauled himself over the side of the roof and took two steps toward her before stopping.

She raised her head slowly, her hand with the letter dropping to her side. Her heart thudded wildly with the joy of seeing him, and then stopped cold when she realized why he looked at her as he did.

"Princess Aliyabeth? What are you doing here?" He took another step closer, yet watched her with wary eyes.

She tried to recall the princess's light laughter, but it came out forced. "It's a long story, Jaemin. But unfortunately, I can't tell it now. I must—"

He closed the distance between them, raising his sword to her throat. Her back slammed against the aviary door, and the thin wood rattled on its hinges. His hair stood on end, as if he had been running angry fingers through it all night, and his eyes glittered with a fury Alanna had never seen.

He leaned as close as his drawn sword would allow. "Where is she?"

"Jaemin—"

He spit out the words. "Where. Is. Alanna?"

She gently shifted her head, but his sword stayed firmly pressed against her skin. "She's fine. Alanna's fine. Please, Jaemin—"

"I don't believe you." His voice held none of the casual

politeness he usually offered the princess. "Where is Drazen?"

"I haven't seen him, I swear!" Her voice rose in pitch with desperation to get him to believe the one answer she could give honestly. "I haven't seen or heard from him since last night in the library, when I was with you."

He shook his head, hissing his words at her. "I believed in you, Princess. I thought we were well-suited. Not a love match, but friends who could have a pleasant marriage. But this? I can't figure out what you stand to gain. There's no benefit to Naermore to kidnap them." His eyes sharpened, boring into her. "Who do you work for?"

She opened her mouth to speak a lie, any lie, but she had none left. "Her name is Geeni." She swallowed the bile rising in her throat. "She said she's the queen's cousin."

Jaemin blinked, and his sword faltered before he jerked it back into place. "Ginevere? You work for Ginevere?"

Her mouth moved, but she could barely form the words. "I didn't know who—I just found out ... She asked me to steal the diary, but I didn't know why ..."

Jaemin's eyes deadened, and he adjusted his fingers on his sword as if he might swing it. "Were there no easier ways to get the diary than to seduce me for it?" He gave a barking laugh. "Hawthorne would have taken you to the library anytime you asked. Why did you choose to torment me instead?"

The tears falling down her cheeks were her only answer.

He drew in a shaking breath. "The punishment for espionage is death, but I will ask for leniency if you tell me where I can find her."

"I don't know where Geeni—"

"No!" he roared. "Where is Alanna?"

A trembling sob wrenched its way up from her core. Even now, he chose Alanna. But when he found out who she truly was … She had wanted to keep his illusion of Alanna pure, but his twilight eyes searched her face for the answer, the desperation and longing written clear.

She took a deep breath, and the sun shifted behind a cloud, softening the harsh mix of sun and shadows on his face. As she blinked the tears from her lashes, a breeze danced lovingly across her cheek. Her fingers clung to the aviary door at her back, but she curled her trembling fingers and beckoned the wind.

A wind, warm from its time at Mount Qira's peak, floated to her side, swirling around her wrist, while a cool ocean breeze slipped across her palm, twirling around each finger. Though the wind touched her gently, she felt the raw power in her hands: with a single word, she could coax the wind to do her bidding. She cradled the tiny storms, and when they understood her wishes, she said the word.

"Jaemin." Her whisper summoned the storm.

The warm wind from her wrist and the cold wind against her palm joined with the breath from her lungs to form a very precise storm. The wind went no further than the edge of the roof, cold and warm wind spinning around each other in a playful game. The storm slipped inside the aviary, scattering Alanna's remaining possessions and sending Bibi darting up into the perches to hide.

The wind ruffled their clothes and blew Jaemin's hair into further disarray, but he closed his eyes and whispered, "Alanna."

Her name on his lips intensified the storm, until her possessions floated in the circling wind. Jaemin opened his eyes and looked around the roof, trying to find Alanna. She sent a sliver of the cool breeze to trace a line across his neck and summoned a handful of warm breeze to caress his cheek. He shuddered with the conflicting sensations, and his sword lowered, the princess forgotten.

Alanna pulled herself away from the aviary door, and looked at the prince, a smile on his face as a warm wind flowed over his stiff shoulders in an embrace.

"I didn't lie when I said it." She spoke quietly in the middle of the raging storm, and he drew closer to hear. "I love you, Jaemin. That's the truth."

The princess's declaration of love confused him enough that he didn't pull away from her kiss.

She gasped at the dripping cold of shedding the princess's skin. The storm disentangled itself from the playful dance, and the breezes fluttered away as fast as they had appeared. She blinked open her eyes to find Jaemin staggering away from her, his sword hanging loose in one hand, the other hand touching his lips as if they were to blame.

"I'm sorry, Jaemin." Her own voice had returned, but it quavered with the same emotion as the princess.

His hand fell from his lips. "You are ..." A shadow passed across his twilight eyes. "You *both* betrayed me?"

She ducked her head, doubly guilty.

He walked in a circle, raking his fingers through his hair. "This whole time ... you've been both." He stopped, and his eyes shot to hers. "The first day in the marketplace, you brought me here, showed me your Spark ... It was all a setup."

"No!" She raised a hand, and he took a step backward. "I didn't know anything then ... That day was real."

He took another step backward, his sword dragging limply on the ground. "You knew I fell in love with you that day. You knew, and used it against me."

Her breath caught in her chest. "No, Jaemin, I—"

"You played me for a fool twice over. Are either of your identities even real?"

"I—"

He held up a hand. "No. Don't tell me. If I've met you in another disguise, just don't tell me." He sucked a slow breath through his teeth. "Just tell me what you've done with Drazen."

"I haven't done anything with him, I swear! I didn't even know he was gone until I heard you looking for him at the monastery."

He laughed bitterly—he probably thought she had been one of the scholars, too. Bibi the monkey chose that moment to hop out of the aviary and begin licking herself like a cat.

He sheathed his sword and, without another word, walked to the edge of the roof and swung his leg over to begin the climb down.

Alanna ran to the edge. "Wait! Don't you want to take me in for questioning or something? I don't know where Geeni is or if she has Drazen, but maybe I can help—"

"No." His harsh voice cut her off. "I don't want help from any of your personalities. Take whatever money you earned from betraying me and spend it while laughing at the twice-fooled prince."

She watched him climb down the theater and walk away without ever looking back.

PART III

33

Alanna sat poised on the ruby wingback chair and summoned the next maidservant. The girl carried a gown of amethyst gossamer that fluttered as she scurried forward. Alanna rubbed the delicate fabric between her fingers.

"Yes, I'll take it." She steepled her fingers, resting her elbows on the red velvet chair. "But add pockets."

The girl smiled at Alanna in adoration and clutched the dress to her chest. "Of course, miss! Whatever you want!"

Alanna pressed her lips against her steepled fingers to hide a grimace. Yes, she could have whatever money could buy.

Whatever money could buy, and nothing more.

Her hotel suite was the finest Isandine had to offer. Expensive wallpaper, elegant tile, sumptuous rugs, and a private bath larger than her aviary. When she first arrived, the hotel staff had eyed her filthy clothes and bedraggled appearance with a fair amount of hesitation. But when she plunked a gold coin on the counter, they'd become remarkably attentive.

Maidservants had drawn her a hot bath with rose petals

scattered on the water. They'd rubbed warm argan oil through her hair, straightening the tangles, until her locks shone. They massaged a coconut and orchid balm over her skin—a luxury she could never enjoy as the princess.

The maidservants didn't know why she cried at their gentle touch, but she paid them well enough that they didn't ask.

Bibi had received just as much pampering. Her white fur gleamed after a team of girls bathed and brushed and trimmed her. Bibi luxuriated in the attention and pranced around displaying her diamond collar to anyone who would coo at her. Her shrine of buttons and feathers had grown to contain sparkly jewels and expensive trinkets. After two days of unimaginable luxury, Bibi rearranged the items in her shrine, looking almost bored.

As Alanna counted how much money she had spent over the last two days, she realized at this rate, she would never run out. Geeni had given her a fortune, a true queen's ransom, and she couldn't buy enough frivolous trinkets to spend it. She considered buying the hotel, except owning a business meant she had employees who depended on her, and she didn't want that responsibility. She could buy land, yet the thought of owning land in a queendom that might soon fall to a civil war made her sick to her stomach.

"Miss?" A young valet removed his cap and bowed to her, which seemed ridiculous considering she wasn't a princess, not even a fake one. However, the attendants at the hotel were even more attentive than those in the palace. Probably because she tipped better than the queen.

Alanna waved an impatient hand at him, signaling him to rise. "What is it?"

"I have the woman you asked me to seek. Shall I send her in?"

Alanna sat straighter. "Yes, send her in and everyone else out."

Hidalsa approached Alanna with hesitant steps, staring at the face of a stranger. "Princess?" she whispered, clasping her skirt as if she might curtsy before Alanna's throne.

Alanna sighed. "No, it's just Alanna."

Hidalsa blinked as recognition lit her face. "I've seen you hanging around the theater ... You're an actress, too?"

"I hesitate to associate your profession with mine." She stood up from her chair and took Hidalsa's hand.

The actress stared at Alanna's hand on her own. "Was it makeup? Or an elaborate mask?"

Alanna bit her lip. "Um ... kind of? It's complicated." She led Hidalsa to a seat at the end of a long dining table, then ducked to fiddle with Bibi's shrine. When she returned to the table, she slid a stack of gold across the table to Hidalsa. "Payment for your services."

Hidalsa stared at the stack of gold as if it might bite her. Alanna understood the feeling—Geeni paying her too much money had made her suspicious, too. "Princ— Miss, that's a lot more money than Geeni promised me."

"Yes, but I can spare it. I hope it's less burdensome to you than it is to me."

Hidalsa looked around the extravagant suite. "You'll spend through it quickly enough at this rate."

Alanna shrugged. "What else do I have to spend it on?"

Hidalsa raised her eyebrow. "I didn't take you for the pouty type, even when you were a princess."

Alanna rested her head in her hand, slumped over the table. "I made a real mess of things, Hidalsa. Like 'the queendom's in serious trouble' kind of mess."

Hidalsa leaned back in her chair. "When you came running back to your room, shoving money and jewels into my hand, I honestly believed you had assassinated someone in the royal family, despite your claim otherwise. Yet there are no rumors about anyone missing other than the queen's royal advisor." She narrowed her eyes, peering into Alanna's face. "Is that who you killed?"

"I didn't kill anyone!" she huffed. "And I had nothing to do with Drazen's disappearance." She'd thought Drazen would have returned by now, but perhaps something really had happened to him.

Hidalsa twisted a ringlet of her blond hair around her finger as she thought. "Other than that, I heard the princess sailed back to Naermore after finding no prince to her liking. So, I'm not exactly sure what you did, but the queendom hasn't fallen to pieces yet."

Alanna sank her head into both hands. "Give it time."

Hidalsa patted her on the shoulder. "Now, now, sulking isn't a good look for a princess. Or for a ..." She waved her hand around the glamorous suite. "... for a whatever you are now. It's time to pick yourself up and fix things."

Alanna shook her head morosely. "I can't fix it, Hidalsa. I've ruined everything."

"Everything? That's unlikely. I assume you can think of at least one thing you could fix if you tried hard enough."

Alanna chewed on her lip as she thought. "Well ... I am curious to know what happened to Drazen. I had no part in his disappearance ... at least not that I know of."

Hidalsa gave her one sharp nod. "That's a good start. Working out that little mystery will give you something to do other than mope about." She gathered her stack of gold coins off the table and tucked them down the front of her dress. "And money doesn't fix everything, but in some cases, it can provide some very creative solutions." She winked and left Alanna's suite.

Her words stirred Alanna's thoughts, which were sluggish after two days of idleness. She couldn't fix everything, but why not use her money to fix what she could? Even if that was to hunt down a man from whom she had previously hidden.

She stood, summoning her maidservants. "Bring me a dress with deep pockets and a low-cut neckline. And I mean a *really* low-cut neckline." The girls scrambled to her closet, searching for the perfect dress.

Her valet twisted his cap in his hands. "Where are you going, miss?"

A slow smile spread across her lips, the first hint of a smile for days. "I'm going to find me a man."

34

Alanna stalked the streets near Drazen's last known location, her eyes focused on the hunt. Usually she pursued foolish men who possessed an excess of wealth, but today she hunted for information. The monkey at her side had a cheerful hop to her step like she always did when they went hunting together. And thanks to Alanna's ability to ask very nice questions while wearing a strategically low-cut dress, she had quickly found the boarded-up music shop of the man rumored to have magic.

The back door wasn't boarded up, but it was locked. Alanna looked at the chimney. "Think you can make it, Bibi?"

The monkey gave her a judgy look, strangely reminiscent of the cat, and climbed her way up the building, then down the chimney. Alanna leaned casually against the building, hoping no one walked by since she didn't know what character to play. Her dress was too glamorous for her to be a prostitute in a back alley and too low-cut for her to be a respectable business owner.

She bit her lip anxiously until the door's lock clicked. She turned the knob and found Bibi inside, covered in soot.

The monkey tried licking herself but spit out the soot with a shake of her head. Alanna hurried inside, closing the door behind her.

The shop had been destroyed. Beautiful lutes lay broken on the floor, their bodies smashed and necks hanging by the strings. She couldn't imagine the Queen's Guard coming in and smashing up the place for no reason, which meant the destruction had happened before they arrived. But why? She picked up one of the cracked lutes, turning it over in her hands.

On the neck, where the crafter's symbol would be, was a small gold plaque with an engraved rune.

"Geeni," she breathed.

Alanna checked the other lutes and found more rune-engraved plaques. "Check the other lutes, Bibi, and tell me if they've all been used."

Bibi vaulted onto a lute hanging on the wall, and confirmed Alanna's assumption with a tail flick.

"Drazen came here because he heard this man had magic, but maybe the man didn't have a Spark. Maybe he used runes to transform."

Bibi continued hopping between the hanging lutes on the wall, while Alanna picked up every broken lute on the floor. Each one had a used rune.

"But why did Geeni give so many runes to this man? If he transformed this many times, the rumor about him having magic was bound to get out."

Bibi sprang onto another lute, but it twisted against the wall, and they both came crashing down. The crash was so loud, anyone out on the street would have heard the noise. Her pounding heartbeat in the echoing stillness told her the answer.

"It was a trap," she whispered. "Geeni knew Drazen

hunted those with a Spark, so she set a trap, and he walked right into it."

Bibi scrambled off the now broken lute, and poked at the cracked neck. The rune still shimmered with unused magic. Alanna popped off the gold plaque and stuck it in her pocket. "Come on, Bibi," she whispered. "Let's go somewhere I can think." They snuck out the back door, then walked to the café across the street.

Alanna sat at an outdoor table and ordered a cup of coffee, then forced herself to consider the question she dreaded: was Drazen dead? If Geeni believed Drazen would detect her, she might have eliminated him. Although Geeni had let Alanna keep the lamp that counteracted Drazen's Spark, saying she had several of those runes. If she wasn't worried about him detecting her, then why capture him?

Alanna sipped her coffee and considered the other clues. The bartender in Ylara had said a pink-haired woman had "saved" the magistrate's daughter. And Drazen had told the queen a woman had snatched people with Sparks before he could. But why would Geeni capture Drazen or anyone else with a Spark if she could just make a rune instead?

Unless she needed someone with a Spark to make a rune.

And what better way to find more people with a Spark than to capture Drazen, then use his Spark to make runes to do the job herself.

Alanna had assumed Geeni had fled once she had the diary, but if she'd captured Drazen to make runes that could find others with a Spark, she might still be close. But where? Probably close to the music shop so she could keep an eye on the trap she had set. And somewhere she could craft the runes.

Alanna pulled the unused rune out of her pocket and

brushed a finger over the carving. She had no idea what tools Geeni used to carve the runes in these gold plaques, the lamp, Geeni's bracelets and necklaces …

She turned to a table of five guys and didn't waste time with subtlety. She leaned toward them, and all ten eyes noticed the very precarious nature of her top. "Can any of you boys tell me if there is a jewelry store nearby?"

The fellow closest to her was the first to answer. "Yes! There's a fancy jewelry store just around the block. Should I walk you there?"

The guy to his right slapped him on the arm. "No, you idiot. That pink-haired lady bought it, and it's closed now, remember?"

Alanna winked at them. "Thanks, boys. You're the best."

"What are you doing here?"

She unbent from her strategic lean to find Jaemin standing over her. She smoothed her skirt and tugged her top into the least low-cut position of the day.

"Jaemin, I'm sorr—"

He cut her off sharply, his voice cold. "I asked, what are you doing here?"

He wouldn't approve of the truth, but she couldn't bear to lie to him anymore. "I'm investigating."

His eyes flicked to her precarious top and back to her eyes. "Is that what you call it?"

"I didn't have anything to do with Drazen's disappearance. I'm going to find him—"

He raised a hand to stop her. "The Queen's Guard has the situation under control. We don't need your help." His voice possessed none of the warmth he had shared with Alanna, not even the casual politeness reserved for the princess.

"But I know how Geeni thinks. I'm going to find her and—"

"Alanna, no!" His voice rose in pitch, drawing the glance of other customers. He straightened his uniform, then spoke in a carefully controlled voice. "Ginevere is dangerous. Do not attempt to find her. This is a job for the Queen's Guard, not a common thief."

Though he meant the words to sting, Alanna saw the secret he tried to hide. On the outside, he played the role of a stern Queen's Guard, but anger didn't simmer below the surface—fear did. Jaemin wanted to protect her, despite everything she had done.

The knowledge filled her with a fierce power. She would find Geeni, and steal Drazen and the diary right out of her hand.

She held her euphoric feelings tightly in check, but her lips twitched in a subtle grin. "I am anything but common, Jaemin. And though you try to deny it, a thief is exactly what you need." She gave him a polite bow, then headed back to her suite to plan a theft.

35

Alanna handed her valet two gold coins and a long strip of paper. "Here is the rest of the list. Gather everything and be in the appointed location at sunset. Don't be late."

The young valet tipped his hat with an excited grin, then ran off to complete his tasks.

Alanna gathered her sketches, outlines, and maps, and laid them out in a neat formation on the long table in her suite. Everything had been a flurry of activity since she had returned from her investigation, but she only had a few more hours to get everything in place.

"You appear in better spirits," said Hidalsa. "When your maidservant came right back to get me, I honestly expected to find you crying in your bathroom."

"It still might come to that, but for now, I have a plan. And I need your help."

"Me?" Hidalsa looked at the legion of scurrying valets, maidservants, and other attendants swarming the suite. "Looks like you have plenty of help."

"Not as a maid. I need you in your official capacity as an

actress. Along with as many actors as you can gather by sundown."

"By sundown tonight?" she choked. "Leland won't like—"

Alanna slid a stack of gold coins across the table. "How many actors can you get me?"

Hidalsa blinked at the coins. "Um ... I think that would buy you a dozen for at least a year."

"I need them for a couple hours at sunset. Can you make that happen?"

"I'll see what I can do," she said cautiously. "What exactly are we doing?"

"Geeni has been secretly scheming for some time, and while she likes to wear disguises and keep her true identity a secret, you don't flaunt pink hair if you want to be unobtrusive. I believe she wants to be seen. And tonight, I'm going to make her wish come true." Alanna leaned forward. "Along with actors, I also need a lot of wigs."

"There are several wig shops in the city ... How many wigs do you need?"

Alanna grinned. "All of them."

Several hours later, Alanna sipped her beer in a tavern booth by the window. A gray-haired woman limped forward, pulling her threadbare scarf over her shoulders as she sat down at the booth.

Alanna nodded appreciatively. "The limp is a nice touch."

Hidalsa bowed with a hand flourish. "Playing a lady's maid was a fairly simple role. This time, I wanted a part that would really challenge me."

Alanna brushed a hand over her own gray wig. "This is

not my usual role, so I hope to play my part half as well as you." She lounged in her seat, casually studying the front of Geeni's hideout across the street. "So, while you slowly limped past the jewelry store, what did you see?"

"A guard posted directly inside the front door, and another one casually making the rounds out front."

Alanna nodded. "I saw the same around back—one at the door and another patrolling."

Hidalsa adjusted her antique scarf with a smug grin. "Aren't you glad we went with my plan and not yours?"

Alanna gave a little sniff. "Wearing a low-cut dress is usually the fastest way into any building."

Hidalsa crossed her arms. "Alanna, all those guards are women."

"You shouldn't doubt my skill, honey." Alanna smirked and sipped her beer.

Hidalsa tossed her head back with a good impression of an elderly woman's laugh.

The barmaid came over, smiling warmly. "Can I get you young ladies anything else?"

Alanna patted the barmaid's hand. "Aren't you a sweetheart? The sun is setting, so it's time for us to go." She handed the barmaid a full silver piece, and the girl's eyes opened wide. "Here's a little extra for your service. I'm afraid you won't get much more business tonight. I heard the jewelry store across the street is having a grand opening, and the owner is handing out free alcohol all night."

The girl's eyes widened even further. "The pink-haired lady? Wow ... giving out that much free alcohol will cost a fortune!"

Alanna winked at Hidalsa, who grinned a proper old lady grin. "Yes, it will, sweetie. But a fortune well spent."

❦

The two old ladies walked out of the tavern and began their stroll to the jewelry shop. The street was a little busier than usual, and the women walked slowly, considering the shorter woman's limp. But they made it across the street right on time.

Alanna bent to pat her elderly friend's hand and whispered, "Showtime."

Hidalsa limped to the jewelry store entrance and started banging on the door. "Hello? Are you open? Is this a jewelry store?"

The woman standing guard inside made a shooing motion, and mouthed the words, "We're closed."

Hidalsa kept knocking. "Why is it so dark in there? How can anyone see the jewelry? I need more light to see the jewelry."

Hidalsa had the better impression of an old woman, so she'd won the lead role. She continued with her long script, and Alanna took her cue to play her role of the strange old woman pressing her face against the window to look inside.

Neither of them had been able to examine the layout of the building on their quick reconnaissance, so Alanna peeked inside, looking for the location of the store's vault. That was where she would hopefully find Drazen and the diary.

Hidalsa kept knocking, and the guard rolled her eyes and unlocked the door with an irritated sigh. She stepped outside, pulling the door shut behind her.

"Ladies, the jewelry store is closed. You need to leave." The woman spoke to them as people often spoke to the elderly—with a condescending, bland kindness.

"The jewelry store isn't closed!" said Hidalsa. "It's opening tonight. Everybody knows it."

The guard sighed and lifted her head to call for the

patrolling guard, but Alanna grabbed the woman by the arm, which caused the woman to tense in reflex.

Alanna cooed at the woman, "Well, aren't you strong!" She squeezed the woman's bicep, which was impressive for a woman her size. "Honestly, child, how did you get so strong?"

The woman halted her search for the patrolling guard, and tried to harden her lips to disguise her pleased grin. "It's part of the job, ma'am."

Alanna gave her arm one more squeeze, buying her accomplices a few more moments. "Well, it's very impressive, dearie." As she clutched the guard's arm, Alanna caught a glimpse of gold at the woman's wrist. Alanna pretended to slip, her hand lifting the woman's sleeve enough to reveal a gold bangle with a shimmering rune.

The guard shook herself out of both women's grasp, and said firmly, "You need to go now. My colleague will escort you—" She turned to look for the other guard, only to see her confronting the driver of a large flatbed wagon pulled by two horses. The man driving the horses was directing his men to keep unhitching the horses, despite the guard's protestations.

While she yelled at him, a dozen people riding on crates in the wagon hopped out and began setting up tall tables. They moved with the efficient grace of skilled workers who had been paid a lot of money in advance. Before the horses were even unhitched, bars had been erected on three sides of the wagon, and happy patrons were already sipping their first taste of free alcohol.

The guard at the entrance stared at the situation with wide eyes. Her colleague still yelled at the man with the wagon, but by now, the horses were unhitched and a fourth bar had been erected.

The guard yanked the door open to find backup, but

Hidalsa's cheerful voice rang out. "Oh look! There's another wagon pulling right up front!"

The guard spun back around and ran up to the new driver, shouting, "Get out! You can't park that here!"

The driver shrugged, and his team began unhitching the horses while the bars started assembling. "Sorry, miss. I was paid a lot of money to be here tonight, so unless you're going to haul this bar out of here yourself, I'm staying."

The guard considered her gold bracelet. Wild panic shot through Alanna—the rune on the woman's arm might give her the strength to do just that. Luckily the guard shook her head, apparently thinking of a better solution. "My boss will double your pay if you leave right now."

He laughed. "There's no way your boss will pay more than I already got. That pink-haired lady was extremely generous."

"A pink-haired lady paid you?" said the guard, completely focused on the driver.

Alanna grinned at Hidalsa. "That's our cue to begin the next scene." She grabbed hold of a man waiting in line at the newly erected bar, and whispered, "I hear there are better drinks inside the jewelry store. Don't tell anyone!"

The man's eyes lit up as he began loudly telling his friends, who told their friends. Alanna and Hidalsa followed the mob inside the jewelry store.

36

Alanna and Hidalsa hobbled through the crowd of people swarming through the door. Bartenders with portable carts had already moved inside, and waitresses roamed through the crowd, taking orders. The guard from the back door ran into the room and started yelling for people to leave, though no one heard her over all the talking and laughing. The woman cursed, then ran to the back of the store and slid away a false wall.

Behind it was a vault.

The guard patted the closed vault with a relieved sigh, then moved the wall back into place before sprinting away.

"We have to hurry," said Alanna. "Where's Bibi?"

Bibi scampered up to them, shaking soot off her white fur with each hop.

"Oh, Bibi," sighed Alanna. "I promise you, no more chimneys after this." She slid the false wall away, revealing the large vault inside a room with two feet of clearance on each side. "Both of you, look for air vents. If there are no vents, she's keeping him somewhere else, and we keep searching."

As Hidalsa maneuvered around the edges, Bibi hopped

on top of the vault. Alanna pulled the false wall closed behind them and touched the spinning lock mechanism on the massive door. She would never be able to get Drazen out through the locked door. If he was in there, she had to talk him into her unconventional backup plan.

"Alanna, over here!" called Hidalsa.

Alanna scooted to the back of the vault, where Hidalsa and Bibi had both discovered the air vent. "Drazen! Are you in there?"

"Who are you?"

Alanna recognized Drazen's voice, weaker than usual, but he was still alive. "We're here to get you out, but you'll have to trust me." Alanna hadn't done much to prove her trustworthiness recently, but her only comfort was that Drazen had been captured by Geeni before finding out about the princess's betrayal.

"You're Jaemin's girl," he said.

Her breath caught in her lungs. "Jaemin's girl ..."

"The one who nearly blew me away outside the theater."

"Um ... yes, I guess that was me. How did you know?"

"I can sense you now, the same as I did then."

Alanna dug through the old woman's flowing shawls and pulled out her lamp. The large rune had finally stopped its shimmering. "The magic's gone. We have to hurry." She dug in her pocket again. "Bibi, you know what to do."

Bibi took the small gold plaque from the musician's shop and squeezed her way through the vent.

"Listen to me, Drazen. Is there a diary in there? An old leather-bound book?"

"No ... Why?"

She thumped her head back against the vault with a sigh. Of course, Geeni wouldn't keep the diary in the same place as Drazen. She straightened up again and spoke in a clipped voice.

"There's only one way I can get you out, and I'm not even sure it will work, but it's the best we've got. Take that rune from the monkey, rub a tear on it, and climb your way out of the vent."

A noticeable silence came from the other side.

"Did you do it? Are you coming?" she asked.

"Do you work for her?" he asked warily. "Geeni already tricked me into crying once and stole a tear from me to craft a rune with it."

"That's how she makes them?" Some runes required a tear to activate, but Geeni also needed the tears of someone with a Spark to create them. Alanna turned her face up to the grate again. "I don't work for Geeni, but I see how it looks suspicious. However, one of two things are true: either I'm tricking you, and you'll stay trapped while I give Geeni another tear, or I'm telling the truth, and I'll get you out of here."

A shorter silence this time, then, "Fine. I'll do it."

Hidalsa leaned against the vault and whispered, "You said the rune turns him into an animal, but you didn't say what kind."

Alanna shrugged. "I have no idea."

Hidalsa's mouth dropped open as she looked at the narrow vent, and she hissed, "What if it's a horse or a cow or anything bigger than a small dog?"

Alanna forced a smile. "I'm trying to be positive, okay?"

After a seeming eternity, Bibi hopped out of the vent, followed by a frog.

Alanna sighed in relief. "Thanks be to Qira! Okay, Bibi, take him on a safe path out the front door and—"

Drazen suddenly stood before them. His dark skin had a grayish cast, and his black robes were wrinkled and soiled. He coughed, spitting the rune out of his mouth into his hand.

"No!" said Alanna. "You need to be a frog to escape unseen."

He shook his head. "I didn't do anything." He turned the rune over in his palm. "It looks different."

Alanna growled. "The magic's gone. Geeni probably only gave each rune a short duration."

"Good thing it didn't wear off while he was halfway out," Hidalsa mumbled.

Drazen looked closer at Hidalsa, who was still in her old lady costume. "You look familiar … Do I know you?"

Hidalsa looked at him in terror, but Alanna jumped in. "It's a long story, Drazen. Time for Plan B … or Plan C, or whatever we are on now. Hidalsa, you and Bibi go out through the front door, then wait for me outside. I'm going to find another way to get Drazen out unseen." She put her hands on the false wall, then paused, turning back to Hidalsa. "Oh, and see if you can find him a pink wig."

Drazen's eyes widened as Hidalsa smothered a laugh.

Alanna slid the door open, letting Bibi hop out and Hidalsa limp away. Then she took Drazen's hand and pulled him behind a tall display case. She ripped off her gray wig and replaced it with a pink one, then removed her outer shawl and used it to start wiping off her old lady makeup. "So, Drazen … now would be a good time to tell me if you really are a wizard. Other than that whole 'magic sniffing' Spark of yours, can you wizard our way out of here?"

He gave her a flat look. "If I could, I would have done it long before you arrived."

She sighed. "Once Geeni realizes you're gone, she'll activate that rune with your tear and find us both. We need to know where she is so we can avoid her until I get you out."

"Simple." He pointed at the back staircase. "She's coming down the stairs."

Alanna sucked in a breath and yanked him over to

another display shelf, then peeked around it. Geeni stomped down the stairs, a thunderous expression on her face. The loud party at the front of the shop made it hard to hear their conversation, but the sheepish expression of the female guard at Geeni's side explained enough.

"I don't care how quickly they got in here," said Geeni. "I want them *out.*"

"Yes, of course." The guard slid a pair of knives from sheaths at her side.

Geeni growled. "You can't just stab them until they leave! If the Queen's Guard gets called, and starts poking around ..." Geeni took a deep breath and rubbed her temple. "Get them out. Pay them any amount to leave—"

"I tried that—"

Geeni fixed her with a furious look.

"Yes, Miss Ginevere. Of course." The guard ducked her head, then waded into the crowd.

Geeni watched her go, her eyes scanning the crowd, when she locked gazes with a dancing woman wearing a pink wig.

The woman looked at Geeni, pointed at her own pink wig with a big smile, then gave Geeni two thumbs-up, before she started dancing again.

Geeni's eyes narrowed in fury, but before she could murder the woman in the pink wig, another pink-haired woman bumped into her, spilling a drink down Geeni's leather vest.

"Sorry, ma'am! I've had *way* too much to drink!" She giggled, then stared at Geeni's hair. "Your pink wig is much cuter than mine."

The only thing that prevented the drunk woman's murder was Geeni's attention on the drink spilled down her vest. Geeni wiped her hand across the leather, flinging away any excess liquid, before feeling inside her vest, then sighing in relief.

"Oh great," mumbled Alanna. "That's where she keeps it?"

"Keeps what?" asked Drazen, his eyes following Geeni through the room as she hunted down her other guards.

"I'm going to get you out of here, Drazen, then come back and get the diary from her. Come with me." She grabbed his hand, but he shook her off.

He crossed his arms, then gave her an imperious look. "I will have you know, child, that I have done a fair amount of sneaking around in my day. I don't need you leading me like an invalid."

She raised her hands. "If you know a good way out, I'm more than happy to follow."

He nodded proudly, took two steps forward, and then his knees buckled.

"Drazen! What's wrong?"

He staggered against the display case, rattling its contents. "I appear to be weaker than I thought from my time in the vault."

She looped his arm around her neck and pulled him further into the shop. "Quickest way out is the back door, let's—"

A guard stood at the back door talking to the patrolling guard, pointing inside.

"We've only got one other direction, then," she said, supporting his weight as he hobbled at her side. "We go up."

37

Alanna threw open another door and peeked inside. Two neatly made beds lined the wall beside a table with an orderly assortment of daggers, knives, and swords. But the room didn't contain roof access or a balcony. She dragged Drazen into the next room and gasped. Tables full of gold glittered like a true jewelry store display, some jewelry with shimmery runes and some that remained unmarked, waiting to be crafted with a rune of their own.

Drazen whispered, "If she finds people with the right Spark, she could arm an entire battalion."

She gave him a nervous look and kept moving.

The tall windows faced the street, and music and laughter from the party still raging outside was barely dampened by the frosted windows. If she could just get Drazen out of the building, he would be lost in the crowd, and if Geeni wanted to use her rune, she'd have to choose whether to go after Drazen or Alanna. If Alanna came back for the diary, she knew who Geeni would choose.

She lowered Drazen with a grunt, and he leaned against the windowsill for support. "I'll be faster if I check the rooms and then come back for you, Drazen. Just wait right there and yell loudly if you sense Geeni coming." She headed to the door.

He coughed and said in a weak voice, "Um ... Pretend I'm yelling."

Geeni opened the door, and Alanna stopped in the middle of the room.

Geeni's eyes widened as she took in Alanna wearing a pink wig and Drazen slumped against the window, but she recovered her cool expression and crossed her arms. "What are you doing, dear? I thought I paid you enough to ensure your loyalty. I didn't think you'd be greedy enough to come back and try to extort me for more."

Geeni had no guards with her. Their angry shouts drifted up the stairs, yelling at the partygoers to leave. Alanna could see no way to get Drazen past Geeni, so her only choice was to surrender. Or at least appear to.

Her shoulders slumped, and she gave a little shrug. "It's like you said. I'm a con artist and thief. It's what I do."

Geeni clicked her tongue as she stalked closer. "Yes, but if you wanted a paying job, I could have found you one. One that wouldn't have cost you as much as this diversion."

It took all of Alanna's will to not back away from her. "I thought that if you wanted Drazen so bad, you'd pay me a lot to hand him back over." She huffed a laugh. "Though I'm surprised to see him able to stand at all. I assumed you would have tortured him to get what you want."

Geeni frowned in profound disappointment. "Don't you listen to anything I say? When I gave you the lamp, I told you the tears had to be freely given, not from torture."

"So, you're holding him indefinitely until he decides to give you his tears?"

Geeni shrugged. "Or he dies first. Either way, the queen doesn't have access to him, so it's a win-win."

"And ... what about me? Can we just forget you ever saw me?" She offered Geeni her most flirty grin. "You keep Drazen and let me walk out of here?"

Geeni's eyes sparkled dangerously. "I'm afraid we're past that, dear. I'm just waiting for my guards to deal with you. I could use a rune to crush you myself, but I like to make my guards work for their pay."

The guards had gotten more than they'd bargained for tonight, paying off partygoers instead of roughing people up. Alanna didn't want them coming upstairs and doing the job they'd been hired for.

"Maybe we can come to some other arrangement?" Alanna asked, a hint of desperation in her voice. "Tears. You want tears. I'll give you mine."

Geeni bit her lip on a smile. "That's adorable. Creating new runes is extremely difficult work, Alanna. I need Sparks valuable enough to be worth the time it takes to carve the rune into gold. What am I going to do with an army of soldiers who stir up clouds of petals when they walk?"

Alanna's mouth fell open. The only time Geeni had seen her use her Spark was on the day they met. She had come storming out of the monastery, upset from another sad encounter with her mother, and Geeni had noticed her because of the petals floating around her. And other than assuming Alanna had blown the doors open at the ball, which Alanna had later confessed was the queen, Geeni had no idea what else Alanna could do.

Alanna took every bit of that knowledge and poured it into a perfectly executed quivering lip. "Is there nothing else I can do?"

Geeni stalked another step closer until she could almost reach out and grab Alanna. "You should have been satisfied with your fortune, dear."

Alanna sucked in a shaky sob, and the air around her

trembled in response. The warm wind from the volcanoes had followed her inside, nipping at her heels like an adoring pup, and now it hovered around her left wrist, sleeping but aware of her wishes. And the cold wind from the sea had nestled against her side, twisting around her wrist in drowsy awareness.

The cheers and laughter from the street intensified, ringing out, along with a steady thrumming beat. The unrelenting rhythm magnified until Geeni finally tilted her head. "What in the Goddesses' names is that?"

Alanna whispered, careful not to wake the wind. "It's a parade."

Geeni blinked, then leaned closer to Alanna. "Did you say a parade? Coming here?"

"Yes." Alanna said the word out loud, and the winds roused, their awareness stirring to sharp attention. The winds floated on her indrawn breath, waiting for their cue. "It was very expensive."

Alanna grinned, then snatched the diary out of Geeni's vest, and shoved it in her pocket.

Geeni's eyes widened as she grabbed for Alanna in fury. But not before Alanna took a step back and clapped her hands together.

Two winds met at once. Instead of the circling storm Alanna had formed on her roof, the winds collided in an explosion. The windows shattered, sending glass soaring onto the crowd on the street below. The wind slammed Geeni against the wall and scattered the runes off the table, while Alanna grabbed Drazen's arm as they hurtled out the window.

38

Alanna landed on her feet with a thump, which was better than she'd expected after being blown out of a second-story window. Drazen slumped against her side, gasping for air. They stood on broken glass among screaming people covering their heads with their hands.

Alanna adjusted her pink wig and yelled, "Thanks for coming to the party! I hope you liked that performance! And now, enjoy the parade!"

The crowd slowly straightened from their crouches and, realizing they had seen something amazing, raised their glasses and cheered.

"Can you walk?" She lifted Drazen's arm over her shoulder. "We have to find Hidalsa and disguise you."

He allowed her to pull him into the swarming crowd, which had become more boisterous as the approaching parade grew louder. "She has my tear," he wheezed. "She can use it to find us."

"I know. That's why we have to split up. And hopefully her guards won't recognize you if you're in disguise."

"You believe she'll come after you?"

Alanna tucked the diary further into her pocket. "I know she will. I have the diary that proves her birthright, and the only place it's safe is in the palace with the queen. Geeni won't go near her for fear the queen will steal her Spark."

Drazen turned his head to look at her. "Do you think the queen will let you just run up and hand her a book?"

Alanna jerked him out of the way of a spinning pink-haired dancer. "If not, I'll move to my next plan and destroy it."

He stumbled, almost tripping over a man waving his glass of beer in the air. "You can't destroy a royal artifact! The queen won't allow it!"

She shifted his arm higher on her shoulder, difficult because of his taller height. "I think she would prefer it over the alternative. You saw those runes Geeni crafted. She's building an army, and I won't be the cause of the downfall of the queendom."

"Alanna!" Hidalsa ran up and took Drazen's other arm. "In that alley. Just avoid all the people making out."

They helped Drazen into the alley and found Bibi guarding their stash. Hidalsa grabbed a fuchsia robe and wrapped it over Drazen's tattered black robe, then handed him a pink wig with downcast eyes. "Sorry, Drazen, sir. This is the best way to hide." He grumbled, but tucked his long gray hair inside the pink wig.

Alanna shed the rest of her old lady costume, revealing her own clothes underneath, and adjusted the pink wig tighter on her head. "Get him to the first member of the Queen's Guard you can find. Bibi can help you look. I'm sorry I can't help, but I know she'll follow me instead."

Hidalsa gave her a sharp nod, then looped Drazen's arm over her shoulder.

Alanna's throat threatened to close as she grasped Hidalsa's hand. "I've never had an accomplice other than Bibi. I enjoyed scheming with you."

"Maybe we'll do it again someday." Hidalsa winked, then hauled Drazen into the churning crowd.

Alanna waited until the crowd swallowed them, then headed the opposite direction. She couldn't use the wind to speed her footsteps because the crowd pushed in the opposite direction as new people headed toward the center of the party. She needed to move onto a side street and begin her mad dash to the palace.

A strong hand grabbed her arm. She shoved her hand into her pocket to protect the diary as she was spun around to face her assailant.

Jaemin didn't remove his hand from her arm as he yelled over the crowd. "What are you doing?"

The sight of him sped her already racing heartbeat. His Queen's Guard uniform looked rough with spilled beer on one sleeve and dirt on the lapel. She turned her face up to him. "How did you find me?"

He gave her a flat look. "Alanna, there's a parade marching toward a raging party near the location of Drazen's last-known whereabouts. Obviously, the Queen's Guard would come."

"I mean, how did you find *me*?" She could count at least twenty other people in her immediate vicinity with pink wigs or pink dye in their hair.

His lips tightened, and his hand finally dropped from her arm. "I guess I've finally learned to recognize your disguises."

She swallowed another useless apology, then said, "Drazen is free, but he's very weak. If you head that way, hopefully you can find them, or Bibi can find you. I told Hidalsa to hand him off to the first Queen's Guard she saw." Alanna bit her lip. "Hidalsa was the princess's—my maid, but she knew nothing. She helped me rescue Drazen, so please don't blame her for anything I've done."

Alanna wasn't sure if Jaemin understood everything she said, because he just stared at her without moving. She pressed her hand against the reassuring outline of the diary in her pocket and turned into the crowd.

He pulled her back to him. "Where are you going?"

She didn't want to tell him, in case she wasn't successful and Geeni escaped again with the diary. "I have one more thing to do tonight."

He drew her closer. "You're not thinking about facing Ginevere alone, are you?"

She heard it again. The barely disguised fear below the surface. After all the lies she'd told him, she was grateful she didn't need to lie to him again. "I hope I never see Geeni again. In fact, I'm in the process of running away from her." She looked down at his hand on her arm. "If you let go, I promise I'll keep running."

He studied his hand as he considered her words. Then he removed his fingers slowly, one at a time. He inhaled a deep breath, closing his eyes, and when he opened them, his twilight eyes fixed on hers.

She couldn't move, even though he'd released her. Pink-haired women swarmed around her, any of them possibly Geeni, and yet she still couldn't move. The first wave of the parade passed around them, twirlers and acrobats and fire-breathers, and yet she couldn't pry herself away from his eyes.

A gymnast painted entirely gold tumbled into Alanna, finally breaking her concentration. "I have to go, Jaemin. I'm sorry ... so sorry."

The gymnast straightened her glittery costume with a glare at Alanna, and the gold triggered an important thought. "Clear every scrap of gold out of the jewelry store right now, while she's gone, otherwise she will use it to build an army."

He blinked as he processed the strange information, then asked, "Wait ... while she's gone? Where is she now?"

She bit her lip as she considered the truth. "I don't know where she is. But I need to go. Now." She backed away from him, then fled into the parade as it parted around her.

If Geeni caught up to her and stole back the diary, Alanna would be to blame. She cursed herself a fool for wasting so much time talking to him, even though it had been his eyes, not his words, freezing her to the spot. Alanna twisted out of the way of an approaching elephant, then tripped over the "foot" of a stilt-walker, before she made it through the parade onto an empty side street.

She looked up at the palace in the distance, and sucked in a deep breath. Using the wind, she could run fast, and hopefully arrive in enough time to convince a guard to let her inside, or at least to take the diary inside. She took two steps, then pulled herself to a halt, the summoned wind swishing uselessly around her feet.

One of Geeni's guards walked across the street one block ahead.

Alanna ducked, hiding behind some empty alcohol crates. If Geeni's guard was patrolling this area instead of protecting the jewelry store, it meant Geeni had sent them after Alanna with the assumption she would run toward the palace. And if Geeni had sent them out knowing the strength of Alanna's Spark, she would have equipped them with runes to challenge her.

They might be able to outrun her, or if they worked together, they could corner her. She had no doubt they would have the strength to crush her if they laid hands on her, and she didn't know if she would be able to call the wind quick enough to stop them.

She wouldn't make it to the palace. Destroying the diary was her only option. And she knew only one place nearby with a fire big enough to destroy the diary instantly.

She waded back into the parade and headed to Qira's shrine.

39

The air around Qira's shrine simmered with power. Though Alanna had been to the shrine many times, offering sacrifices of paper and wood to keep the flame burning, she had never recognized the power before. The heated air expanded in ever widening circles, billowing out from the flame at the center of the obsidian shrine. She let the hot wind wrap its arms around her shoulders and coax her inside.

Black volcanic stone pillars stood at the four corners of the shrine with the sides open to showcase the flame burning within. A fluted chimney at the center carried away the smoke, but the heat radiated through the black stone tiles, sending prickling heat through the soles of her shoes. Rugs surrounded the flame where penitents could kneel and sweat out their sins, though the shrine was empty of everyone but a few roaming monks tonight.

Everyone else was at the party.

An old monk in flowing red pants bowed to Alanna with folded hands before leaving her alone with her prayers. Alanna walked closer to the flame at the center, removing her wig as the heat formed sweat along her brow. She removed the diary from her pocket, then whispered a prayer to Qira.

"Goddess Qira the Trickster, this diary belonged to a queen, one descended from the First Queen, Twice-Blessed. I would rather not see it destroyed, but I must do it to protect the one I love. I stole this book twice over, both times through trickery, so I pray you accept this offering from one of your own."

"Alanna! What are you doing here?"

She spun around at the sound of Jaemin's voice, diary still clutched tightly in her hand, heart pounding as if he'd caught her doing something naughty.

She clutched the diary tighter when she saw Geeni beside him.

Jaemin firmly gripped Geeni's arm, while her hands were tied with thick ropes across her wrists. Despite Jaemin holding her prisoner, Geeni grinned as if she were the captor.

"What are you doing, Jaemin?" Alanna whispered. He walked toward her, pushing Geeni ahead, but Alanna raised a hand. "Stop! Don't come closer."

He paused suddenly, a now familiar look of betrayal ghosting across his features. "What's going on, Alanna?"

She kept her eyes focused on Geeni. "I'm destroying the diary. Keep Geeni away ... I don't trust her."

"Alanna, I captured her. It's over. You don't need to destroy the diary. We'll put it back in the library to keep it safe."

Despite the roaring fire at her back, cold suspicion trickled down her spine. "How did you find her?"

"Oh ... I sensed a gentle breeze coming from the shrine, and I followed it, knowing you were here."

She stared at him, understanding how the chain of events made perfect sense to him. Jaemin thought Alanna was the only one with the ability to summon the wind. He would never suspect Geeni could use the wind as a trap, because he didn't even know what runes were. The best time to explain everything would have been before Alanna betrayed him, but after that, she hadn't found the chance.

Jaemin cleared his throat as if ashamed to admit he had followed a breeze to find her. "Anyway, I happened to find Geeni sneaking around. I overpowered her and tied her up, then brought her here so the monks could summon more Queen's Guards."

The gold around Geeni's neck and wrists flared in the firelight, and Alanna trembled. Could her skill with the wind challenge whatever Sparks Geeni had at her disposal? Alanna flexed her fingers, stroking the warm wind at her side for comfort.

"You made a rune with my Spark." Alanna leveled her accusation at the bound woman.

Jaemin blinked, confused at the statement, but Geeni's lips curled in a grin, as slow and smooth as if she had her pipe in her hand. "The day we met, you ran out of the monastery with tears in your eyes, and I wiped them away. I never waste tears, even if they're weak. And they were weak —you hadn't come into your full power yet. I didn't realize you'd been practicing until you slammed me against the wall. If you'd let me know you could do that, I would've bought the tears you offered." She glanced over her shoulder at Jaemin. "However, your weak tears were enough to get the job done."

The words were unspoken, but clear: the job of luring Jaemin to find her. Alanna took in a shaking breath as she stared at Jaemin standing at Geeni's back, his brow furrowed in confusion. Geeni knew. She knew how much Alanna cared for him. And she knew he would be the only thing she could use as leverage to get the diary back.

"What do you propose?" Alanna forced her voice to be calm, yet the trade was obvious. And she would make it, though she hoped Jaemin would forgive her once he understood what was happening.

Geeni bit her lower lip in delight, confident in her victory. "You'll trade me the diary for this ring." She raised her bound wrists and wiggled her pointer finger. The rune on the ring's surface glimmered.

Alanna tilted her head, studying Geeni's delighted grin. Her offer was unexpected, which made her even more wary.

Jaemin tightened his grip on Geeni's arm. "What are you—"

Alanna spoke over him. "I don't want your runes, Geeni."

"You'll want this one, dear." Geeni flexed her arms, and the rope around her wrists shredded. Before Alanna could blink, Geeni spun, grabbed Jaemin's dagger from its sheath, stabbed him in the side, then pulled him close, blade at his throat.

It was only a heartbeat—so quick that Jaemin's first gasp of pain came after Geeni already held him in her rock-hard grip.

Alanna sucked in a breath, and the wind billowing out of the shrine flew back in, as if in a giant inhale. The great flame at the shrine's heart flickered uncontrollably as the wind's held breath battered against it. A storm surged around her, vibrating the air with an unsteady pulse that made her hair stand on end.

So much power under her command, a single heartbeat too late.

Alanna stared at Geeni with a wild fury, wanting to use the burning wind to sear her alive, but could find no way to separate her from Jaemin. His mouth gaped as he struggled to pull in a breath within Geeni's arm clasped firmly across his chest, while his blood gushed down his blue uniform, onto Geeni's shiny boots, and onto the rug at their feet.

"What's your decision, dear? Do we have a deal?" Geeni craned her neck to look at the prince's face. "He's cute, but maybe you'd prefer the diary. He's a prince, which doesn't mean much around here, plus the queen does have six more ... Perhaps you want a healthy one instead?"

Alanna's wind whipped through the shrine, blowing Geeni's hair into her eyes, but the woman's stance never shifted. Jaemin's left leg buckled, his eyes fluttering, and the only reason he stood was Geeni's arm across his chest.

"I will gladly fight you, girl." Geeni grinned, squeezing Jaemin even tighter. "But this one doesn't have much longer. Do you truly want to battle me? To test your Spark against all the Sparks I've gathered? You might win. You seem determined enough. But look in my eyes—I have that same determination. I will have that diary, no matter who dies. Can you say the same?"

Alanna looked deep into Geeni's eyes—it was the truth. Geeni would relish a fight with her. She'd drop Jaemin dead at her feet and savor the battle as she fought for the one thing she wanted. But there was only one reason Alanna wanted the diary.

The wind dissipated on a warm exhaled sigh, and Alanna held out the diary with a shaking hand. Geeni grinned and dropped Jaemin unceremoniously onto the rug at her feet. Alanna lurched forward, then slowed, watching Geeni with careful eyes.

Geeni pulled the ring off her finger and held it out to Alanna. "Do we have a deal?"

Alanna clasped the ring in a firm grip as she released the diary. She thought Geeni might overpower her and take both, but instead, Geeni released the ring and tucked the diary back into its home near her heart. She gave Alanna a little bow, as if to a business partner. "It was a pleasure working with you again, dear." Then she strode out of the shrine without a backward glance.

Alanna ran to Jaemin, skidding to a halt beside him. He barely clung to consciousness, his eyes not focusing on her. Blood poured out of the wound in his side, and she pressed a hand against it, before changing her mind, and pressing a warm wind against the wound instead. She took the ring in her trembling, bloody fingers, and slid it onto Jaemin's smallest finger. She brushed a tear from his eyes, and rubbed it across the rune.

"Jaemin!" She pulled him across her lap so she could take his face in her hand. "Look at me! Can you feel that? Use the rune ... I don't know how ... but use it to heal yourself."

He blinked at her, finally focusing on her face. "The rune?"

"Yes! This ring contains the tear of someone with a Spark. This one is from a healer. You have to use it to heal yourself." His eyes fluttered again, and she clutched him tighter. "I can't lose you! Please, focus on the rune. I love you. I love you more than anything, Jaemin, and I need you to heal."

His eyes refocused, and his mouth slowly opened in wonder. "The rune ..."

She caught her breath. "Is it working? Can you feel it?" She looked down at his wound, but blood continued to leak from the edges of the wind. "It doesn't look like it's healing you."

He whispered, "It's not a Spark from a healer." Though his words shot terror through her, his lips curved in a soft smile. "Just say you love me again, Alanna. That's all I need."

"That is *not* all you need, Jaemin!" She grabbed his

uniform and tugged him closer. "You need to *live*! I love you, and you have to live!"

He smiled, and his eyes fluttered shut. She screamed his name as she ripped the ring off his finger. "I'll heal you! That's how the rune works. Geeni didn't betray me. I'm supposed to heal you with this ring. She gave me a fortune with our last deal, and she wouldn't betray me by giving me the wrong rune." Tears flowed down her face, so she had plenty to add to the ring.

She didn't know if runes worked the same as the Sparks themselves, but she sought her own Spark and sent the wind's power into Jaemin's side. She imagined flesh reknitting and veins sealing and skin repairing, yet when she opened her eyes, his wound looked the same.

Her voice came out as a shaking sob. "Jaemin, I'm so sorry. I traded for a useless ring."

His eyes reopened, and she didn't deserve the look of love she saw there. His voice was weak, but sure. "The ring works. It's the magistrate's Spark."

As he said the words, a low gong resonated within her heart. Jaemin told the truth. She looked at the ring, and a scream threatened to burst from her lungs. "She tricked me? This is the truth detector's Spark?"

Jaemin looked at her with a steady gaze, his mind beyond the recognition of pain. His hand floundered until he clasped her fingers, then he spoke clearly, carefully enunciating each word. "I love you, Alanna. I always have and always will."

The gong sounded, rattling her bones with the strength of Jaemin's true words.

40

Alanna's scream summoned the winds from the four corners of the shrine and from the four corners of the world. Her call wasn't the playful coaxing she had used before, but instead, a beseeching wail ripped from her soul, a desperate plea to the wind for help.

The world switched to the strange double vision of air currents flowing around her. Instead of just feeling it, she could see the hot air flowing away from the center of the shrine and the warm wind still pressed to Jaemin's side. And because of her cry for help, she could see tendrils of wind summoned and awaiting her command.

A cool breeze that had blown inside the aviary on a lonely night hovered around the fingertips of her left hand. A warm wind that had sped her little feet after she stole her first loaf of bread now floated around her shoulders. And the held breath she exhaled every time she left her mother lingered near her collarbone.

Geeni had said Alanna's Spark was weak when they first met, but Alanna saw the truth laid out before her: The wind had always loved her. She could have seduced the wind and used it to get what she wanted at any time. But now she recognized the difference between love and seduction, and finally knew who she truly loved.

Jaemin.

Her mother.

The devoted wind.

And herself.

She rose onto her knees, careful of Jaemin's barely breathing form at her side, and gathered each thread of loyal air into a whirlwind above her head. Then she pressed her hands down to her sides, until the wind was thinner than the bloodstained rug where she kneeled. The wind slid under the edge of the rug, the golden tassels along the borders shivering, until the rug lifted from the floor, hovering a handsbreadth above the black stone.

She clasped Jaemin's body, wobbling until she realized the wind wasn't unsteady. It responded to each tiny movement, cushioning his body and shifting as she moved. She took hold of Jaemin's hand and aimed her body and mind at the monastery.

The rug lurched into motion, and she leaned over Jaemin's still form, protecting him from the wind rushing by. They flew over buildings and trees, causing both screams and cheers from drunk partygoers who happened to look up. Terror pulsed through her veins, not at the height or speed, but at the thought of watching Jaemin's last breath escape his lungs.

They sped out of the range of the party, and the city quieted, until all Alanna heard was the rushing wind. She raised her head, and the breeze fluttered her hair, flying it behind her as a flag, and her breath caught in her throat. The wind speeding past wasn't trying to batter her—it just wanted to run its fingers through her hair. Through her panic, a gentle laugh escaped her lips, and she leaned her head back and let the wind caress her, running loving hands across her face and drying her tearstained cheeks.

She blinked open her eyes as the rug curved in a slow descent and lowered them directly into the center of the monastery's courtyard.

Alanna wanted to scream her need again, but instead, she trusted the wind and whispered, "Ethelwin! I need you in the courtyard! Please hurry!"

The wind carried her whisper through hallways and into bedrooms with sleeping scholars, and within moments, Ethelwin appeared. She ran to the center of the courtyard, still tying on a robe, her long gray hair messy from disturbed sleep, yet her sharp eyes took in the situation in a moment. Ethelwin dropped to her knees on the rug, pressed her hand against Jaemin's bloodstained uniform, and closed her eyes.

Alanna's double vision had cleared, but she still sensed the wind hovering around her, waiting. The air in her lungs burned with the pain of her held breath. She couldn't release the air until she knew what it would become: sigh of relief or howl of grief.

Ethelwin opened her eyes and turned immediately to Alanna. "He will live."

The breath escaped her lungs in a shaking sob, and she curled herself around him, pulling him close. Ethelwin's hand rested on her shoulder, and warm sunshine flooded through her, knitting together sore muscles fatigued from her night of jumping out windows and flying across the city.

Ethelwin tilted her head as she studied Alanna. "You were the blond girl, but this is your true form."

Alanna's head snapped up. "Don't worry about me! Heal him more instead." She touched a hand to Jaemin's face. "Why hasn't he opened his eyes? Is he—"

Ethelwin clasped Alanna's other hand. "He'll live, but

his body is exhausted. I'll send Melora to add her healing as well, but he will still require rest." She stood slowly and looked around the empty courtyard. "I'll go find someone who can help us carry him to an empty bed."

"Oh ... I can manage it myself." She adjusted Jaemin's arms into a peaceful pose, then stood and stepped off the rug. She didn't call every current of wind at her command, but asked a few breezes to lift the rug to hover at her side.

Ethelwin's eyebrows rose as Alanna rested her hand on Jaemin's arm, then looked up, ready to go. The scholar snapped her jaw shut, then led Alanna deeper into the monastery.

Ethelwin helped Alanna move Jaemin into a bed in an empty room. The scholar lit a single candle as Alanna carefully removed Jaemin's boots and uniform jacket before tucking him into the small bed. Ethelwin laid her hand against Jaemin's forehead, and gave Alanna one last comforting smile before she left the room, closing the door quietly behind her.

The scholar hadn't suggested Alanna should leave, which was good, because Alanna would have refused. The bed was small, probably designed for one of the women scholars, so Jaemin's muscular form took up almost the full width. But Alanna curled up beside him, resting her head against his chest, and fell asleep listening to the air moving in and out of his lungs.

When she woke, Jaemin still slept. He didn't stir as she uncurled herself from her uncomfortable position, but she reassured herself with the steady rhythm of his breath. She quietly closed the door behind her and made her way to the courtyard.

Her mother sat at her usual spot in the courtyard, but Alanna didn't approach. Her clothes were covered with Jaemin's blood, and Alanna didn't want to distress her mother. She stood in the shadow of the cloister and watched her mother gaze peacefully at the birds, until Ethelwin approached her.

Alanna gasped, "Is he—"

"He's still sleeping. I sent Melora in, and she's doing what she can. He will recover, child. You can relax."

Alanna exhaled, but she couldn't relax. The guilt about everything she should have told him still lingered, and she couldn't shake the blame for his injuries that still snaked its way around her heart. "I need to go take care of some things. When he wakes, will you tell him ..."

What should she tell him? There was too much she should have said long ago, so now she was only left with the words that would never be enough.

"Tell him I'm sorry." She turned to leave, her sigh a heavy breath that floated away.

Ethelwin held up a hand to stop her. "He will want to see you, child."

"It's complicated between us." Alanna shook her head. "It's better if I'm gone before he wakes."

"You rescued this young man by flying him across Isandine on a magic carpet. He would have surely died if you hadn't summoned me as quickly as you did. Prince Jaemin owes you his life, child." Ethelwin gave her a stern look. "He will want to see you."

Alanna rubbed a hand across her trembling lip. "But I'm the reason he almost died."

The scholar's eyes opened wide. "You're the one who stabbed him?"

"No! Of course not! But I—"

Ethelwin waved a hand in dismissal. "Whatever the circumstances leading up to that moment, the fact is, he is breathing because of you." She aimed a pointed look at

Alanna. "You need to give him the chance to say how he feels about you."

"I know how he feels about me." Alanna twirled the ring with the truth detector's rune. Jaemin's words had rung with the truth. He loved her. She couldn't dispute his feelings, and yet, it changed nothing. "He plans to marry a foreign princess and leave the queendom." Then a whisper. "And leave me."

Ethelwin placed her hand on Alanna's arm and tilted her head to look her in the eyes. "He'll have to decide if running away is still the answer. I've seen many people pulled back from the brink of death. It often changes their perspective."

Alanna had no words for her, so she gathered a cloak of warm air around her shoulders and set off into the city with the wind by her side.

41

Alanna stood in the middle of her aviary bedroom and surveyed all the changes she had made in the three days since her showdown with Geeni. That was how she calculated her time—from the moment she had watched Geeni escape with the diary. Not that it had been three days since she'd left Jaemin in the monastery and hadn't gone back.

She fluffed the pillows on her actual bed, not the thread-bare mattress she used to sleep on. The room was more cramped than it had been, now that it had a real bed and a nice wardrobe full of clothes, but with the furniture she had added outside on the roof, she had more usable room than before.

After leaving Jaemin in the monastery, she had returned to her suite at the hotel and counted her remaining gold. After a conversation with a lawyer and then a valet sent to the monastery, Alanna had walked into the theater with a contract for its purchase along with a large stack of gold. She'd told Leland, "This is where I will live, so you need to leave." Leland's breath had rattled in his chest as he eyed the money greedily, and when he appeared to consider haggling, Alanna revealed the rest of her offer. Ethelwin had laid a hand on his shoulder, and Leland had pulled in his first unrestricted breath in decades.

The theater was hers by the end of the day.

Hidalsa had done a good job working with the actors to strategize about the theater's future, and Alanna trusted her enough to leave her in charge of the decisions about their upcoming productions. Between the two of them, they needed to make sure the theater made enough profit to support them and all the actors for the long term.

It had to, because Alanna had spent all Geeni's gold, down to the last coin.

Alanna walked onto the roof outside the aviary and found Bibi curled up on the couch in the last patch of sunshine as the sun set. The monkey still exhibited catlike behavior from time to time, but she had mostly returned to normal. Normal except her tummy, which grew rounder each day. Alanna suspected Bibi had made a good "friend" on their trip to the jungle.

Alanna considered an empty portion of the roof. Would the theater generate enough money for her to build a monkey nursery?

A familiar scrape drifted on the wind, and she ran to the edge of the roof. Jaemin was climbing up the back of the theater, using all her familiar handholds, yet he was slower than on previous climbs. When he heaved himself up to the top and swung his legs over, Alanna extended her arms, then pulled them back, unsure if she should assist.

He stood straight, wiping sweat from his brow. "I can't believe you'd make a sick man climb a building to find you."

She ducked her head shyly. "Well, since I own the theater, technically you could have come in the front door."

A hint of a smile tugged at his lips. "Are you not going to offer me a seat?" He looked at the furniture arranged into a living room outside her aviary bedroom. "You've made your-self comfortable up here."

She waved him to the couch and fetched him a glass of water. Bibi opened an eye at him, then stretched and curled up in a new position with one paw touching his leg. It appeared unintentional, though Alanna knew Bibi was just showing confident ownership. Judging by Jaemin's smile, he didn't mind.

Alanna handed him a glass of water, then sat in the chair next to the couch with her own glass. As he watched her drink, she recalled the day they met, when she brought him home and shared her only glass with him. Though dark circles from uneasy rest ringed his eyes, he appeared much as he had that day, in the same neatly pressed work clothes. He had climbed up to see her as Jaemin, not the prince in full uniform, and she appreciated the distinction.

She couldn't ask the question burning in her lungs, so she asked a simpler one. "Has anyone found Geeni?"

"No. After leaving the shrine, she disappeared along with her guards. But we won't stop looking for her."

Alanna frowned. "What about her runes at the jewelry shop?"

"A lot of the jewelry was crushed by the explosion you caused when you rescued Drazen, which ruined the runes. The ones that still glisten with magic were handed to Drazen and the scholars to examine." He took a sip of water. "They are somewhat hesitant to test out runes when they don't know what they can do ... although I heard you made Drazen test out a rune himself so he could escape."

Her lips twitched. "I always thought Drazen would turn me into a toad, but he actually turned himself into a frog instead."

"Perhaps I'll be lucky enough to see something like that for myself. While I was recovering, the scholars unlocked the laboratory and let me inside, and Drazen has been more forthcoming about magic. Especially now that rumors are spreading wildly across Isandine about a girl who rescued the prince with her flying carpet."

Alanna bit her lip. "I think Sparks will be a difficult secret to keep from now on."

"Yes, and after your party, pink-haired women are everywhere. I imagine Geeni will be forced to dye her hair if she wants to stay hidden."

"I don't think she'll change her hair, though I'm sure she wants to murder me for that trick alone. She wants to be seen. She will reveal herself." She sighed, tapping her finger on her chair. "She's still here—scheming—but we just don't know where."

Jaemin nodded soberly. "We will find her. She won't win. I'll be here to make sure she doesn't."

Alanna's breath stilled. "You'll be ... here?"

Throughout their conversation, his eyes had held a warm familiarity, the friendship she'd felt with him as both princess and Alanna, but now his eyes shifted into a gaze he had only given Alanna. "I'm not leaving, Alanna. I won't leave Isandariyah to marry a foreign princess." He leaned forward and whispered, "I won't leave you."

The truth detector's ring on her finger tingled. The shimmer had faded from the rune, but a faint trace of magic had remained, revealing Jaemin's true feelings once again.

He stood and offered her his hand. "Would you dance with me, Alanna?"

His words echoed what he'd asked the night they danced in the jungle, and though she allowed him to pull her to her feet, she hesitated. "Are you sure you're strong enough?"

"The last time we danced, you held me up when I felt

the world was falling. I trust you to do the same again, if necessary."

He spun her in a quick circle, then they settled into a soft sway. The heat from his body, warm but not fevered, soothed her soul, and he held her close, yet with enough space to stare into her eyes.

She blurted out, "I'm so sorry, Jaemin. I should've—"

"I met Sunah. Ethelwin told me she's your mother."

Her jaw snapped shut, and she swallowed an unsteady breath while she nodded. "I had planned to take her and flee the city. But I realized I can't take her from her home. And I don't want to leave ..."

His eyes watched her with an intensity that froze the words on her tongue. She had so much to say, but had no idea how to say it. All her scripts failed her, and she had no lines prepared. "I don't know what to say to make things right."

"You know exactly what to say, Alanna." His eyes twinkled as the wind of his soft words floated around her. "Since you aren't a princess, I could technically be the one to ask, but you know me ... I'm old-fashioned." He pulled her closer and whispered against her ear, "Just ask me, Alanna. You know my answer."

The currents of wind that always surrounded her suddenly stilled. Every breeze and gust and storm held their breath, waiting for the question, if only she was brave enough to ask it.

She breathed the words out on a sigh. "Will you marry me?"

"Yes." The wind of his exhaled reply caressed her temple, brushing the hair just above her ear. Even after the sound had faded, the breath floated above her brow, another current added to the collection of winds that would never leave her side.

She looked into Jaemin's eyes, the same color as the twilight sky surrounding them. She didn't know if tradition demanded she be the one to ask her next question, but she asked it anyway.

"Will you kiss me?"

Jaemin brushed his hand along her face, his thumb resting on her cheek, then bent his head and pressed a soft kiss against her lips. In the past, Alanna had claimed to find chaste kisses boring, but his gentle kiss nearly buckled her knees. Her inhaled breath blazed like the sun in her chest, and her eyelids fluttered as if she might faint. He had asked her to hold him up if he grew weak, yet his strong arm around her back was the only reason she kept her feet.

He slowly pulled his lips away, and a shuddering breath escaped her lungs. He bit his lip, and a playful glint twinkled in his eyes. "Thank you for allowing me to be old-fashioned, even though tradition can be quite boring."

"Yes," she whispered, still out of breath. "That was so boring."

He grinned, and brushed a lock of hair behind her ear. "It's quite ... cozy up here. Are you sure you can make room for me?"

She blinked at him. "Make room for you? You'd choose to live here instead of the palace?"

He batted his lashes. "I assumed with a proposal, you were also offering me a place in your home and bed."

"I ... uh ..." She stuttered, once again reduced to the lovesick fool in his presence.

"I admit, your roof is smaller than the palace, but it has an amazing view." Instead of looking at the darkening sky, he looked directly into her eyes.

She caught her breath, then cleared her throat, her stuttering suddenly broken, and slapped a playful hand against his chest. "You don't need to use sappy pickup lines on me, Prince. I've already proposed to you, and now you're mine."

"Yes, I am yours." His solemn voice wrapped around her like a vow. "I knew I loved you from the day we met, but I never imagined I'd ever be yours. You stole my breath that day, as you've stolen it many times since. I would live with you in this aviary, in the jungle, or follow you across the sea just for the chance to hear you say you love me."

The wind drew close on her inhale, and she breathed, "I love you, Jaemin." Then she used both hands to pull him by the collar of his work shirt and drag him into a passionate kiss. She threaded the fingers of one hand through his hair as the wind curled loving tendrils across the back of his neck. Her other hand kept tight hold of his lapel, reminding him that she desired every type of kiss, not just the chaste ones. He slid his strong hands up her back, supporting her, though the wind dancing around their ankles meant they barely touched the ground at all.

She relaxed her fierce grip, her hand sliding to rest directly above his heart. As she slowly pulled away, she took the thud of his heartbeat and wrapped it in a gentle breeze circling the roof. His eyes never left her lips as she wet them, then whistled a short melody, which she set to spinning through the rhythm of his heartbeat. She sent a wandering breeze down to the streets below, and it plucked yellow petals from the trees, then carried the petals back to the roof to scatter them in a fragrant rainfall.

Alanna leaned her head against his chest, savoring his heartbeats, both in his chest and roaming around the roof. He breathed in deeply through his nose, and Alanna mirrored the inhale, savoring the scent of the petals.

He gave a contented sigh. "It's not quite the same as running away and marrying a foreign princess."

She let out a self-satisfied huff. "I should think not." She lifted her head. "I will allow you to live here with me, Prince, but someday you will dance with me at a real ball. We didn't get to dance at the last one."

He smiled and squeezed her closer. "Consider your wish granted." He glanced at the palace in the distance. "The queen has called the other princes home. Maybe one of my brothers will throw a ball to find his own wife."

She looked into his eyes, happy to see her love echoed back. "All my wishes came true, and I hope theirs do, too." She rested her head back on his chest, and continued their slow dance around the roof.

PART IV

EPILOGUE

Geeni adjusted the hood of her cape as she ducked into the alley behind the monastery. The pale blue silk flowed elegantly around her calves with each step down the filthy alley. Geeni was always fond of a good cape—they were the perfect mix of drama and disguise. However, she didn't like being forced to use the hood to cover her hair.

After Alanna's irritating parade, pink hair had become entirely too common and yet very noticeable. Now anyone who noticed her pink hair gave her a thumbs-up like they were co-conspirators for the greatest party of all time. If Geeni had thrown the party herself, she might have found it amusing. As it had been Alanna's idea to ruin Geeni's plans, she found the whole thing distasteful.

Her only comfort was the diary tucked inside her vest, kept safely next to her heart at all times. But she'd learned the hard way, even that location wasn't safe when it came to a thief.

Geeni found the girl sweeping the back entrance of the monastery. She wasn't Geeni's newest spy since she had been inside the monastery months before Geeni even met

Alanna. The girl had done little more than clean since Geeni had wanted the diary in hand before activating all her spies.

Although this girl was a far cry from being a true spy.

Geeni shook her head as she studied the poor thing. Elliya was covered with ashes, the same as when Geeni had discovered her, working as a servant in her own home.

Geeni didn't know the full extent of the cruelty Elliya had experienced at the hands of her stepmother. But when Geeni offered gold in exchange for the girl, the stepmother had accepted it with a gleeful grin, and Elliya had wept.

The girl wept tears of relief.

When Geeni told the girl she would not serve in her own household, but in the monastery, the girl wept again, both in gratitude and trepidation. Geeni reassured her that the job would be much the same as when she lived with her stepmother, except with no abuse. All Elliya had to do was sweep the ashes in the monastery.

Sweep and listen.

As Geeni approached, the girl looked up and fumbled her broom, unsure if she should curtsy. Geeni rubbed her forehead and mumbled a prayer to the Twin Goddesses to save her from simpletons. But then she reminded herself to be grateful for finding such a gift as Elliya, even if the girl was tedious.

"Good morning, Elliya. You look well." And by well, Geeni meant less bruised, though the girl was still unhealthily thin.

"Thank you, Miss Geeni." She did curtsy then.

Geeni cleared her throat. "It's best if you don't speak that name." She felt the queen's presence like a looming shadow. Despite Geeni's protective rune, she worried the queen might still find a way to steal her Spark. If the queen gained Geeni's Spark, the woman's power would be unimaginable.

Elliya ducked her head as if Geeni had struck her. "Yes, miss … You're right. I apologize."

Geeni tried to restrain her eye roll at the profuse apologies that always spilled from Elliya's lips. She told herself to be grateful she'd found the girl exactly like she was. Elliya was a real treasure.

"Of course, I forgive you, dear. If you need to refer to me, just call me your godmother." She brushed back the girl's messy blond hair. Elliya flinched, then leaned into her touch. Geeni smiled. "Have you heard any interesting gossip lately?"

"Yes, Miss—Godmother, yes." Elliya stood up straight as if giving a report in school. "The queen has called all the princes home. It will take some time before they all arrive, but I've heard she has important matters to discuss with them."

Geeni raised an eyebrow. Perhaps the queen had finally decided to reveal her secrets to the princes. Geeni assumed the queen would have already told her sons everything about magic, but perhaps the queen had even less respect for princes than Geeni did.

"Very good, dear. That's exactly the fascinating gossip I enjoy." The girl bit her lip to hide her proud smile. Geeni prowled closer. "And you will continue to work hard, will you not? Sweeping every hearth, quiet as a mouse, listening to every word. That's how you can show your gratitude to me for rescuing you from your stepmother."

Tears sprang to the girl's eyes, as Geeni had known they would. "I owe you my life, Godmother. I promise I won't let you down."

Geeni gave her a warm smile and gently wiped away each tear. "I believe you, dear. The day I found you, I knew you were a blessing from the Goddesses."

While the girl lowered her head to hide her embarrassed smile, Geeni rubbed the tears on her bracelet. Even though Alanna had destroyed most of the rune stockpile, Geeni had managed to save quite a few. And with a prolific crier like this girl, she'd have a new stock built up in no time.

"Continue your work, and I'll be back to check on you." She shook a finger at the girl in mock sternness. "And don't you let any of those princes seduce you, do you understand?"

The girl's eyes widened, and a furious blush stained her cheeks.

Geeni chuckled. "I'm just teasing you, dear. You're much too smart to fall for any of their tricks, right?"

Elliya nodded, looking younger than her twenty years. Geeni patted the girl on the head, then left her to sweep up.

The oldest prince falling for a con artist thief was bad enough, but the thought of one of the other princes with this mousy thing was truly laughable. If a prince fell in love with this scullery maid, it would probably make the queen even more insane than she already was.

Geeni pulled out her pipe and lit it as she considered the idea. Perhaps she'd try to get one of the princes to fall in love with the girl after all.

To be continued in
A Spark of Nature: A Cinderella Retelling

ACKNOWLEDGMENTS

Kent, thank you for being my partner in love, life, and world building.

To my family, thanks for cheering on a lifetime of my wild ideas.

Jamal, thanks for being the best fan an author could wish for.

To my dance teachers, thank you for creating brilliant roles like Eleanor Scrooge, Aunt Drosselmeyer, and Lady Sith Lords. Why shouldn't girls have a chance to play all the fun roles?

And you, dear reader, thank you for escaping into a fairy tale with me, then re-entering the world, stronger than before.

ABOUT THE AUTHOR

Susannah Welch lives in sunny South Florida with her brilliant husband and a magically hypoallergenic cat. She enjoys singing and dancing and showing off. She likes her stories with a little bit of drama, and a whole lot of sparkle.

facebook.com/susannah.welch.author

instagram.com/susannahwelchauthor

Ingram Content Group UK Ltd.
Milton Keynes UK
UKHW010821260623
424053UK00004B/245

9 781958 568095